Praise for Gabi Stevens

"Charming."
—*Publishers Weekly* on *The Wish List*

"An incredible story filled with romance, suspense, and some utterly delightful magical beings."
—*Huntress Reviews* on *The Wish List*

"*The Wish List* is an entertaining read, which drew me in and had me rooting for the characters. I'll be looking forward to the next book in the series."
—*Once Upon a Romance*

"Will appeal to fantasy fans and contemporary romance lovers alike."
—*RT Book Reviews* on *The Wish List*

"It sucked me in and I read it in one sitting, and that's all I need to give it a recommendation."
—*All About Romance* on *As You Wish*

BOOKS BY GABI STEVENS

The Wish List
As You Wish
Wishful Thinking

Wishful Thinking

GABI STEVENS

A TOM DOHERTY ASSOCIATES BOOK
NEW YORK

WISHFUL THINKING

A Tor Book
Published by Tom Doherty Associates, LLC
175 Fifth Avenue
New York, NY 10010

www.tor-forge.com

Tor® is a registered trademark of Tom Doherty Associates, LLC.

ISBN 978-0-7653-6505-7

First Edition: May 2012

Printed in the United States of America

0 9 8 7 6 5 4 3 2 1

This one is for the readers, all of you:
the ones who write me, the ones who befriend me,
the ones who "get" me and my stories.
Having an audience makes the whole experience of
writing so much sweeter. I hope you like this one
as much as (or more than) the others.

ACKNOWLEDGMENTS

I've said it before and I'll continue to say it: While an author writes alone (unless part of a team), no book arrives without help. This time I have several people to thank.

To Melissa Frain for editing this book to a strong final version, teaching me a lot in the process.

A huge thank you to Marlene Stringer, agent extraordinaire, for having the ability to talk me off the ledge whenever I need it. Your belief in my writing helps more than you know.

Thank you to Faren Bachelis for copyediting me with a beautifully light but correct hand.

To Cassie Ammerman, a delightful publicist whose unwavering support and enthusiasm is greatly appreciated.

To Tamara Baumann, the turn-to woman for beta reads. The book is very different from when you saw it, my friend, thanks to your input. I'm just afraid one of these days you'll start charging.

To Alessandra Anderson for once again taking the time to read an early version. Nice to have an expert in the house.

And, of course, to Bob always, not just for being the Grillmaster and Cocktail Guy, but for being perfect (despite his faults).

Wishful Thinking

1

JUSTIN'S GUIDE FOR THE ARTIST

•

Art, like life, is filled with choices.

CARLSBAD, CALIFORNIA

STORMY JONES-SMYTHE winced as the floorboard squeaked under her footstep. Silence was essential.

She checked the archway to the kitchen. No one came through the opening, and the low murmur of conversation hadn't ceased. Good.

Exhaling gently, she chanced another step. Her bare foot produced no sound. Just a few more yards and she would be on the rug, which would muffle her tread further, and then she could ease out through the front door. Of course, she still had to make it past the kitchen.

A quick dash might work. On three. She held her breath and counted. One . . . two . . .

She stilled as she heard her name. Her fathers were talking about her. Again.

"You're not disappointed? I know you did the math." Justin Jones's usually booming bass voice held a note of softness.

"No. You know I love her just the way she is." Ken Smythe sighed. "But I'd be lying if I said I hadn't thought about it."

About what? Stormy leaned against the wall. Eavesdropping was wrong, but curiosity trumped manners. This time.

"She just turned twenty-seven a few days ago," Justin said. "It might still happen."

And what did turning twenty-seven have to do with it? God, she hoped they weren't talking about her getting married. Just because she'd recently broken up with a boyfriend, didn't mean she would end up an old maid. Besides, there was nothing wrong with staying single. She didn't need a man to be fulfilled. She twisted her mouth with impatience.

"I hope not. I wouldn't wish it on her," Ken said.

Wait. They didn't want her to get married? She was confused.

"Well, she isn't, and it's for the better this way. We wouldn't want her involved in the whole mess."

"Absolutely. I'd never stop worrying," Ken said. "What kind of life would she have? She could never be normal."

Her fathers' words stunned and hurt her. Were they ashamed of her? Her fathers were wizards, Arcani. But she? She was a Groundling. She had no magic. Never had. No number of lessons, tutors, or bribes had produced even a puff of smoke.

Despite her lack of powers, her life was happy just as it was. She had gone to Groundling schools, attended a Groundling college, and majored in fabrics, textiles, and weaving. Her tapestries sold for hundreds, she had collectors talking about her work, and she loved weaving. Loved the feel of the thread in her fingers, creating the fabric, playing with texture. Her life was meaningful and creative, and she was on the verge of major success. And she had believed her fathers supported her in her lifestyle.

Fighting back tears, Stormy sought resolve. She needed time to think. If her fathers believed her so inferior, she couldn't stay with them. She needed to rethink her plans. And the best place to do that was her studio. Her loom waited. She could send the shuttle through the yarn and organize her thoughts with the repetitive motion.

She turned, prepping herself for the dash past the opening.

Her elbow banged against the wall.

Clearly sneaking wasn't her forte.

"Stormy? Is that you?" Justin's voice bounced off the walls.

She cringed and swiped her cheeks. Head held high, she walked into the kitchen. "Yes."

"Were you listening?" Justin placed his hands on his hips.

"You *were* talking about me." Her eyes burned as tears threatened again, and she clenched her teeth.

Ken looked abashed. "Baby, I don't want you to think that I'm in any way disappointed in you."

Stormy lifted her hands in front of her. "Well, what did you expect? You don't want me to get married. Why? You don't want me to infect children with my inferior genes?"

Her fathers looked at her with matching blank expressions.

Stormy stopped at their reaction. "Weren't you talking about me getting married?"

"No." Ken looked at Justin, who shrugged. "What did you think we were talking about?"

"That you're disappointed I'm a Groundling."

"You jumped again, Stormy." Justin said. "What have we said about not getting all the information?"

"That conclusions are reached by logic, not leaping." She felt stupid and embarrassed. "So what were you talking about?"

When Ken hesitated, she crossed her arms over her chest. "I am an adult."

Ken sighed. "Well, there was a chance you might have received powers when you turned twenty-seven. According to Arcani history—"

"Which we are not allowed to tell you," Justin interjected.

"I know." Stormy gave a little sniff of a laugh. "I'm a Groundling."

Ken cocked his head and shot her a pained look.

She threw her arms around Ken's neck and gave him a quick squeeze. "Really, Dad, I don't mind being a Groundling. I don't need magic. Why would I when I have you?"

Ken appeared mollified. "Well, in Arcani history, new fairy godmothers are chosen every seventy years. It's called the Time of Transition. This is one of those years. Two new godmothers were chosen about a month ago."

Ohhhhh. Their conversation made so much more sense now.

Ken continued. "This time there's trouble. The aunts have gone against the Council and are considered fugitives, and the two new godmothers have joined them."

Justin pointed to the Arcani newspaper on the kitchen table. "The paper is calling them dangerous renegades and asking people to notify the Council if they see them. They're saying the godmothers want to take over the Council."

That was crazy. The three old women known as the

godmothers had brought her presents throughout her childhood. She called them aunts. She couldn't imagine them as power hungry or subversive criminals.

"And if you were one of them, one of the new ones . . ."

She took Ken's hand. "Don't worry, Dad. No magic here."

"And I love you just the way you are."

"Yeah, sorry about that. I love you guys. You are the best parents a girl could have."

Ken placed his hand over Stormy's. "Yeah, we're a good team, aren't we?"

Justin boomed, "What do you mean, 'good'? We're the best."

Stormy chuckled. "Yeah, we are. Now I'm going to my studio before I lose all the light." Emotional outburst resolved, she still had to appease the desire to create.

"You can't go out now. Dinner's in half an hour." Ken drew his brows together. "I know you. If you start working at this hour, you'll forget all about the time and work until two or three A.M."

Thus the reason for her earlier stealth. "I'll grab a bite when I've finished." Stormy walked to the door.

"Leave her alone, Ken. We told her we wouldn't bug her if she moved back home. You can't schedule brilliance." Justin smiled at his partner.

Ken shot a look of disgust at the ceiling, then muttered, "As if I haven't put up with enough of this kind of behavior from you."

Justin just laughed, then turned to her. "I'll put a plate in the fridge for you."

"Thanks, Daddy." She stepped through the back door onto the sprawling property they called their compound.

They were always thinking of her, watching out for

her. When she was small and showed no signs of magical ability, they called in experts. And when those failed, they simply shrugged and enrolled her in the best Groundling schools they could. Oh, they had cried a little—she'd heard them—but she never felt as if they loved her any less for being a Groundling instead of an Arcani. Well, until a little while ago. Idiot. She laughed at herself. She was their daughter, and her place in their lives was secure.

Her bare feet slapped the flagstone path to her studio. Shoes were optional in the warm August evening, and she seldom wore them in the summer. Carlsbad had perfect August weather. Air-conditioning was seldom necessary, but she could wear shorts and a tank top without feeling a twinge of cold. Until night, anyway, but she had several hours before she would need her hoodie.

A soft breeze carried the faint hint of the sea to her nose, tinged with the ceramics firing in the kiln on their neighbor's property. She paused for a moment to breathe it in. Their neighborhood housed seven artists and their families, all Arcani, and they lived like kin in this artists' enclave.

As usual, she paused before entering her studio door to admire the intricately carved door. She ran her finger over the design. Justin had created it. It depicted the myth of Arachne. Between the lead filaments of the spider's web, translucent glass created a window. The door itself was a work of art. To be expected, since Justin was himself a renowned artist. He'd even written a book.

The vast property housed three separate buildings: the house where they lived and two studios, one for Justin and the other for her. Her studio was a gift from her fathers on her twentieth birthday. As she pushed open the door, she smiled. This was her space. A large skylight let natural light pour into the room. Beneath it, she had her looms set up on the gleaming hardwood floor. Racks and bins held her wools, threads, and yarns. Surrounded by shelves that housed her many books on patterns and textiles, a computer desk occupied one corner, and a MacBook sat on top. There was even a small bathroom hidden behind a protruding wall dotted with moving and adjustable pegs. Right now they held a half-finished piece of hand weaving and some skeins of yarn. Had the studio contained a bed and a kitchen, she could have lived in here.

The large loom in the center of the area waited for her. She had set up the warp threads that morning, then had taken a break, letting the idea for her project gel in her mind. Now she was eager to start.

She plucked several skeins of yarn from the pegs and loaded her shuttles. Then taking her seat in front of the loom, she touched her feet to the treadles, working out the pattern with her muscles before starting the actual weaving. Closing her eyes, she visualized the image of the fabric as it grew. Her toes danced across the bars of the treadles; her hands twitched in an imitation of sending the shuttle through the shed, then back from the other side.

And then she threw the first row. Strand by strand, inch by inch, color bloomed on the weft. The shuttles flew from her fingers and the cloth grew in front of her. Her fingers barely touched wool or wood, almost as if the loom reacted to her thoughts rather than to her movements. At some point she must have turned on the lights, for the skylight was dark but her studio blazed with brightness. The cloth grew longer; patterns twined in the fabric.

She paused only to reload the shuttles. Her mouth

dried out, but she didn't want to stop for water. She licked her lips instead, which did nothing more than dry them out further. Still she didn't stop. The pattern spoke in her mind, pressing her onward, pushing her. Energy filled her, drove her, sustained her.

She had never worked like this before, but she didn't want to question it. She passed the shuttle across the loom again and again.

And then she stopped.

Stormy looked at the fabric in front of her. The colors glowed, and the pattern danced. One more row would complete the work. One less would diminish it, one extra would ruin it. She passed the shuttle through the shed one last time, making sure she missed one thread of the warp on this row. The deliberate mistake was the reminder that no one is perfect.

She stood and stretched. With a shock she realized that the skylight let in a pale pink glow. Had she worked all night? Her neck felt none of the strain of bending for hours over the loom.

"It's beautiful."

Stormy yelped and spun around, heart pounding. When she recognized the three women standing in her studio, she let out a breath of relief. "You nearly scared me to death."

"Sorry, dear," Aunt Lily said, "but we had to be stealthy."

They weren't actually her aunts, but that's what she called them. "I can't believe you're here. I didn't think I'd see you with all the trouble."

"You've heard?" Hyacinth said.

"A little. I don't really understand what's going on. You're taking over the world?"

"Ha!" Hyacinth barked.

"That's nonsense," Lily said, but faint circles under

her eyes betrayed the stress of the past month. Taller than the rest of them, Lily stood watchful and graceful. Her iron gray hair was pulled back into a tasteful and neat coil.

"You are looking so beautiful." Aunt Rose touched Stormy's cheek and smiled at her. Rose's bobbed white hair bounced on her head. She usually looked as if she was ready to fly into the air with joy, but even she looked a little less bubbly today.

Aunt Hyacinth stood beside the other two, her feet splayed as if waiting for someone to push her. Her short-cropped silver hair gave her an air of toughness and practicality that Stormy knew masked a generous and sensitive heart. Hyacinth touched the cloth still on the loom. "You've got talent, kid. This is incredible."

"Thanks." Stormy yawned. "I think I worked all night on it."

"You think?" Hyacinth cocked an eyebrow.

"It was really strange. I came out to work for a couple of hours, but I couldn't stop. It almost felt like the piece was weaving itself."

The three old women exchanged glances.

"What?" Stormy wrinkled her brow.

"Like magic?" Lily asked.

"I wouldn't know." Stormy studied the three women with a hint of misgiving twisting in her gut. Stormy paused for a moment. "It felt right, though. And the piece did turn out well, if I do say so myself. I've never captured my vision as completely before."

"Perhaps there's a reason for that," Rose said, her eyes twinkling.

A reason? Her stomach clenched. Stormy didn't want to explore that idea too deeply. She was afraid she knew the purpose of their visit, and she wasn't ready to acknowledge it. She shoved her suspicions to the side.

"Should you be here? I mean, isn't half the Arcani world looking for you?"

"Probably," Hyacinth said. She glanced around the room. "But they won't find us here. Not yet anyway."

"And it won't help you to try to change the subject," Lily said with a sad smile. "You've already guessed why we're here, haven't you?"

Attempted evasion: fail. Stormy nodded. "It would be hard not to. Dad and Daddy just told me about the Time of Transition. I'm assuming you're here for me."

Rose clapped her hands together. "Isn't it exciting?"

"Honestly?" One corner of Stormy's mouth drew up. "Not really."

Rose's eyes widened. "Why not?"

"You can't blame the girl," Hyacinth said. "This isn't exactly the celebration it's supposed to be. Not now."

"Well, no, but that doesn't mean it's not exciting." Rose's whole face crinkled in joy. "And Stormy is the perfect candidate."

"That is why the Magic chose her," Lily said.

Yeah, lucky me. But Stormy didn't speak. She gazed at her studio, the place where she had spent so many satisfying hours. Would she have to give up her weaving? Dumb question. Of course she would. Especially with the trouble the godmothers were in. "Do I get a choice?"

Lily said, "Certainly, but you must consider the consequences carefully." In a smooth movement, Lily brandished her wand.

Any unsuspecting Groundling would have flinched at the display of the magical implement, but Stormy had seen similar flourishes from her fathers for years.

Lily flicked her wand. A slim case appeared in her free hand. "You can turn this down, but the Magic picked you for a reason." She opened the case.

Stormy stared at the supple length of ebony that lay in the case. The dark wood gleamed under the lights of her studio and the rising sun. Silver filigree encased its handle, and geometric shapes in the pattern allowed the wood to peek through. Here and there round diamonds added a sparkle to the handle. Stormy caught her breath. She couldn't explain it, but the wand called to her. She wanted to hold it, to grasp it in her hand. Her fingers twitched in anticipation of touching it.

Hyacinth placed her hand on Stormy's shoulder. "You don't have to choose this life. We would all understand if you didn't want to."

"Boy, you guys are sure making this easy." Stormy let out a mirthless laugh.

She stared at the wand. Her fathers had never pressured her to do anything that she hadn't wanted, but neither had they let her ignore what they considered her duty as a member of humanity. How could she ignore what the Magic had planned for her simply because it meant her life would become complicated?

The fabric on the loom almost glowed under the growing light of the sun. As she looked at it, she realized why it was so vibrant, so perfect. Magic. She had poured parts of herself into this piece that she hadn't even known existed.

Her heart sped up, and excitement bubbled within her. Although she had found her way in the Groundling world—attending school, making friends—not having magic troubled her. She had wanted to be like her dads. Oh, she had accepted fate, but when she was younger she had borrowed her fathers' wands and tried more than once to do a spell or two. With zero success. Now she had the chance.

Hell, she had always enjoyed complicated. It made life fun.

She reached for the wand.

"Wait." Rose placed her hand over Stormy's.

Startled, Stormy jerked back from the case.

"Sorry, dear," Rose said. "But as soon as you touch the wand, the Council will find out who you are."

"What do you mean?"

"As soon as you choose the wand, your name will appear on the wall of the Council Hall, and they'll send someone to try to catch us." Lily sighed.

"They'll try, but they'll fail." Hyacinth grinned.

"You really need to know what's happening before you accept." Lily shook her head. "The newspapers haven't exactly been accurate."

Hyacinth snorted, and Lily sent her a chiding look.

Hyacinth didn't look the least bit sorry. "It was either snort or cuss, and I thought the snort would bother you less. Those idiots are just printing what the Council tells them to."

"Be that as it may, we still need to tell Stormy our side," Lily said.

"You mean you're not trying to take over the Council?" Stormy nearly smiled. The idea that these three sweet old ladies were the most dangerous threat to the Arcani was preposterous.

Lily's somber expression checked Stormy's levity. "Part of the story you've heard is true. Someone is trying to overthrow the laws and rules we've lived by for centuries."

"But it isn't us," Rose said.

"No, it's a scumbag named Lucas Reynard." Hyacinth chuffed out a breath. "He wants the Arcani to reveal themselves and essentially rule the world as the superior beings."

"But that's . . . that's . . ." Stormy sputtered for words.

"Barbaric," said Hyacinth.

"Ridiculous," said Rose.

"Impossible," Lily said. "And that's the point. The Groundlings would react with fear, and some Arcani with arrogance and glee, a sure recipe for hostility. He's going to drag our worlds into a conflict that will make both sides suffer."

Stormy would have fallen into a chair had one been near. The consequences already whirled in her head. Even if they wanted to, the Arcani didn't have the numbers to defeat the Groundlings. While magic was powerful, using it cost energy. More than one Arcani had died by using too much magic—her fathers had told her that much. And dead was dead; she'd learned that when she had begged them to bring a beloved dog back to life. If they started a battle and lost, the Arcani world would be exposed, and the Groundlings would hardly allow them a peaceful existence. History had proven that. Hell, the fairy tales proved that. And the Salem Witch Trials, and God knew how many more examples there were. The Arcani world and the Groundling world didn't mix well.

She looked at the three godmothers.

"Godmothers have gone bad in the past," Rose said. "You shouldn't believe us just because you know us."

"You need to see for yourself and decide for yourself," Lily said.

"And the Council will try to persuade you that we're crazy and the other two godmothers are dangerous," Hyacinth added.

Stormy didn't know why the mention of the other two new godmothers surprised her. Her fathers had told her about them. "Will I meet them?"

"In time," Lily said. "First you have to practice your magic."

Questions whirled in Stormy's head. She settled on

one. "You're telling me there's some guy trying to take over the world?"

"Lucas is growing in power daily. But we might still be able to stop him." Hyacinth's gaze bored into hers.

She looked again at the fabric she had just woven. Hard to believe that last night her greatest concern was making the pattern come out right. Now she was supposed to step into some sort of conspiracy theory?

The wand still waited for her.

She took a deep breath and decided. Her fathers had not raised a coward. She took the wand into her hand.

The handle fit into her palm as if molded there. Her hand blazed with a comforting heat that spread through her as if infusing her every cell with power. She smiled at the exuberance that filled her. She lifted her arms and let the feelings trickle through her.

Rose clapped her hands. "I may cry."

"Don't you dare," Hyacinth said, her own eyes already brimming with tears.

Stormy laughed and hugged Hyacinth. "You fraud."

"Harrumph." Hyacinth squeezed her.

With a smile on her face, Lily said, "As happy as I am right now, I need to remind you that the Council is probably on their way. We have to get going before they arrive."

"Be careful if you meet a man named Luc LeRoy. That's the name Lucas was going by last we heard," Rose said. "I hope you don't run into him."

"She will," Hyacinth said.

"We'll try to keep in touch," Rose said.

Try? Stormy drew her brows together. "Can't I call you?"

Hyacinth shrugged. "Sorry, girl, we've given up our cell phones, and since we're in hiding, it's best you don't know where we are. That way you don't have to lie. Yet."

"We'll come again soon," Lily said. "Until then, work on your magic. You'll need it."

Hyacinth glanced toward the door. "Our time is up here, ladies."

Stormy looked through the glass to see several figures approaching. "But what about—"

"Trust in yourself, Stormy," Lily said.

The three women bunched together, and a moment later they vanished from the room. Stormy stared at the spot where they had stood and then at the wand she still clutched in her hand. A mix of elation and trepidation churned in her. What had she gotten herself into?

"Stormy?" Ken's voice called through the door. "Are you in there?"

She crossed to the door and opened it. Dad, Daddy, and five other men stood on the flagstone path. Four of them were huge. Two of the large ones pushed into the studio, wands drawn, and searched the room.

"If you're searching for the godmothers, they aren't here any longer," she said.

The smallest of the unknown men stepped forward. "We knew there was only a slim chance we'd catch them. Go see if you can find their trail."

The two men nodded and transported on the spot. For an instant, the air shimmered in a ghostly footprint of their presence.

Stormy looked at the three remaining strangers. Who were they? The small guy seemed kind of wormlike compared to the other two. One had a grin on his face and looked like a beach bum. The other's dark, intense gaze never left her face. She shivered.

Ken's brow furrowed, and then his eyes grew wide

as he saw the wand in her hand. “It’s true then. My baby girl’s a godmother.” Apparently his earlier qualms had disappeared.

Justin stepped to her and pointed over his shoulder with his thumb. “And these three guys are here to talk to you about it.”

2

JUSTIN'S GUIDE FOR THE ARTIST

•

Conflict creates interest or frustration.

SHE COULDN'T BE taller than five foot six. And *she* was supposed to be an all-powerful fairy godmother?

Hunter Merrick ignored the way his pulse sped up as he examined her. Blue eyes refracted stars when the light hit them. The chin-length blond hair danced every time she moved her head. Shorts exposed long legs and hugged her hips below her waist, a good expanse of which was bared by her short T-shirt, although he wondered if you could still call such a bit of fabric with nothing more than two thin straps holding it up a T-shirt. Her shoulders were as bare as her waist, showing off her tan. And right there on her left shoulder blade was a tattoo of a storm cloud with a lightning bolt jagging from it. A reference to her name, he supposed. What kind of name was Stormy anyway? He hoped it wasn't an omen for the future.

Nah. How much trouble could there be in such an

attractive package? Though no one could have guessed the old godmothers could cause as much turmoil as they had, and they looked sweet.

As usual, Hunter's partner, Tank, was grinning like a drunkard. Tank enjoyed chaos and noise. He hadn't taken his gaze from their charge. Hell, Stormy was just Tank's type.

Ian Talbott sniffed slightly, drawing Hunter's attention. The prig eyed the new godmother with some disdain. Ian's gaze traveled over Stormy's scantily clad body, and his lip curled in revulsion. Not surprising since the stiff wore a Brooks Brothers suit. Probably would have kept the price tag on if he could have gotten away with it. Hell, it wasn't like it was an Armani.

Hunter didn't know which bothered him more: Ian's pompous attitude or that he knew the difference between Brooks Brothers and Armani.

From the amused expression on Stormy's face, he would guess that Ian's ill-disguised disdain at her apparel entertained her rather than insulted her. She might have hope, this one.

"You two need to check on security." Ian flipped his hand as if dismissing them.

Tank shot Hunter a look, but Hunter just shrugged and cocked his head in the direction of the house. They did have to survey the perimeter. Now was not the time to remind Ian that he and Tank were Guards, not Ian's employees. They worked for the Council, not the putz.

The eleven remaining Council members were in an uproar since the godmothers had killed one of their members, and the Guard felt the consequences. Some of his colleagues had been assigned to protect individual members. The majority of the Guard hunted the godmothers with a small unit on patrol at the Council Hall in case of attack.

He focused on his task. Their job was to protect the asset. The Council had already lost the other godmothers and wasn't taking any chances with this one. Which was why he had been chosen for this assignment before the Council had even learned her identity. He and Tank. They complemented each other. His ability and Tank's personality.

Although he doubted he'd need it, Hunter kept his wand at ready. The latent power flowed through him as it always had. The wand was a natural extension of his arm. It felt right in his hand, and his senses opened to the Magic. He was good; that's why he became a Guard. He had top skills, dexterity, and brains. It wasn't bragging if it was true.

Okay, maybe it was bragging. Nevertheless, he and Tank had great reputations, and he was proud of his role in protecting the Council.

And if the Council wanted him to babysit a fairy godmother, then he'd do it.

Hunter scrutinized the compound. The house should be easy to secure, despite its rambling layout. The neighborhood was a little more problematic. Although fairly secluded, the Arcani artist colony lay a little too open for him. The inhabitants didn't make the slightest effort to hide from Groundlings. If they didn't even protect themselves from Groundlings, an Arcani would have no difficulty getting in.

Inside, the house proved well suited for the assignment. The asset's room was easily defendable: wide hallways—room for fighting; hardwood floors for the most part—carpeting muffled steps; a unique layout—a couple of twists and turns to throw off any intruders. The atmosphere meant to evoke warmth and friendliness, but with a shudder Hunter evaluated the eclectic mess that he would call home for the next indefinite period. The house was clean, but the lack of cohesion in the decorating, the brash colors competing for attention, the mismatched furniture, the odd paintings and posters on the walls . . . they all offended his sense of order and logic. It was an artist's house.

But at least the house was better than that studio.

The unfinished projects trailing balls of yarn stuck up all over the wall, the desk covered with papers piled in no perceptible arrangement, the floor littered with bits and ends of string, the explosion of colors, the looms set up all over—it had given him a headache and left him wondering if their asset enjoyed chaos.

Tank nudged his shoulder. "I'll flip you for the day shift." Tank held up a large coin.

Hunter eyed his teammate with skepticism. His lids narrowed slightly. He'd trust Tank with his back, but not with this.

Hunter held out his hand. "We aren't doing the day-shift, night-shift thing."

"I know, but we can't be on twenty-four/seven. Winner gets to decide schedule." Tank tossed the coin to him.

Silver, two sides, good weight. It looked clean, but that meant nothing. Tank was known for giving himself the advantage.

Hunter concentrated on the coin for a moment, then handed it back. "Agreed."

"Heads, I've got control; tails, you do." Tank grinned. He tossed the coin. Its edges blurred as it flew through the air. Tank caught it and flipped it onto his arm. He lifted his palm. Without looking down, he said, "Too bad, Hunt."

"Look again, idiot."

The tails side faced up, and Tank's mouth tightened. "You cheated."

"No, I just counted on you to. If you tried to magic the outcome, the coin would do the opposite."

"Asshole." Tank looked annoyed for a moment, then he laughed. "It was worth the risk. You know me too well."

"Well enough. And I still own the schedule."

"I said it before. Asshole." Tank grinned. "Let's get back. The putz is bound to be near the end of his speech by now." Tank headed toward the kitchen.

As they entered the room, Hunter steeled his expression. He glanced at their asset and then at her fathers. They didn't look too happy. Well, why would they be? Their kid just landed in a mess not of her own making.

Stormy herself blinked heavily as Ian spoke to her. She scrunched her eyes shut for a moment then nodded at something the putz said. In fact, Hunter had seen her repress at least one yawn since they'd come into the kitchen. Hell, he'd be hiding yawns too if he had to listen to Ian Talbott for long.

Ian, the Council kiss-ass and putz assigned as her arbiter, droned on. He probably saw this assignment taking him one step closer to becoming a Council member himself. If there was any justice in the world, the Magic would never choose Ian for the Council. Hunter might be loyal, but he wasn't blind.

"Because of the danger we now face, we've assigned two Guards for your protection. They will be with you at all times to protect you."

The larger father, Justin, leaned in. "Is Stormy in danger?" This dad's volume was more appropriate for a basketball game than a house.

"We're here to make sure she's not," Hunter said.

Ian looked surprised that he had spoken. His eyes widened for an instant, then his lips set into a thin line.

That was fine. Hunter's job wasn't to make friends with the putz but to protect the asset.

Tank winked at Stormy. "Don't worry, Miss Jones. We'll keep you safe."

"It's Jones-Smythe." She leveled her gaze at Tank.

Tank didn't miss a beat. He just grinned. "Forgive me. Miss Jones-*Smythe*."

"Do I really need baby-sitters?" Stormy asked.

Hunter's eyes widened. He had used that exact word when he complained to his commander. Not that his commander had cared. Hunter had received the assignment anyway. Maybe she was more perceptive than the state of her studio led him to believe.

The other dad, Ken, took her hand. "I'm happy the Council is thinking of you. It's for the best. I couldn't stand it if something happened to you."

She smiled at him, and for an instant Hunter wondered what it would feel like to be the recipient of such a love-filled expression. "I'll be fine, Dad."

"Yes, you will because we shall see that you are," Ian the putz said. "The Council wants to assure you that we are taking this situation seriously. The Council has also decided to relax the rules a little. I shall be your arbiter during the Time of Transition. I shall also serve as your tutor in magic."

"I thought godmothers were supposed to learn on their own," Justin said.

"Extraordinary times call for extraordinary measures," said Ian, "so we shall teach you magic without delay."

Stormy held up her hand. "But not today. I've been up all night—"

"What?" Ken frowned at her. "I knew it. I knew you would do something ridiculous if you went to work last night. Stormy, that's not healthy or—"

"She's a big girl, Ken. Leave her alone." Justin smiled at her. "Did you finish your project?"

She nodded. "And it turned out great. The aunts said I used magic—"

"Did they say where they were going? What they were planning?" Ian leaned forward, his chin quivering with indignation.

Hunter saw the brief roll of her gaze. She said, "I already told you what happened. They said I was the next godmother and gave me my wand."

"Yes, yes, of course." Ian sat back, restoring his expression into a semblance of dignity.

Stormy stood up. "Look, I need some sleep. Can we continue this later?"

"Of course we can," Justin said, ignoring the disapproving glance from Ian.

The front door banged open. Hunter drew his wand and placed himself in front of Stormy. Tank, grin missing, lined up beside him, effectively making a wall shielding her.

"Where's our girl?" A woman with a long, gray-streaked braid swinging over her shoulder sauntered into the kitchen. She saw the wall and drew back. Her eyes widened, and her mouth curved into an amused and appreciative smile. "Oh, my."

Justin stepped forward and took the woman's hands in his. He kissed her cheeks. "Barbara. Good to see you."

Barbara tried to peer behind them. "I just came to congratulate Stormy. I heard she's the next godmother."

Hunter heard the squeak of the chair against the floor as Stormy stood. As she walked around his right shoulder, his arm shot out to stop her. "Who is she?" he asked, cocking his head toward the woman.

Stormy blew out a puff of air in disgust, pushed at his arm, and ducked beneath it. "Barbara Cross. My birth mother."

Birth mother? He wasn't judging them—at least he didn't think he was—but these family relations were getting complicated.

"Wait. How did you know?" Ian glared at Barbara.

"We don't keep secrets here." Barbara hugged Stormy.

"How *did* you find out so fast?" Stormy asked.

"I called her." Ken shrugged. "I thought she needed to know. She did give birth to you."

"Well, of course she needed to know," Justin said. "This is a big deal."

"And we've already planned a celebration for tonight." Barbara wrinkled her nose. "Conrad is making his sauerkraut. You'd think after thirty-five years together he'd know better."

Wait. Barbara had a husband of thirty-five years? But Stormy was only twenty-seven. More ties to unravel.

"No celebrations, Barbara," Ken said. "Stormy might be in danger." The man's face seemed to have aged since they had arrived this morning.

"Danger?" Barbara's face paled.

Stormy took Ken's hand. "I'll be fine, Dad."

Justin took his partner's other hand. "We'll keep her safe."

Ian wrinkled his nose when he saw the clasped hands. "*We* shall keep her safe. That's our job. The Council wants nothing to happen to Stormy."

Barbara smiled. "So we have our little party, just the neighborhood. They're family too, you know. And you should come too, Mr., uh . . ."

"Talbott. Ian Talbott." Ian waited for the recognition of his name, and when it didn't come, Hunter nearly laughed. “Yes, I suppose I can come to your little party. Stormy’s gift should be celebrated.”

“Excellent.” Barbara clapped her hands. Ken looked reluctant, but resigned.

“Then you’d better let me get some sleep, because I won’t make it much longer without falling over.” Stormy stretched her arms above her head as a yawn engulfed her. Her shirt lifted, exposing more of her stomach. Yup. Tank’s gaze had taken in every new inch of skin. Okay, he’d noticed too.

“But it’s morning,” Barbara said.

“I know,” Stormy said. “I worked all night.”

“On a new piece? You have to show it to me.” Barbara started for the back door.

“Stop. You’ll just encourage her never to sleep,” said Ken.

“She’ll show you later.” Justin pushed Stormy gently in the direction of the hallway. “You can show her before the party.”

“Perhaps it is best if the neighbors get to know me first. They shall see quite a bit of me as Stormy’s arbiter.” Ian stood and straightened his tie. “Our lessons shall start tomorrow. Shall we say nine o’clock?”

“Better make it ten. Stormy isn’t a morning person.” Justin clapped the arbiter on the back.

The look of outrage on Ian’s face was the best part of this visit. Hunter kept his amusement to himself, but he wished Justin would hit the man again.

“Fine. Ten o’clock. I shall see you at the party later, Stormy.” Ian jerked his head in a stiff nod, shimmered for a moment, and then transported.

“What about you two?” Ken asked.

“We’re staying,” Tank said.

“For how long?” Ken asked.

"As long as she's our job." Hunter saw a look of resentment flash across Stormy's face.

Ken shook his head. "But I don't know where we'll put them."

"Don't worry about that, Mr. Jones," Hunter said.

"Ken, please." Ken pursed his lips. "There's a guest room, but it's on the other side of the house . . ."

"We'll take care of things, Ken," Tank said.

"Let me know what you decide. I'm going to bed." Stormy walked down the hallway.

Hunter moved in behind her, Tank following in line.

She whirled on them. She placed her hand on Hunter's chest. The contact was warmer than he expected. Her gaze narrowed on him. "Whoa. Where are you two going?"

Hunter raised one brow. "Wherever you do."

"It's why we're here, pretty lady." Tank's grin was back.

"Oh, no, you're not." Stormy crossed her arms over her chest.

Her breasts pressed up, and Hunter looked. He couldn't help it. He was a guy after all.

She reached out and flicked his chin up. "I'm up here, bucko."

To his mortification, his cheeks started to burn.

Tank chortled. "Don't worry, Hunt. I looked too."

"We, Miss Jones-Smythe, are here to protect you. That can't happen unless one of us is with you at all times." He leaned over her. "At all times."

She didn't flinch. She didn't step back or blink. She just stared up at him. A wind blasted through the hallway. Her hair whipped around her face. The light fixtures flickered. Her hand tightened on the handle of the wand she held. "Well, I hope you like hot water, because I like my showers scalding, and I'm not about to change the temperature for you."

Tank reached out and placed his hand over hers. When she whipped her gaze at him, the wind died and the lights remained dark. Tank nodded. "Now that was impressive."

For a moment she seemed disoriented, then she smiled. "Was that me?"

"Uh-huh." Tank smirked at Hunter. "Now, why don't you show us where your room is?"

She examined both of them. "I don't even know your names. You're called . . . Hunt?" She pointed at him.

"Hunter Merrick."

"What kind of name is Hunter?" She drew her brows together.

"What kind of name is Stormy?" he said.

Her eyes lit up for the first time that morning. "Fair enough. I was born in the middle of a thunderstorm, and my parents couldn't decided who sounded angrier, the storm or me. Don't tell me you came out ready to blast someone." She pointed to his wand.

"It's a family name."

"Although he does show an aptitude for using that thing." Tank held his hand out to her. "I'm Tank."

She shook his hand, but gave him a sideways glance. "Really?"

"Well, my name is Oliver. Oliver Bryant. But the guys nicknamed me Tank because of the way I look." He drew himself up.

Tank was broad and wide, but no bigger than Hunter was. Hunter cast an uninterested glance at his posing friend. "And it had nothing to do with that unfortunate incident with the commander's aquarium."

A laugh burst from Stormy. Tank scowled at him.

Hunter shrugged. "You want to explain why the commander's wife has banned us all from their house?"

"Vicious rumors."

Stormy said, "Well, I'd say we have the odd-name market cornered with the three of us."

"Speak for yourself," Hunter said. "I'm from a long line of proud Hunters."

She looked at him and then laughed again.

"That didn't come out right."

"Give it up, he-man," Tank said. He pounded his chest. "We find room now."

Still smiling, Stormy pointed to the next door. "It's over here."

She reached for the doorknob, only to jerk back when Hunter grabbed her wrist. "From now on, we enter rooms before you."

He released her and pushed the door open. Unlike the studio, her room was meticulous. The bed was made, nothing cluttered the floor, and everything looked in its place, with the exception of an open book lying on a small round table beside a comfortable-looking chair. Hmm, this room showed a different side to this woman. Not that he needed to analyze her personality. This new detail about her wouldn't distract him from his job.

His gaze raked the room, then he stepped inside. Tank stood in the doorway, wand at the ready, arm barring her from entry.

"Is this really necessary?" she asked, the annoyed tone back in her voice.

"Yes," Tank answered. "It's our job."

Hunter checked the closet, the bathroom, and then under the bed. "Clear."

Tank lifted his arm and she came in. She frowned. "This is going to get old fast."

"The Council wants you safe." Hunter stood against the wall and crossed his arms.

She placed her wand beside the book. "Look, gentlemen, I don't have the energy to argue with you right now. The room is . . . clean, is it? You can leave."

"Clear," Hunter said.

"Whatever."

He nodded to her. "One last thing."

He walked to the window and touched the glass with his wand. *"Imperviam."*

"What was that?" She placed her fists on her hips.

"Just made the window impervious to attack. No one can see in from outside, and it'll take a bazooka to break it." He pushed Tank out the door. "We'll be right outside if you need anything."

"I won't." Her voice followed him into the hallway.

"That's where we'll be anyway." Hunter closed the door.

Tank looked at him and grinned. "I like her."

"What a surprise." Hunter took a position beside the door. "You'd better get some rest too. You have primary tonight."

"Asshole."

3

JUSTIN'S GUIDE FOR THE ARTIST

•

Never anticipate what the future will bring.
The future has an odd sense of humor.

KRISTIN MONTGOMERY CARRIED a sandwich on a plate and a large glass of iced tea into the back bedroom that served as Tennyson's study. The man himself was at the desk, poring over a large tome. A sad smile curved her lips. He worked as hard as the rest of them to defeat Lucas Reynard, only his work involved the *Lagabóc,* the mystical book left by Merlin to guide the Arcani.

"How's it going?" she asked as she placed the sandwich and drink beside him

Tennyson Ritter leaned back and pushed his fingers through his hair. "Slowly. I may know Latin and Old English, but that doesn't make this book any shorter."

Kristin draped her fingers across the back of his neck and started to knead. The muscles were taut and tense. A low moan of appreciation floated from his mouth, but he shook her off a moment later. "It's not that I don't enjoy your touch, but I'm not the only one who's working hard."

"Yes, but you're the only one I'd give a neck rub to. You are so stubborn, and you missed lunch again."

"I did?" He laughed. "I guess I am hungry. Thanks for the sandwich."

"Well, someone has to watch out for you. I'm glad it's me." She kissed the top of his head.

"What's the news with Stormy?" He grabbed the sandwich and took a bite.

"She was reluctant to take her wand. Not surprising, seeing as being a godmother isn't exactly popular these days."

"But she took it?"

"Yeah. Helps that she was raised in an Arcani family."

"Unlike you, who didn't even know there was magic two months ago."

"Hey, I've learned a lot in that time." She flexed her arms. "I thought being a Rare One would make things easier. Like I had superpowers or something."

"You do. You just don't know how unusual you are."

"Try telling me that after one of your magic workouts and Callie's flying lessons."

Tennyson just grinned.

She pointed to the *Lagabóc*. "Have you found anything more in there?"

"The description of Merlin's Gifts."

Kristin's heart sped up. Merlin's Gifts were three treasures left by the great magician to the Arcani. "What have you learned?"

"Each piece augments the abilities of the user. The orb grants greater power, the staff gives strength, and the tapestry wisdom." Tennyson tapped the book. "But Merlin also writes about using the three together."

"Right. Together they form some kind of weapon.

According to legend, the last time the Gifts were together they caused the White Ship to sink and threw English succession into chaos."

"They also say it caused a certain tower in Pisa to lean. Rumors." His tone indicated he didn't believe the story. "So far I can't find the details."

Kristin nodded. The orb, a beautifully cut ruby sphere, had fallen into her possession; Reggie had summoned the staff, an intricately carved rod that extended over her head, to herself; the tapestry belonged to Lucas. "Fat chance we'll have to use them together with Lucas hanging on to one."

"True. And our chances won't get better unless I get more of this translated." Tennyson tapped the book.

"Is that a hint?" she asked. She slid her arms over his shoulders.

"Kristin, if you don't leave now, I won't get back to work for an hour." His eyes glinted with something other than annoyance.

"Promises, promises." Kristin bent over and took a lingering taste of his lips.

"Like I'm supposed to concentrate now." But his hand had already reached for the *Lagabóc*.

She loved this man. "Later, Professor. Don't forget to eat."

Kristin walked back to the living room. Regina Scott held a note in her hand. "He's recruiting. I just got word from my parents."

"And how are they, dear?" asked Rose.

"They're fine." Reggie chuckled.

"Don't you think we have more important things to worry about?" Hyacinth drew her brows together.

The chiding didn't fluster Rose in the least. "Nonsense. The day we forget about the mundane is the day Lucas wins."

Hyacinth shrugged. "You have a point."

"Well, yes." Rose patted Hyacinth's hand. "I usually do."

Kristin shook her head at the two and then turned to Reggie. "What did they tell you?"

"He's dining out all over town meeting possible supporters. So far he's been a very popular guest. He's regaling whoever will listen with the story of how he lost his eye." A note of pride sounded in her voice. "My parents are hosting a dinner for him later this week." Reggie wrinkled her nose as if she smelled something rotting. "I hate that my parents are throwing him a party."

"It's quite logical really," Kristin said. Instead of the usual pad of paper in front of her, she sat with a modified iPad that responded to the touch of her wand. The screen was filled with notes. "No one can suspect them of helping us if they're also helping Lucas. After all, they've lost two daughters to the rebellion. The Council must suspect their loyalty."

"I know. But these dinners are actually helping him." Reggie blew out a breath. "Mother sounds like she's having the time of her life."

"Hidden depths, that woman," said Hyacinth with an approving nod. "I like her."

"You won't when all this is over and she schedules you for a makeover." Reggie cast a cool glance at Hyacinth's short silver hair, as she pulled one of her own curls in emphasis.

Hyacinth's hand flew to her hair. "She wouldn't dare."

Reggie just smirked.

Lily lifted her hand. "Ladies, we have to stay focused. Stopping Lucas is our prime objective."

"Right," Reggie said. "How's Tennyson coming with the *Lagabóc*?"

"Slowly, but I have faith in him." Kristin hated the note of frustration in her voice.

"So do I," Hyacinth said.

"In the meantime, we need to deal with Lucas ourselves," Lily said, "and try to spread the truth as far as we can."

A sad smile curved Reggie's lips. "Jonathan is in New York speaking with some of his business acquaintances right now."

Kristin squeezed Reggie's hand. "He'll be fine."

"I know. He's proven himself stronger than most people think." She let out a chuckle that in no way masked her worry. "You don't want to mess with Jonathan when he gets riled up. You could lose an eye."

Hyacinth's laugh was filled with admiration.

"And so we plan." Kristin moved the iPad, lifted her wand again, and poised it over the device in front of her. "What is our next step?"

"You stay safe until the bond of three is complete," said Lily.

Kristin nodded. "And to complete it, we need Stormy."

"If she'll join us." Reggie looked at Kristin.

The three older women had nothing to say.

SHE SHOULD HAVE been asleep.

Stormy stared at the ceiling, unable to still her mind.

Maybe she had made a mistake moving home, even if it was convenient. Since her fathers had built her the studio, she had worked here daily. Now she lived here, but they hadn't redecorated her room since she was a girl. While the fairy motif had been cute when she was eight, especially when her parents had made the pictures fly around the walls, her tastes had changed, and these days she would prefer something a little more dignified.

Their house had always been a refuge for her, a place where she felt safe and loved. The love remained, but now her world had changed. She had been thrust into something she didn't fully understand. And her safety wasn't guaranteed either. The Council had placed a bodyguard on her. Actually, two of them. She puffed out her cheeks. That alone made this whole godmother thing annoying.

The worst part was that she might be placing her fathers in danger whether she sided with the aunts or Ian. Of course her dads wouldn't have stayed out of her life even if she hadn't moved home.

She flopped onto her side and stared at her hands. They had magic. The only magic they had created before was in her weaving.

Who was she kidding? She couldn't sleep.

She swung her legs off the bed and focused on the wand that lay beside the book on the table.

In the next instant, the wand flew from the table into her hand. Her eyes widened as her fingers closed automatically around the handle. She had magic. She really did.

The wand felt so right in her hand. She twisted her wrist from side to side, admiring the view. It looked good. Too good, in fact, it was trying to suck her in to the idea of magic.

Still, how much could it hurt to try?

Sending her gaze around the room, she wondered what she could zap.

Duh. The book, of course. It was lying on the table facedown where she'd left off. Simple, but effective. She could levitate the book to her.

For a moment she hesitated, then she realized she had seen her parents do the same trick hundreds of times. She pointed the wand at the book, squinted her eyes slightly, and said, "*Veni.*"

The book twitched a little, then rattled on the table. She furrowed her brow and pointed harder, if that were possible. The book bounced once and rose above the tabletop. It hovered like a flying carpet.

Yes! She held her breath.

In the next moment, the book shot at her. The drapes flew out as if blown by gale-force winds. She flung her arms up to block the flying novel from her face. A crash reverberated through the room, rattling the floor. She peeked around her elbows. The book lay spine open, pages fluttering on the floor, the table had overturned along with the overstuffed chair beside it, and the drapes swished against the window.

Whoa! Thank God it was a paperback.

And immediately after that thought, the door flung open. Hunter jumped into the room, wand at the ready. He shoved her down onto the mattress and held her there. "Stay down."

Whoa, again.

His gaze scoured the room.

She pushed against his arm. It didn't budge.

"Stay down." The words hissed through clenched teeth.

"Uh, Hunter?"

"Not now."

"Hunter." She shoved against him again.

"Stop that." His fierce dark gaze blazed down at her for an instant.

Why hadn't she noticed how much depth his chocolate eyes had? Suddenly she had visions of warm dark sweet liquid enveloping her. And that dimple in his chin? Her tongue wiggled in her mouth at the thought of playing in it.

She had to turn off her imagination.

From her angle on the bed, he loomed above her. As if he wasn't tall enough just standing. And he still hadn't gotten off her. Since pushing wasn't working, she'd try pulling. She grabbed his sleeve and tugged. "I'm not in danger."

His brow furrowed. "I heard a crash."

"That was me." She pointed at the overturned table.

His gaze followed the direction of her finger. He narrowed his gaze. "You did this?"

"Not on purpose." Stifling a laugh, she pushed against his arm one last time, and this time he released her. She rolled off the side of the bed.

"I thought you were sleeping." He rose from the mattress and stowed his wand in a pocket.

"Yeah, well, clearly that wasn't working for me."

He cocked an eyebrow. "What happened?"

She shrugged. "I tried magic."

His eyebrow never lowered.

Her dander up, she said, "Because you were perfect the first time you tried magic."

"Close enough. Magical aptitude is one of the requirements to become a Guard."

Arrogant SOB. Ignoring him, she righted the table and placed her wand on it. He grabbed the chair.

"I can do it."

"I know, but my mother raised me with better manners." He set the chair beside the little table and adjusted it into its original position.

The corner where the table stood contained the mural of a willow tree with pixies and fairies fluttering in its branches. They waved at him. His eyes widened. The unicorn Daddy had painted into the scene walked around the tree and bowed its head. Hunter pointed at the scene. "Really?"

"They painted it for me when I was eight. Then they cast the spell to make the figures move."

"And you haven't redecorated?" The eyebrow was back.

"I haven't lived here in years. I only moved home about a month ago. Remember the earthquake? My apartment was damaged."

Six weeks earlier, a strong tremor had rolled through North County. It had been an odd one, since it hadn't centered on a fault, but the aftermath had been that her apartment complex had suffered some damage. "My parents hadn't painted over it, and I'm not sure I can. It's kind of hard to paint over creatures who were your friends when you were a child."

"They aren't real, you know."

She'd known he wouldn't understand. "I know that. But I gave them personalities, and we talked."

"You talked?" The look of skepticism on his face made her want to punch him.

"I provided their voices. Usually in my head, but yeah, we talked."

His lips jerked as if he restrained a laugh. "Really?"

"It's a girl thing."

"I wouldn't know about that." A smile appeared for a moment and then vanished just as quickly.

The pixies released a shower of petals over the unicorn. His lips quivered again. "Do they do that all day?"

"No, only when someone is close enough to see them." She put her hand on the mural, and the pixies flew down from the tree onto her fingertips. When she lifted her hand, they returned to the tree.

"Okay, I can see how this could be pretty cool." He

lifted a finger. "If they had used dinosaurs and monsters. Or trucks."

His approval sent surprise surging through her. She peered at him. He looked less intimidating as he examined the painting. He placed his hand against the wall, and the unicorn strode over to it and nudged it with its horn. She knew he couldn't feel the point—it was an illusion—but he smiled. The fairies circled his fingers. His expression was the most open she had seen it since they had met. He looked less the warrior now and more like a big kid. Of course that didn't change his appearance. His dark hair was cropped short against his head in the style of the Guards. Probably for combat purposes. A pity. He would look like a medieval knight with long flowing hair. His nose was slender and long, and his lips were unexpectedly full for a man's. And he had that dimple. His shoulders were broad, and beneath the dark T-shirt he wore, she could see the definition of his muscles.

As she was about to move her gaze even lower, he straightened. The pixies scattered back into the tree. She shook herself. While she appreciated a fine male body as much as the next female, he wasn't here for her appreciation. He was here to confine her. She wasn't supposed to be admiring his external qualities.

He turned to her. A frown had replaced the smile. "You were a Groundling. They shouldn't have used magic to entertain you."

Her moment of warm thoughts evaporated. "My fathers love me, and they painted me a magical mural. Big deal. It's not like I didn't know they were wizards."

"The Council laws state—"

"Do all rules excite you so much, or is it just the ones my fathers bent?"

"We have rules for a reason."

"And it's your job to point out every little infraction thereof."

"Obviously." He pointed to the insignia on the sleeve of his T-shirt. It was a wand crossed with a sword. "That's why I'm a member of the Guard."

"So you'd follow the rules even if they were wrong?"

"I am not having a philosophical or ethical debate with you."

"Why not?"

"Because what I believe is irrelevant." Hunter propped his shoulder against the wall. "Rules exist for a reason. They provide order and peace. And I'm here to enforce them."

"And for a moment I thought you were human," she muttered.

"I heard that." His frown deepened. "You should paint over this."

She placed her hand on her hip. "It's too late now. I'm a godmother, and not a Groundling after all."

"And you're not a child anymore either, even if you are living at home." He pointed to the mural again. "You can't tell me that you want fairies on your walls."

Her annoyance with him grew. And it didn't help that she had had that same thought earlier. Not that she would admit that to him. "I think it defines the room."

He shrugged. "It's your room, but it would give me the creeps to sleep here."

"Do you sleep? I thought you were supposed to guard me twenty-four/seven."

"That's why there's two of us. Tank'll be on soon and give me a break." He retreated to the door and clasped the knob. "I'll return to duty now. You should get some sleep. You're getting cranky." He shut the door behind him as he left the room.

Ooooo. She gritted her teeth and searched the room for something to throw at the door. He was unbelievable. And to think for a moment she almost thought him nice.

A little voice niggled at her that he was technically right. Her fathers shouldn't have painted her the magical mural. Groundlings weren't supposed to be exposed to more of the Arcani world than was necessary, but really, was it that big a deal?

She didn't know much about the Arcani. Oh sure, no one at the compound had ever hidden their magic from her, but she had attended Groundling schools, had Groundling friends, and had lived in the Groundling world since she had been out on her own. She came back to the compound every day to do her weaving, but she didn't know much about the Arcani. For all their artsy ways, her dads adhered to the rules of the Arcani. For the most part.

What was it that the aunts had said? Someone was trying to expose the Arcani to rule over the Groundlings. She knew little about Arcani-Groundling relations. She needed to find out more.

But not now. Hunter was right about one thing. She was cranky.

She climbed back onto her bed and rolled over. Her wand beckoned to her. That had to be her imagination, but the urge to hold it again filled her.

She flopped over to her other side, ignoring the urge.

4

JUSTIN'S GUIDE FOR THE ARTIST

•

Life is messy. Revel in it.

AS STORMY STRETCHED the next morning, she felt languid and lazy, and well rested. Until she spotted her wand lying on the table in her room. Damn. Her world had changed yesterday, hadn't it?

With a groan she pulled on shorts and a tank top. Then, remembering whom she was meeting with, she changed into jeans and threw on a blouse over the tank. Her arbiter was a bit of a prig.

At the party last night, Ian had paraded about as if their neighborhood was beneath him. Until he had spied Kazuo Masuda, the noted Arcani artist, who was a part of their community. She'd encouraged Ian to introduce himself. Kazzy would never forgive her.

She still had time before Ian arrived. Eager to have some time to weave, she pulled her door open. A wide back met her gaze. Tank turned around almost at once.

"Good morning, pretty lady." His grin gave no indication of any awkwardness at the situation.

"Hi, Tank. Where's Hunter?"

He clutched at his chest. "I'm crushed you're even thinking of him when I'm here."

His antics brought a smile to her face. At least he wasn't as stoic as Hunter. "I just thought he'd be here. I'm not saying I want him."

"That's okay then. Hunter's taking a break. He'll be back at nine." Tank glanced at his watch. "You're up early. It's only seven thirty."

"I thought I could get a little work in before my magic lessons." She felt her wand poke her from her pocket. Clearly it was impatient. So was she if she was honest with herself.

"I may have to take my break then."

"You guys don't like Ian much, do you?" she asked.

Tank shrugged. "Not my place to like or dislike him."

She examined his deadpan expression. "What do you know about him that I don't?"

"Ma'am, it's not my place to say."

Ma'am? Tank sounded awfully formal. It roused her curiosity. "Sure it is. Your job is to protect me. Don't you think I need to know about my arbiter to stay safe?"

A corner of Tank's lip curled up. "I like your thinking, pretty lady. He's a poser."

She arched her brow. "Should you be talking about your employer that way?"

"He's not my employer. Hunter and I work for the Council. Ian is just a lap dog. He thinks he's a hero, when all he was was lucky."

"What do you mean 'lucky'?"

"He likes to say he played a major role in the discovery of the second godmother's treachery. Really he happened to be in the right place. His fiancée was her sister."

"Whoa."

"Jonathan Bastion and Reggie Scott were holding her parents hostage. Jonathan has a dual personality. He's a beast by day, a real live monster. Talbott escaped when he sneaked out of his fiancée's house to call the Council."

"Sounds kind of brave to me."

Tank shook his head. "According to his own report, they didn't take the parents hostage until after they discovered he was gone. He walked out."

She headed toward the kitchen. "So he abandoned his fiancée when he believed she was in danger?"

"And her parents. Turns out his fiancée was a traitor too and part of some plan, but he didn't know that when he ditched her." Tank entered the kitchen first, blocking her entrance until he surveyed the room.

She placed a hand on her hip. "Do you really think someone is hiding in my kitchen?"

"Sorry, but I don't skip procedures." Tank let her pass.

She was beginning to realize what a pain in the ass being protected would be. "Then you'd better check the yard too, because after breakfast I'm heading for my studio." She grabbed a banana and headed for the door.

"That is not breakfast."

"It's enough for now."

"You should take a cookie or something."

"I don't eat sugar."

"Ewww. And here I thought you were the girl of my dreams."

She chuckled as he crossed to the door and pushed it open. He scoped out the yard, and then nodded. Shaking her head, she stepped onto the stone path that led to her studio.

As soon as she pulled the key from her pocket, Tank grabbed it. "Me first." He opened the door and peered inside. "Looks safe."

"No kidding. It was locked all night."

"Locks don't keep Arcani out."

She'd forgotten. "Well, can't you put a hex over this place like you did to my room?"

"I'm already on it." His wand drawn, Tank outlined the door with the tip, followed up with a tap on the middle of jamb.

She stepped into the studio, and as she passed through the door, she felt a tingle, like a soft breeze that blew down her body. Her steps halted, until then she realized that she was feeling the magic, the spell that Tank had placed on the studio. She strode to the center of the room.

Tank followed her in. "So this is where you work."

"Obviously." She ran her fingers over the piece that she had just finished the previous day. It still hung on the loom. It was perfect. Her best work. She began the process of unhooking it.

"So you make . . . what do you call this?" He pointed at the weaving.

"Fabric."

"Really? You don't have a fancy word for it?" Tank scrunched up his eyes at the cloth.

"No, we call it textile art. Mixed media if we use other elements, but essentially I just weave cloth."

"Interesting."

"Really?" She mocked his earlier tone and arched an eyebrow.

He grinned. "No, not really. I don't get the whole artsy thing, although I like statues. Naked ones."

She laughed. "You're honest. I like that."

"There's lots of me to like." He winked at her.

"But are there any brains behind that brawn?"

"Plenty. Just because I'm blond doesn't make me dumb."

"Uh, hello?" She pointed to her own head. "I don't do dumb blond jokes." She hung the weaving on the peg wall, and grabbed a broom. After she finished a piece, she cleaned. All the bits, threads, and fluff that weaving left on the floor needed to be swept up before she could start her next project.

He looked at her. "You know you can use magic to do that."

She looked at the mess on the floor, and then at the broom in her hand. It might just be a good idea to practice before Ian got there. Her arbiter was sure to be impatient if she couldn't do anything. She pulled her wand out and felt it lengthen as it left her pocket. "What do I do?"

Tank held up his hands. "Don't ask me. Magic is a personal thing. You have to figure it out for yourself."

She knew that. Before her fathers had realized she had no powers, they had encouraged her to try her skills and always told her to just do whatever felt right. She examined the studio. How hard could it be to clean the floor?

She pictured the mess swirling together into a single pile, beads that could be reused rolling into their own area, yarn that could be employed in other pieces sorting themselves by length. She lifted her wand.

"Well, what are you waiting for?" She swirled her wand in a wide arc.

Okay, those words were pretty lame, but they had felt right. Probably, with more time, she'd become more eloquent, but she felt the power surge through her and down the wand. Nothing stirred for a second, then a wind circled around her ankles, lifting the debris from the floor. The bits of string and yarn entered the stream of moving air and flowed toward one spot.

The air flowed faster now. It rolled the loose beads toward one corner, and sent the longer strands of yarn aloft. The litter and fluff on the floor gave the airstream color. Satisfaction gripped Stormy and a smile stretched her lips.

Uh-oh. The wind was growing stronger. Her smile slipped from her face as she realized the wind was now lifting the half-finished hand-weaving project from its pegs. The air roiled. Spools and bins bounced on the shelves, papers were airborne, colors aloft.

"Uh, Stormy?" Tank lifted his hand to block a skein of yarn from hitting him.

Her hair blew into her eyes, a bead pelted her arm, and still the wind increased.

One of the plastic bins thunked to the floor, spilling its contents. Several more bins followed, then clunked around as the air pushed them across the parquet. Crotchet hooks and knitting needles tinkled as they joined the chaos. Balls of yarn unrolled, yards of wool unfurled and tangled in the looms and their legs.

"Uh, Stormy?" Tank said louder.

The looms started to rattle, as the wooden parts banged against one another. She could no longer see much of the room with everything flying, but the noise was growing.

"Stormy!" Tank shouted.

"What?" she shouted back. A bin banged her in the shin.

The door flew open. An instant later, the wind died away. Through the curtain of hair that hung over her eyes, she saw Hunter holding his wand in front of him.

He stood in the doorway, his expression one of disbelief.

"What the hell happened here?" Hunter asked, stowing his wand.

Tank looked at Stormy, then laughed. "She was cleaning up."

Her studio was . . . well, the word *mess* didn't come close to describing it. The shelves were empty; her computer was in place, but no papers lay on the desk; and the looms clattered one last time and stood still. Everything else was on the floor. The whole storm hadn't lasted longer than thirty seconds, but it would take hours to clean up.

"You couldn't have stopped it sooner?" As soon as she said the words, she shook her head. "No, I'm sorry. I didn't mean that. This is totally my fault."

Hunter picked up the fabric at his feet. It was the piece she had just finished. He shook it, and a puff of dust rose from it. "Cleaning, huh?"

For a reason she couldn't quite recognize, his words brought tears to her eyes. She felt humiliated. She snatched the material from him and folded it. "I would appreciate it if both of you would leave so I can clean up."

"We could help," Tank said.

"No, you'd put things in the wrong place." She stuffed her wand into her pocket, picked up the bin at her feet, and shoved a hank into it. She turned her back to them.

"You're here early," Tank said to Hunter.

"I thought I would spell you. I had no other plans." Hunter paused for a moment. "Looks like I should have come a few minutes sooner."

She clenched her teeth and hissed out a breath. "Why don't you two take your conversation outside?"

"We can't help from out there." Hunter crossed his arms over his chest.

"I don't want your help. You'll just slow me down." She picked up another bin and crossed to the shelves. "You can guard me from outside. Tank has put that hex over the studio. You can even keep the door open. I think I want the fresh air." She picked up the wool at her feet and placed it into a bin.

She felt warmth at her back first. She whirled around and found herself facing Hunter's chest.

"Hey." He touched her shoulder.

Her vision was still blurred, and she didn't want to let him see the tears, but she lifted her gaze anyway.

"It's pretty obvious you've got a lot of power." He gave her a crooked half smile. "All you need is control and practice."

"Ya think?" She indicated the mess with a sweep of her hand.

He chuckled. "It'll get easier. You'll see." He turned to leave, then stopped. "Sure you don't want help?"

"No," she snapped. Then she paused. "But thank you. I've got this." A tear dripped down her cheeks, and she swiped at it. Why she was crying, she didn't know, but she was crying. Embarrassment probably.

"Okay. We'll be right outside if you need us." Hunter left.

The door was still open, but she was alone. She shoved another bin back onto the shelf. A length of yarn tangled on her foot, and she grabbed the end and started wrapping it into a ball. "I wonder how much more I'll destroy before I'm any good."

"A lot if you're anything like me," said a woman's voice from behind her.

Stormy whirled around. Hyacinth stood in the studio. The godmother took out her wand and waved the door closed. Hyacinth looked around at the mess. She smiled and picked up a basket. "I see you've been practicing. I used to do the same things when I first started."

"Are you telling me that you couldn't . . . Wait." Stormy lifted her hands. "I saw Tank put a spell on this place. How did you get in?"

Hyacinth shrugged. "We made a back door. We had to be able to talk to you, and we knew they would put a spell over you to keep us out."

Stormy glanced at the door. "The Guards are right outside."

"That's why it's called a 'back door.'" Hyacinth waved her wand. As if the room blurred, the mess swirled around the room, then settled into place. "There. That's better."

She made it look so easy. Stormy let out a sigh.

"Don't worry, you'll get it." Hyacinth's expression grew earnest. "I wish this could be a happier time for you." And then she laughed. "'I wish.' That's your job soon."

"It's only been a day, Hyacinth." Stormy rubbed her cheeks in an attempt to erase the feel of her final tear.

"I know, but I . . ." Hyacinth shook her head. "The others don't know I'm here. I came to talk to you. You're a lot like me."

"I am?"

"You feel things so deeply, you try to protect yourself from your emotions. At first."

She was right. Stormy looked at Hyacinth and saw the love that glowed in her eyes. "You didn't want to be a godmother either?"

"God, no. We were in the middle of a war in Europe. I saw the limits of our powers. My parents were exhausted trying to keep our family safe and trying to keep from killing themselves by expending their energy on all the horror that was around us. Granting wishes seemed so trivial at the time."

A solemnity washed over Stormy. "What changed your mind?"

Hyacinth gave her a sad smile. "I couldn't turn my back on what was right."

The words stunned Stormy. Hadn't she thought the same thing yesterday when she picked up the wand? Even after the minor disaster, the urge to try again swelled in her.

"It wasn't an easy choice. So many friends died at that time." Hyacinth sighed. "I don't think there's ever been a good time for the world."

Shock jolted through Stormy. She had never heard Hyacinth so negative.

Hyacinth took her hand. "Forgive me. I'm getting maudlin in my old age. But that's why our job is so important. We give hope. We give magic to the world, and the world needs it so often." Hyacinth let out a puff of air. "Listen to me. I sound like Rose. Sheesh. And I promised myself I wouldn't preach."

"Well, I'm glad you did." Stormy realized she wasn't just saying that. "I guess I was just mourning the passing of my old life."

"And you have every right to. Take the time to be a little selfish. You deserve that."

"But everyone is so excited for me, and all I can think about is giving up my weaving."

Hyacinth nodded. "I gave up writing. I still scribble on occasion, but I didn't have the time once I became a fairy godmother. Hmm, maybe now that we're retiring I can get back to it. Once the Lucas mess gets cleaned up."

Stormy paused. "Did you regret it?"

"Regret is a strong word. I'll admit to pangs on occasion, but not regret. Being a fairy godmother fulfilled me in ways I didn't know I wanted and brought me fame too. I met so many amazing people, and that's not even counting Rose and Lily. Don't you dare tell them I said that." Hyacinth's eyes sparkled.

Stormy laughed. "I wouldn't dream of it."

"Can you imagine the grief they'd give me if they knew I love them?"

Stormy guessed that the other two godmothers knew, but she refrained from saying that. "The two others are waiting for me too, aren't they?"

"Kristin and Reggie are good kids. You'll like them."

"I expect I will." Stormy sighed. "It just all seems like predestination or fate or something. Don't I have control over my life anymore?"

"Did you ever really?" Hyacinth shrugged. "When you think about it, the stuff we can actually control is minor anyway. You can't control illness, or economics, or natural disasters, or other people."

A crooked smiled curved Stormy's mouth. "When did you become such a philosopher?"

"I've been hanging out with Rose too long. I have to counter her platitudes with actual depth." Hyacinth lifted a finger. "Don't you dare tell her I said that either."

"I won't."

"I guess what I'm trying to tell you, in my own inept way, is that this life is worth it." Hyacinth nodded. "It's hard work, but nothing worthwhile is easy."

"You're philosophizing again." Stormy chuckled.

"Damn. There has to be a cure for that." Hyacinth scowled. "I'm showing my age."

A shadow passed in front of the window in the door. The doorknob rattled, then the door shook. The two women jerked their gazes to the opening.

"Stormy?" Hunter's voice called from outside. "Open this door."

With panicked glance at Hyacinth, Stormy yelled, "I'm coming."

"Gotta go." Hyacinth gave Stormy a quick kiss on the cheek. "Things are going to get crazy for you. Hang in there. And watch out for Lucas. You can't trust him." Hyacinth shimmered and popped out.

Going to?

"Stormy, open this door now, or I'll break it down."

"Don't you dare!" she shouted back. She walked to the door and unlocked it. As soon as the bolt clicked, Hunter shoved the door open. It banged against the stop.

"My father made that door. Be careful. It's mostly glass." She examined the milky glass of the artwork.

"Who were you talking to?" Hunter strode into the studio.

"Nobody."

"The door was supposed to be open." Tank stood in the doorway. "We heard voices."

"You heard voice. I was talking to myself. I do that sometimes." She wouldn't think about how easily the lie came to her. "I don't know what you think you heard, but"—she swept her hands in front of her—"it's just me."

"Wait a minute. Who cleaned up?" Hunter looked around the studio.

"I did." She shrugged. "I guess I had more control than I thought."

"Excellent." Ian spoke from the doorway.

Oh crap. She had forgotten that her arbiter was coming. And, crap, he had heard her.

Ian strode in. "Perhaps you can show me your abilities in our session today. The Council wants you to appear at a function tonight. They want to reassure the Arcani that they have this minor rebellion under control. It would be, hmm . . . impressive if you could already perform magic."

The Council wanted to show off her powers? Great. She was starting her career off with lies. Not that she minded lying when necessary, but she was afraid she would wreck the venue. That's all her magic had done for her so far.

"So shall we begin?" Ian flicked his wand and moved her loom to the side of the room.

Who gave him permission to rearrange her stuff? She felt a pinch of indignation.

"Gentlemen, we shan't need you any longer. You may protect us from outside." Ian made a shooing motion with his hand.

"Yup. Time for my break." Tank rubbed his hands together. "She's all yours, Hunter. See you in a bit, pretty lady." He walked through the door and transported.

Hunter said nothing, but sent a sideways glance toward Ian and stood in the doorway.

"Now let's see what you can do." Ian pressed his fingertips together. "Shall we start with something simple? Bring that ball of yarn to me."

From the corner of her eye, she saw Hunter duck behind the jamb. She drew in a deep breath, focused on the bright green yarn, and said, "*Veni.*"

The yarn lifted from the shelf and floated toward her. She didn't breathe; she didn't look away. *Just the one, just the one.* Her chant made no difference. In the next moment, the other yarn balls followed, as well as the loose skeins, hanks, unspun wools, the bins, the needles, hooks, threads, materials, and papers. Even the loom flew at them. She covered her head with her arms.

Ian let out a shriek.

She didn't peek even when she heard him yell, "Oh my God, I think I've been stabbed!"

5

JUSTIN'S GUIDE FOR THE ARTIST

•

New ideas are like divas; they require attention.

FORMAL GATHERINGS WERE among Hunter's least favorite assignments. The sala, the most public part of the Council Hall, was crowded. Hunter stood beside the wall and observed the Arcani glitterati and illuminati mingling, chatting, posing, and preening, trying to impress one another. Such evenings always proved challenging, not because of the danger, but because of the boredom. He ignored the temptation to lean against the wall. One did not lean on duty—at least not in public. Luckily Tank would be here soon to take over. A job like this required working in shifts to stay alert. He covered the first half, Tank the second. And then he could go home and get some sleep. Tank had the night shift.

He watched the asset as she schmoozed with the Council members and other Very Important Persons. Her dress seemed black, but every now and again shone a deep purple, reminding him of liquid night. The darkness hinted at secret pleasures. The long, one-shouldered gown clung to her in all the right places and somehow was more tantalizing than the barely there shorts and shirts she usually wore.

He frowned. That thought definitely lacked professionalism. Eyes off the body and on the crowd.

The Council members appeared thrilled that Stormy . . . the asset . . . was there. He could identify relief in every expression. A touch of her arm, an overloud laugh, a straightening of the posture, an expelled breath—all signs that Stormy was the star of the evening.

The asset, damn it.

And through the throng Ian paraded her as if he were responsible for choosing her as a godmother. Certainly a change in his demeanor from the knitting needle episode this morning.

Hunter swallowed a snort at the thought of the panic on Ian's face when the he emerged from the studio with knitting needles stuck in his hair. Trails of yarn hung from him like tentacles and streamed from his shoes. He hadn't been hurt, but from his yelling you would have thought so. Even Stormy had hidden her smile as Ian had bounded through the yard demanding help. By the time they'd removed the needles, his hair looked like two hedgehogs had taken residence on his head. His face was red as a baboon's ass, and he clutched his chest as if he had just run the mile in middle school. Hunter wondered how the pretentious prick would enjoy the evening if that story made the rounds.

Stormy . . . *the asset* looked comfortable and poised. She handled each new introduction with aplomb. Except for the stiffness in her smile. It couldn't be easy to be on display like that. Her eyes lacked the usual glint of emotion, whether irritation or happiness. He'd certainly experienced plenty of the former.

An attractive and sharply dressed middle-aged woman stepped over to Stormy. Hunter recognized Sophronia Petros, a member of the local Council. She had played a starring role in the previous godmother's defection. Her celebrity had grown since she had been kidnapped by Regina Scott and Jonathan Bastion. They had released her, but not before regaling her with conspiracy theories and outrageous claims of a plot to take power in the Arcani world. He had only heard the stories secondhand—rumors flew fast in the Guards—but Sophronia had returned with disdain for the rebels and used her position to denounce the former godmothers.

"Ian, it is good to see you again." Sophronia kissed the air by his cheek, then eyed Stormy like a raptor spotting a rabbit. "Introduce us."

Ian nodded. "Sophronia, this is Stormy Jones-Smythe. I am her arbiter."

"Indeed." Sophronia clasped Stormy's hands in hers.

Hunter recognized Sophronia's type: a woman who sensed weakness, and manipulated and used others' strengths and faults to propel herself forward. A new, untried godmother would make a perfect victim. She had certainly taken advantage of her position as Regina Scott's arbiter. Despite the disastrous outcome of the whole episode, Sophronia had emerged with a stellar reputation. Accounts of the events called her heroic, brave, and loyal. He reserved judgment.

The woman's gaze assessed Stormy. "Well, well. So you are the third godmother. I hope you fare better than the first two."

Stormy's eyebrows arched. "Thank you, I think."

Sophronia's laugh tinkled with a practiced lightness. "As long as you understand what the Council expects of you, you'll do fine. You haven't met them yet, have you?"

"Met whom?"

"The other ones. The godmothers."

"I got my wand from—"

Sophronia flapped her hand. "No, no. The old ones gave you the wand. I'm talking about new ones. They're who you have to worry about."

"Thank you for the warning." Stormy gave her an uncertain smile.

"Don't worry. I'm keeping my eye on her." Ian brushed a fleck of dust from his coat. "I won't let anything happen to her. We've already suffered enough disappointment."

"We? I wasn't aware you'd been appointed to the Council, Ian."

Ian's face reddened, and with a triumphant twist to her lips, Sophronia turned to Stormy. "Your safety is imperative."

Stormy's expression brightened. "How kind of you to care for my welfare. I didn't realize how complicated my situation was." She let out an audible sigh. "So nice to know that the Council cares so much about me. I can't tell you how nervous I was." She clasped her hands to her chest.

Hunter nearly laughed. She had to be acting. Stormy was not that ditzy.

Sophronia blinked at her. "Yes, well, the fairy godmothers are an important part of our world."

"That's what I've been told. It must be devastating to have lost . . . how many is it now? Five of them?"

He snorted then. He couldn't help it. The earnestness of her expression couldn't be real. Could it? If it was, he'd have to question the Magic's choice of her. If it wasn't, she had more temerity than he thought.

Sophronia's brows drew together as if she couldn't decide whether to be irritated or pleased with Stormy's reaction. "As long as you're aware of the situation."

Stormy let out long breath. "There's just so much to know, isn't there?"

Before Sophronia could respond, a murmur rippled through the room. On alert, Hunter edged closer to Stor— . . . the asset, damn it, and searched for the source of the disturbance. A well-dressed gentleman had just entered the sala. Greeted on all sides, he had stopped to smile, clasp hands, and chat with many wizards near the entrance.

As the man turned to the room, Hunter saw a black eye patch. He'd heard of this guy. Luc LeRoy. He'd lost his left eye a month ago when Jonathan Bastion had gouged it out.

Sophronia glanced at the door and frowned.

"Is something wrong?" Stormy asked.

"No." Sophronia's wide public smile reappeared. "Nothing to disturb yourself about."

Ian looked more animated. "Excellent! I hoped he would get my invitation. You have to meet him." Ian grabbed her upper arm like an excited child. "Excuse us, Sophronia."

"Of course. I shall speak with you later, my dear." Sophronia gave a little wave of her hand and melted into the crowd.

Ian steered Stormy toward the door. Hunter followed as unobtrusively as he could, which wasn't easy since he towered over many of the guests. His gaze never left her. Her dress, now black, now purple, swished over her hips as she walked, drawing his attention. *Not good, Hunter. Keep your eyes on the crowd.*

Ian waved his free hand. "Luc. Luc."

God, the putz sounded like a praise-deprived acolyte.

LeRoy turned at his name. Hunter noticed a jagged red scar extending above and below the eye patch. The scar still looked angry and raw. That wouldn't heal for a while. It looked as if a beast had removed his eye. Of course, that's exactly what had happened.

"Ah, Ian, my friend." Luc shook Ian's proffered hand. "And who is this lovely creature?"

Smarmy bastard. Hunter didn't like him already.

Ian waved her forward. "Stormy, I'd like you to meet Luc LeRoy. Luc, this is Stormy Jones-Smythe. I'm her arbiter." He threw out his chest.

Luc's remaining eye widened. "So you're the new godmother. We've been waiting for your arrival." He bowed over her hand.

Stormy raised an eyebrow at Luc's action. Hunter wondered whether she was surprised or amused or flattered. That French accent would probably impress a lot of women.

Luc straightened. "My dear lady, such a pleasure to meet you. And to find that Ian is your arbiter brings more satisfaction."

An odd choice of words.

Ian bounced on his feet, the eager twit. "We shall have to acquaint her with your philosophies, Luc."

Luc held up a hand. "All in good time, all in good time. Tonight is a social gathering." He offered her his arm. "May I get us some champagne?"

Stormy slipped her arm into his. "That would be lovely. I haven't had any yet."

Luc turned to Ian. "For shame. Allowing this beautiful woman to go thirsty."

Red crawled into Ian's face. "We were . . . She didn't . . . I had to introduce her—"

Luc laughed. "Ian, my boy, I was merely pulling your chain." He turned to her. "That is the correct term, is it not?"

"Yanking, but close enough," Stormy said.

As the Frenchman led her to a standing bar, irritation coiled in Hunter's belly. Good God, this Luc guy was more arrogant than Ian. Hunter hadn't thought that possible. Couldn't Stormy see that?

He wove through the crowd following the trio—trio, because, of course, Ian had tagged along—watching Stormy smile up at Luc. They looked good together—his dark hair, her light, his refinement, her elegance.

The irritation wound tighter.

"Dude, what's up? You look ready to kill someone." Tank appeared at his elbow.

With some shock, he realized his eyes were squinting and his brow had wrinkled. He relaxed his forehead. Damn, he hadn't even noticed Tank approach him. "Nothing. Is it nine o'clock already?"

"Yeah." Tank drew himself up with a false salute. "Reporting for duty, sir."

"Idiot."

Tank surveyed the room. "Where is the asset?"

"By the bar." Hunter cocked his head in that direction.

"Oooo, looking good. Who's the SOB with her?"

"Luc LeRoy. Some Frenchman who has Ian licking his butt."

Tank grinned. "Can't wait to see that."

"You don't have to wait. Just look."

Sure enough, Ian was gazing at Luc with a look that Hunter could only call love.

"That's just not right." Tank shook his head. "I'd be saving those glances for Stormy."

The tangle of irritation in Hunter's stomach started to

burn. "She's our asset. Quit thinking of her like that." His voice was sharper than he intended.

"Hey, I'm just joking, man." Tank frowned. "What's wrong with you anyway?"

"Sorry." What *was* wrong with him? He looked at Stormy and felt his gut clench. She was laughing at something Luc was saying. His insides tightened further. "We're too far. Can't hear their conversation." Hunter moved toward the pair.

Tank's hand on his shoulder stopped him. "I've got it. Go home and get some sleep."

Hunter ran his hand down his face. Tank was right. He was tired, and his thinking was screwed up. Stormy was the asset, and she had the right to make a fool of herself with anyone. "I'll spell you in a few hours."

Forcing himself not to take a final look at Stormy, he walked toward the entrance. The sala was protected against transporting in and out. He'd have to leave the room before he could go home. Out of habit he moved along the periphery of the room, his eyes watching the crowd. His gut told him to stay and watch Stormy, but logic told him Tank was more than capable of handling this environment.

When he cleared the room, he let out a breath. He hadn't realized he was holding it. Damn it, he knew better than to tense up. He needed a few minutes to shake off this strange mood he was in.

The anteroom wasn't empty. Arcani who worked the event collected the coats and invitations of the late arrivals. Some carried trays of champagne flutes or appetizers, making their way to and from the sala. A few Guards stood on alert, and a few waited against a wall. Those Council members who had requested protection probably hadn't wanted to dampen the atmosphere of the party with Guards hanging around in the room.

Reckless and stupid, if they'd ask him. The point of protection was having the Guard hang around. He acknowledged them with a brief nod.

The one person he couldn't place was a slender man dressed in black. He stood apart from everyone else. His presence stirred Hunter's instinct. Hunter couldn't ignore him. Without another thought, he crossed to the man. "Who are you?"

Despite their difference in size, the man showed no fear. He smiled up at him. "Ah, you are Guard, I see." His accent was thick and guttural.

From this close range, Hunter saw the man had a sinewy strength. He was probably quick too. Hunter knew you didn't need brawn to defeat an enemy. Of course, if you had both, as he did, you'd have the advantage. "Right, and you are?"

"I am Dmitri. I serve Mr. LeRoy."

Serve? Dmitri said it without any embarrassment. In fact, if Hunter could judge by the tone of his voice, he'd say Dmitri was bragging about his position. "You're his bodyguard?"

"I am whatever Mr. LeRoy needs me to be."

Creepy. "So you weren't there when he lost that eye."

Dmitri visibly bristled. "I was. He has forgiven me."

"Good thing. Because you might have been out of a job."

"I am not employee." Dmitri's eyes narrowed.

"Then why aren't you in there with him?"

"I do not need to answer your questions."

"You're right about that." Hunter regarded him with an amused expression. "See you round, Dmitri."

"I doubt that."

"I don't." Hunter leaned in closer. "See, you've aroused my curiosity, and when I'm curious, I make sure I find out what I want to know." He smiled, straightened Dmitri's lapel, and strolled away.

His mind focused on the little he knew. Since Ian was in love with this Luc guy, chances were pretty good that Stormy would see more of him. Hunter knew that the last fairy godmother had attacked Luc; well, actually her lover had, but the semantics were irrelevant. Somehow this Luc LeRoy was tied up with the fairy godmothers. Add Dmitri to the picture, and Hunter's instincts buzzed. He had some digging to do.

He stepped back into the sala and searched for Tank. Finding him only took a moment. It always surprised Hunter to see Tank on duty. His alert stance was so different from the way he usually acted. That was part of Tank's strength. He fooled people into thinking he was a screwup. More than one person had assumed Tank was harmless. They never had the chance to make that same mistake twice.

Hunter knew that Tank had already seen him return. He worked his way along the wall, taking his time, in part not to disturb the attendees, in part to show Tank that nothing serious had happened.

When he reached his friend, Tank spoke first. "Something I need to know?"

"No, not really. I need you to do something."

"Of course. What is it?"

"Keep your eye on Luc LeRoy." He glanced at Luc. Stormy was still beside him sipping champagne with a look of interest in her face. Ian was still there as well.

A single raised eyebrow showed Tank's query.

"I'll fill you in tomorrow morning when I know more."

"Does this have anything to do with our assignment?"

"I think it does." Hunter couldn't explain why he thought this was so important, but he knew he could count on Tank. "Thanks."

Tank nodded.

Hunter left the room again and transported to his condo. He pulled off his T-shirt, tossed it onto the sofa, and opened the fridge. Only one beer left, and he'd be back on duty in a few hours.

With some regret, he screwed off the top of a soda water. His place suffered from a dearth of food and drink. Tomorrow he would have to go shopping for some essentials. Like more beer to celebrate the end of this assignment. He downed half the water in a long draft, then stepped away from the empty fridge. He checked his cupboards. No bread. Not that it mattered. He didn't have meat to make a sandwich with anyway.

He grabbed his phone and tapped it with his wand. A moment later he heard the voice at the other end.

"Merlin's Pizza. Our pizza is magical. How can I help you?"

"I need a large mushroom, ham, and onion pizza. Double cheese."

"Is this for delivery or pickup?"

"Delivery. I've already sent the coordinates."

"Excellent. That'll be $14.95. Would you like anything else?"

Beer, but that would have to wait. "No, I'm good."

"How would you like to pay for that?"

Hunter took out his wallet and pulled out a twenty. He touched his wand against the bill. It vanished.

"Thank you, sir. And here's your change."

A five spot and a nickel appeared on the counter.

"Your pizza will arrive in a few minutes. Thank you for giving us your business."

Merlin's Pizza wasn't the best in the city, but it was

pretty good, and they were definitely the fastest. It helped that Arcani ran the place.

He grabbed his laptop, pressed the on button, and placed it on his tiny dining table. Before the screen had loaded, the aroma of fresh baked pizza wafted from a flat square box on the kitchen counter. He grabbed a slice and stood in front of the screen. Eating the pizza with one hand, he typed with the other, then accessed the Arcani Web search engine, Abracadabra, with a tap of his wand.

He grabbed another water and the pizza and sat in front of the computer. He typed in Luc's name and waited for the results. There were surprisingly few, which roused his curiosity even further. He snagged himself another slice and settled in for some research.

6

JUSTIN'S GUIDE FOR THE ARTIST

•

What lies beneath is often more interesting than what appears on the surface.

DIM LIGHTS AT his back, Lucas peered out of the window onto the golf course. A few streetlamps lit the grass, lightening the night. He allowed that stab of anger that always accompanied the view to tune his senses before he tamped it down again. He had had the perfect house with the perfect view, but *they* had taken it away from him. That house had been destroyed, so he made do with this house and this pedestrian view. How unimaginative to think that a golf course held some sort of cachet. And Groundlings paid extra for their houses in such locations.

Despite his past setbacks, he was making progress. Tonight's event had been an exercise in banality, but he recognized the need for such appearances. He played the game well. Half the Council was his already, and the other half was paying attention. He had been right to start his push here, far from the long history of Europe.

These Americans had short memories. Besides, he hadn't yet taken his full revenge. Those three godmothers were outlaws, not dead. Yet. They would pay for his mother's imprisonment.

He had new scores to settle as well. Kristin would regret playing him for the fool, and Reggie . . . well, that bitch had cost him his eye.

His fingers traced the raised and bumpy scar that slashed over the left side of his face from brow to chin. He avoided the cavity that used to hold his eye. Magic couldn't replace his eye—dead flesh was dead flesh—but the doctors would be able to give him his looks back. Although he was considering leaving his face as it was. The eye patch and scars generated more sympathy and turned ears amenable to his ideas.

A knock at his door drew his attention. "A moment." He secured the eye patch. The open socket generated revulsion in all but his closest associates. "Come."

Dmitri entered the room and gave a short bow. "I drove them home as directed."

Although it was well past two, Lucas felt alert and energetic. "And?"

"It was as you expected. She cannot do magic yet."

A smile curved Lucas's lips. This new one was the worst yet. Vapid and common, she appeared the weakest of the three. And Ian was her arbiter. He couldn't have planned it better himself. The Magic was finally showing him its approval. "What of the Guard?"

"She has two. The Council fears she may go the way of the others." Dmitri straightened. "One is a buffoon."

"And the other?"

Dmitri allowed himself a moment to think. "I met him before he left. He is arrogant and believes he is clever. I have no worries."

For a moment Lucas let his eye narrow. "Don't

underestimate their strength. I've paid twice now for incompetence."

Dmitri clicked his heels together. "No, sir. What I mean is they are predictable. They are Guards. They are loyal to the Council."

Lucas considered those words. "We can use that loyalty when the time comes. Thank you, Dmitri. You are dismissed."

"It is late, sir. Do you need—"

"I said you are dismissed."

The man clicked his heels together, bowed again, and left the room.

Lucas returned to the window and stared out into the night. They were out there somewhere. The godmothers had stolen two of Merlin's Gifts from him and used them against him. He still had the third. The tapestry. He would recover the sphere and the staff and reunite the Gifts, proving to all Arcani that the Magic had chosen him for great things. He would lead them to their rightful position in the world.

Drawing his wand, he strode to a desk in the room, touched his wand to the lamp, and watched as the light illuminated an open manuscript. Ancient illustrations and diagrams shone at him from the open page. He ran his finger over the archaic text. Money had bought him this copy of the *Lagabóc,* Merlin's own words. Money could buy anything if you approached the right person. The copy had been easier to obtain than he had expected, and the translation from the Old English and Latin would simply cost more money. It didn't matter. What mattered was that he could soon read it and learn Merlin's secrets. Somewhere in the pages lay the specifics that turned the Gifts into a legendary weapon, and then he would use it to elevate the Arcani above the animals who shared blood but not power and magnificence. And when they looked for a leader, he would be ready.

This time, he would be unstoppable.

THIS TIME IT would work. A new day equaled new possibilities.

Stormy scrunched up her nose and looked at the pile of stuffed animals, her former playthings. Really, she had to update this room if she was going to stay, but they did make a safe, soft thing to practice on.

She pointed her wand at a small pink octopus, her favorite when she was a child. And she wouldn't think about what that said about her. "*Veni.*"

The toy wiggled its feet, then lurched into the air. It bobbed toward her as if swimming in a gentle current.

"Come on," she hissed out between clenched teeth. Her effort wrinkled her forehead.

The octopus inched closer, closer still, until it shot at her, followed by a purple teddy bear, a green and yellow duck, a red cat, and the rest of the pile of plush creatures. They hit her in the head, arms, chest, legs, hell, just about everywhere.

"Damn it." At least they were soft. She glanced down at the jumble of stuffed animals on the floor, their limbs flung helter skelter.

And then she started to cry.

Every attempt at magic seemed to end in tears. She didn't know why; it was silly really, but the tears slid down her cheeks and plopped onto the fuzzy pile scattered at her feet. She looked for the tissues she kept on her nightstand, but with her vision blurred, she couldn't see them, so she felt for them, knocking her alarm clock to the floor, which caused the tears to flow harder.

She wasn't incompetent—she had achieved so much on her own—but now she felt as inept as an elephant in a ballet studio.

Eventually she found the tissues. Placing her wand on the table, she blew her nose (twice) and sat on the edge of her bed.

As she sniffled, she heard three rapid taps on the door. She averted her face. "Come in."

The door opened. "Uh, Stormy?"

She glanced up to see the door ajar and Hunter's head peeking in. She swiveled her body so she didn't have to see him at all. "What do you want?"

"I heard, um, I thought maybe . . . are you okay?"

If she weren't so caught up in her own misery, she would have found his total discomfort with her tears amusing. "I'm not in danger. You can go now."

"But you're crying."

"Thanks for the update. You can go now." She grabbed another tissue.

The bed beside her rocked as he sat down. "Is there anything I can do?"

"You can go now."

He bent over and picked up the bear. "Why are there stuffed animals all over the floor?"

Which brought on fresh tears. "Because I can't do magic, all right?" She snatched the bear from him and threw it down.

He said nothing, just picked up the pink octopus. Then he spoke. "Sure you can."

Anger seeped into her self-pity. "Do you not see the animals all over my room?"

"Sure I do. But how did they get there?" His voice held a note of patience that riled her further.

She chanced a glance at him. He was looking at her, eyebrows raised in an expression of expectation. She clicked her tongue in disgust. "I know what you're saying, that I had to use magic to launch them all over the floor. But what good is that unless I want to start my own demolition company?"

He laughed. "What did you expect after two days? Perfection?"

"No, but making something come to me is supposed to be easy. I'm not supposed to get pummeled every time I try to summon something." She swiped her cheeks angrily. The tears were slowing now.

"Nobody is good the first time."

She put as much contention into her gaze as she could. "You said you were."

Nodding, he chuckled. "I was hoping you wouldn't remember that."

She glared at him, but the anger drained from her. "Why am I so bad?"

"You're not. You just need—"

"If you say 'practice,' I'll use this thing on you." She waved the wand at him.

He flinched in mock horror. "No. Anything but that."

She chuckled and then sighed. "I guess I just feel so alone, so overwhelmed, and I'm not used to that. My dads always supported me in anything I did, and now Dad seems more scared than anything else, and Daddy is acting all nonchalant so Dad won't worry more. I was raised by Arcani, but I wasn't raised Arcani. I don't know a lot about magic, and the other godmothers are criminals, so I'm on my own. And let's face it, Ian is such a . . . a . . ." She paused looking for a word.

"Twit, snob, ass licker?" Hunter looked almost eager.

"I was going to say 'sycophant,' but your words work too."

He shook his head. "Nobody says 'sycophant' anymore."

"They do if they are trying to watch their language."

"And they know what 'sycophant' means."

"If these were normal times, I'd be learning how to do magic with the other two godmothers. We could encourage one another, laugh at each other's mistakes."

"I'm willing to laugh at you, if you think it will help." He twirled the octopus so its legs spun out.

"Gee, thanks." But her mood had brightened.

Hunter stood, still grasping the octopus, and leaned against the wall beside the door. "Look, you're right. You are in this alone. Well, not entirely. Your parents are there for you, and you have Ian." He made a quick grimace that elicited another laugh from her. "But you're in an awkward situation. The godmothers have broken with the Council—"

"But why? They wouldn't do that unless they had a good reason. Seems to me the Council should look into their allegations."

"The last time a godmother went rogue was in the 1950s. Elenka Liska started a movement to overthrow the Council so the Arcani could rule the world, which is what they're accusing the godmothers of doing now." His voice was impassive.

"If you knew them like I do, you'd know they'd never hurt anyone." Unable to contain her nerves any longer, she jumped off the bed and started to pace. "Besides, they told me that's what this guy Lucas is doing."

"Who's Lucas?"

"That guy I met at the party. Lucas Reynard. Only he's going by the name Luc LeRoy." At the stunned look on his face, she stopped. "What?"

"Luc LeRoy. They told you he has another name? Lucas Reynard? You're sure that's the same guy?" His brow furrowed.

"Yes. I don't know much, but the aunts told me he

was trying to take over the world." She flipped her hands into the air. "I'm exaggerating, but they said he wanted the Arcani to rule the world and he was trying to implement some plan. Just like that Elenka woman."

"You don't know the story?"

"How would I? I wasn't raised Arcani. I went to Groundling schools." Trying to rein in her impatience, she placed her fists on her hips. "You want to fill me in?"

"Elenka Liska was based in Eastern Europe. After the Second World War, the communists took over. The condition in that part of the world went from terrifying to oppressive. Elenka decided she would use her godmother position to gather like-thinking Arcani and end our centuries of hiding. She'd had enough of Groundling domination and ineptitude. She believed the Arcani powerful enough to rule the world."

"Okay, I can see how living through all that could make you mad, but really, what was she thinking? Arcani aren't all-powerful. Even I know that. Daddy is often exhausted after a particularly hard sculpture he's worked on. Besides, Groundlings outnumber Arcani, what, thousands to one?"

"Basically."

"And can you imagine the clamor for magic if Groundlings knew?" She altered her voice. " 'I've run out of sugar. Can you zap me up a cup?' 'Mow my lawn for me.' 'I want a vacation. Put me on a beach somewhere.' 'Get me a Lamborghini.' 'Help me win the lottery.' 'My wife has cancer. Cure her.' The Arcani don't have that kind of power. We can't do all that and survive."

Hunter held up a hand before her arguments continued. "I know. Now, what do you know about Luc LeRoy?"

"Nothing. I only met the man last night. Why do people keep talking to me about him?"

"Who else has talked you about him?"

Oops. She wasn't supposed to have seen Hyacinth. "The aunts told me to find out about him. When I first got my wand." There. That wasn't a lie. Exactly. "Why? What do you know?"

"Nothing. That's what's so odd." Hunter fell silent. An emotionless expression fell over his face, but his grip tightened on the octopus.

"Hey, don't hurt Kitty."

"Kitty?" He looked startled.

"My octopus." She pointed at the animal.

"Kitty?"

"Yes. Oc-to-*pus*. Pussy. Kitty. It made sense to my eight-year-old brain. Give her to me before you rip her."

He started to hand it over, then pulled his arm back. "No."

Before she could say anything, he continued. "Summon her to you."

Disbelief flooded her. "Are you insane? You want me to point my wand at you? After what you've seen me do with it?"

He tilted his head. "Then you'd better be careful." He held the animal in front of him.

"You Guards really do have to be brave." She looked down at her wand, then shook her head. "Uh-uh. I can't do it."

"Yes, you can. You're using too much power. Don't think about it so much. Just feel it." He jiggled the octopus so that its legs fanned out.

She let out a loud breath, then gritted her teeth. Tension roosted in her forehead.

"Relax. Don't think so hard." His voice was soothing.

She forced her brow to uncrease. She focused on the octopus and raised her wand.

"Not so much. Easy." His voice flowed over her like a warm breeze.

She released another breath and closed her eyes. She imagined a heavy weight lifting off her, leaving her light and airy. Her breathing calmed, and she opened her eyes. "*Veni.*"

She felt the tingle as power surged up her arm into the wand, but she pictured it as a trickle of water, not a raging river. She continued to breath, in, out, easy, even. The wand joggled gently in her palm.

Hunter released his grip on the toy, but instead of falling to the floor, the octopus hovered in front of him and then began to float toward her. It flew across the room and landed in her hand.

"I did it," she whispered in awe.

He grinned. The dimple in his chin deepened.

"Woo-hoo, I did it!" She tossed the animal onto the bed and ran to him in celebration. Without thinking, she flung her arms around his neck and hugged him.

His arms closed around her.

Elation coursed through her veins. Silly, really. It was simple magic, but she had done it. She laughed in triumph. And looked up at his face. Right in front of her.

Suddenly the pressure of his embrace was all she could feel. The arms that held her were rock solid, warm, and, oh God, safe. Where did that thought come from?

She stepped back, and his arms released her immediately.

Heat crawled into her cheeks. Impossible. She had never been embarrassed by affection before. She couldn't remember the last time she had blushed. Over a hug? Knowing she blushed caused her to blush deeper. "Sorry. There's probably some rule against hugging."

"Not specifically, but I doubt the Council would approve. So we won't tell them." He looked amused. Amused! He probably thought she was some kind of freak.

"Great. Well, thank you for your help." She held out her hand to shake his. God! What was she doing now? She snatched her hand back to her side.

One corner of his mouth quirked up. He had every right to laugh at her. She was acting like an idiot. Since when had she ever reacted to a man this way? Not even in middle school had she felt this awkward. Must be the magic. She was definitely awkward with magic. It must spill over to the rest of her life.

"You just needed a little confidence. You're not alone in this. There are a lot of people who want to see you succeed."

"Like you?"

"Sure. Now you can practice." He turned to leave, then stopped. When he faced her, all hints of levity had left his expression. "If you hear anything else about this Luc, let me know."

"Why do you want to know?"

He hesitated. "I can't say for sure, but there's something about him. Just doing my job." He left the room.

Right. His job. And that job didn't include hugging her. He wasn't her type anyway. He was too big. Too uptight. His hair was too short, his manner too dutiful. He probably considered that dimple of his an imperfection.

Good thing, because she wasn't interested anyway. No matter how cute that dimple was.

* * *

TANK HAD DUTY that evening, not him, so why had he spent his free hours searching for the invisible? Hunter stared at the computer screen. If the search for info on Luc LeRoy had left him frustrated last night, the search for Lucas Reynard was maddening. There was no information on a Lucas Reynard.

Except one report Sophronia had filed after her kidnapping. In it she stated that the godmothers had woven a story about Elenka Liska's son, Lucas Reynard, and his bid to finish what his mother had started. It was the same story Stormy had related to him. Further research revealed that Elenka had indeed had a son, but the Council knew him under a different name.

His research troubled him. He'd expected the godmothers to maintain consistency in their story—they were smart enough—but that still didn't explain the lack of information about Luc LeRoy. The details hadn't dismissed his unease: Elenka did have a son, despite the inconsistency of the names, and Luc LeRoy had appeared from nowhere with boatloads of money and influence. And the godmothers had had a stellar reputation before his appearance.

Hold on. He couldn't let Stormy's emotional appeal influence facts. Just because the godmothers had never caused trouble before didn't mean they weren't capable of it now.

But a niggling dissatisfaction remained. He wasn't one to buy into conspiracy theories, but neither did he want to dismiss a true threat. He needed more info on the whole mess.

He pushed away from the computer. He wasn't going to find it online. From the start Luc LeRoy had set off a warning in his gut. When he thought back to the night of the gala, his stomach still cramped at the memory of Luc bending over Stormy's hand, of the shared champagne and laughter, of that servant of his. The guy was up to something.

On an impulse he typed Stormy's name into the computer. On the first Web site, a picture of her laughing, head tossed back, popped up. He could almost hear the sound, see her move. The same page showed some of her weavings. Beautiful, bright, vibrant, just like the artist herself. The next site showed a picture of her posing with some people at a gallery, and again her vivacity jumped off the screen. A list of other Web appearances, mostly local, followed, showing her, her work, reviews, and interviews. He hadn't realized the reputation she had started to garner. And now she was putting it aside to take on a job, a duty that was thrust upon her. Admiration for her welled in him and, as he looked at the latest image, something more.

An instant later, memories of Stormy crying at the side of her bed, her elation at summoning that ridiculous octopus, her exuberant hug, slid into his head. Throughout every emotion, her vitality shone. She wasn't one to fear life; she leapt into it. All aspects of it. And she had slipped beyond his sense of duty into his head.

That could be the real problem, not the alleged conspiracy he had just wasted hours on.

7

JUSTIN'S GUIDE FOR THE ARTIST

•

Change is the only constant in life. Embrace it.

STORMY PULLED INTO the driveway and laughed as Hunter unfolded himself from the car. "Don't drive much do you?" Hunter had been less than thrilled to go to the store, but after citing the dangers and not changing her mind, he had accompanied her without too much complaint. She probably shouldn't laugh at him now. Yes, she should. He needed to know she didn't find him intimidating. Yeah. Right. Thus the debacle with the hug.

"Don't need to. Usually I transport where I need to go. But when I do drive, it's in something bigger than a tin can." He pointed to her Mini Cooper.

Popping the back hatch, she gave him a fake glare. "Don't you dare make fun of Fred."

"Fred?"

"Fred Cooper. My car."

"You named your car?"

"Just grab the groceries." Arms full of canvas bags, Stormy turned toward the house. Grocery shopping done, and it was still early enough to get some time in her studio.

With a scowl on his lips, Justin came up to them. "That man is here, and he's looking for you." Justin's normally friendly voice was steely hard.

"Daddy?" Stormy said hesitantly.

"That idiot couldn't find you, so he came to my studio and pounded on the door. Not knocked, pounded. He wanted to know where you were and if I could take a message." Justin's hands balled into fists. "He's lucky my chisel didn't slip."

"Oh Daddy, I'm so sorry."

"It wasn't your fault, baby." His irritation appeared to melt away, although a tic in his left eye betrayed his mood.

Hunter, his arms likewise full of bags from the car, came up behind Stormy. "So Talbott is here?"

"I sent him into the house. Ken had an errand."

"I'm still sorry, Daddy." Stormy tiptoed and kissed her father's cheek. "I'll take care of him."

Justin nodded and walked back to his studio located on another section of the property.

Stormy eyed her studio. So much for a free afternoon. With a sigh, she headed toward the house.

Ian sat at the kitchen table, lips tightened into a thin line. Did that man always look as if he smelled rotting fish? She dumped the bags onto the counter.

"I have been waiting here for half an hour," Ian said. His nostrils flared in indignation. Really? She never realized people actually did that outside of movies.

Drawing upon some reserve ability, she gave him her most serious expression. "And a man of your importance has better things to do than to sit around." She took his hand.

"Yes, well, your . . ." Ian cleared his throat. "Your father said you were grocery shopping. I think it's time you realize your new position and avoid going into the Groundling world." His lip fairly curled at the word.

"We have to eat."

"You don't have to shop at their stores. We have Arcani stores. Then you can avoid contact with . . . them."

She didn't like what his words implied. "I thought as a fairy godmother, my job was to bridge the two worlds."

"Well, yes, but only part of your job is about the Groundlings." A strange eager light lit his eyes.

Something about the exchange bothered her. She wanted to glance at Hunter to see his expression, but didn't dare. She chose her next words carefully. "I still have much to learn. How lucky I have you to teach me."

Ian drew himself up. "Which brings me to the reason for my visit. I wish to take you to a dinner tomorrow night. I think you will find it interesting and educational."

"I look forward to it." She smiled.

"Excellent." Ian clapped his hands together. "I have a few errands to run. I shall return later for your magic lesson." He leaned in and adopted a joking tone. "Unless you have further shopping to do?" He chuckled at himself.

"No," Stormy said.

"Then I shall see you at three. Next time use an Arcani market." Ian nodded at Hunter, and then popped out of the kitchen.

As soon as Ian vanished, Stormy turned to Hunter. Whoa. He stood close, almost touching. The question she was about to ask vanished from her head. Glancing away, she took deep breaths to prevent blushing. This was stupid. Blushing? Again? Just because she couldn't forget the feel of his arms around her, didn't mean she needed to behave like a teenager. It was one hug, one simple hug. Why was she dwelling on it?

"Did he just say what I think he did?" Hunter asked, breaking into her rush of thoughts.

"Huh? Oh, you meant about godmothers and Groundlings?" Thank God he spoke. And he'd asked the very question she'd had. "Yeah, he did."

"Hmm."

" 'Hmm,' that's good, or 'hmm,' that's odd?"

"Definitely odd. Godmothers are supposed to maintain contact with Groundlings." Hunter frowned slightly.

"That's what I thought."

"I wonder what he's thinking." Hunter shrugged. "I guess you'll find out tomorrow on your date."

She held up a finger. "It is *not* a date."

"I don't know. You're going to dinner with him."

"He's taking me to *a* dinner, not *to* dinner."

"It's still dinner."

Her face heated as frustration bubbled. "Well, I *hugged* you. What does that mean?"

Had she really just said that? *Idiot. Stupid. He probably doesn't even remember.*

Before she could make a joke or mask the moment with a witty remark (though what witty remark escaped her), the air shimmered, and Tank popped into the kitchen.

" 'Well met by sunlight, Titania,' or should I say, 'Stormy'?" Tank swept into an exaggerated bow.

A distraction. Thank God. "I don't believe I've ever been misquoted Shakespeare before," Stormy said.

"Not misquoted, just improved for the present situation."

Hunter arched one eyebrow. "Improving Shakespeare? Your ego is enormous."

"Nothing about me is small." He waggled his eyebrows.

Stormy laughed. Her panic subdued.

Hunter said, "You just missed Ian."

"Then today must be my lucky day," Tank said. Then serious, "Time for you to go, Hunt. You need downtime."

Hunter nodded. "I'm going, and since I didn't get a chance to, you can help Stormy unpack."

"Unpack? Unpack what?"

"Groceries. See ya." Hunter shimmered and then popped out.

Tank frowned at the spot, then said, "What did he mean, 'groceries'?"

"You don't know what groceries are?"

Tank just sent her a look.

"I can explain it to you later." She grabbed the first bag and started unpacking, enjoying the camaraderie. "He's right, though. I do have to put them away. And then I'm working in the studio."

"Another exciting day in the life of a Guard." Tank pulled out a box of vanilla pudding and held it up. "This just about describes my life."

SHE STARED AT the loom. She'd been there for hours and had found every excuse not to work. The floor was clean, the yarn was sorted, and the beads were neatly separated in divided trays. There was nothing left for her to clean up or straighten or organize. And still the loom didn't beckon.

Her head was too full. Her world had changed, and she hadn't dealt with the consequences yet.

Something fluttered at the periphery of her vision. She looked up and saw Hyacinth.

"You shouldn't be here." Stormy's voice hissed as she whispered her concern.

"Sure I should. He didn't see me come in. Do you think you can get away for a while?" Hyacinth asked.

Not that she was against breaking rules when necessary, but she didn't usually set out to purposely flout them. Leaving was definitely against the rules. Still, she needed lessons only the godmothers could teach her. And she was curious. Stormy glanced at the door. Tank's silhouette threw a shadow on the glass. "I think so. He thinks I'm working."

"Then let's go, kid. You've got a couple of friends to meet," Hyacinth said.

Those words sent a flutter of nerves to her stomach. Hyacinth meant the two new godmothers. Stormy glanced down at the loom. Well, she certainly wasn't doing anything here. She stood. "I can't pop anywhere yet."

"Pop? Oh, transport," Hyacinth said. "Not to worry. I'll help you."

Stormy straightened her shoulders. "Okay. Show me the back door."

Hyacinth led her toward the rear of the studio. "Here, take my hand."

Stormy did so. With the next step, all light disappeared, and Stormy's lungs couldn't function. Before any panic could set in, however, the light reappeared, and Stormy stood in an alleyway. She drew in a deep breath and shook off a final feeling of confusion. "Where are we?"

"Del Mar. This is the back of the Star Bright Bakery. It's Reggie's."

Right. Reggie. One of the new godmothers. Stormy looked up at the two-story building in front of her.

Hyacinth pulled open the back door. "Come on. They're waiting."

Stormy stepped through to a brightly lit seating area. Gathered at a table were four women.

"I got her," Hyacinth said.

Four pairs of eyes focused on her. She recognized two of them. The other two had to belong to the new godmothers. Stormy examined the two women.

Lily rose from her spot. "Stormy, I'd like you to meet Kristin Montgomery and Reggie Scott."

The woman with beautiful auburn hair waved at the first name. Kristin Montgomery had what looked like an iPad in front of her, but used her wand to take notes on it. Stormy hadn't realized there was an app for that. Reggie nodded at her name, sending the curls spiraling from her crown bouncing.

The room was silent. Not that Stormy could blame them. They didn't know her either. There was a possibility she would turn them in. This tense circumstance wasn't exactly how she pictured meeting the other two godmothers. Maybe some coffee, something to nosh on. She'd expected a little awkwardness, but not AWKWARDNESS. Still, if the clumsy smiles and nervous glances were any indication, genuine warmth and caring lurked beneath the apprehension.

"Hi, I'm Stormy." She held up her hands. "And I've been a fairy godmother for three days."

A chuckle rippled through the small group.

"Not at all what you expected, is it?" Lily said.

"I never expected anything. I was a Groundling and never even heard of the Time of Transition." Stormy shrugged.

"Welcome to the club," Kristin said. "I'm a Rare One."

"What's a Rare One?" Stormy asked.

"An Arcani born to Groundlings. I didn't even know there was magic two months ago." Kristin shook her head.

"This is all very charming," Hyacinth said, "but we can't stay here. They could be watching us right now."

"You're right, of course," Lily said. "Shall we walk, ladies?"

"Walk?" Stormy said.

"It's harder to trace someone if they're moving." Reggie said. "Tommy and Joy will stay here in case the Guards follow you."

"They will. If they're competent, and I bet they are, they'll find the portal." Hyacinth voice held a note of resignation.

"In that case, you'll probably want to leave a note, dear," Rose said. "We wouldn't want your Guards to worry."

"Yes we would," Hyacinth said. "Serves them right."

As she wrote, Stormy realized what life on the run meant. These women were fugitives and had to take all sorts of precautions Stormy had never really considered. What could be so important that they had to risk meeting her now?

"Let's go." Lily hustled them out the door and onto the streets of Del Mar.

HUNTER GRABBED A clean shirt from his dresser and tossed the towel into the hamper. A hot shower made all the difference. He shook the last few drops from his hair. Now some food and he'd be ready to go back on duty.

This job was proving harder than he expected. A real danger existed when a job was too easy. Guards became complacent, lost their edge. Tank was already complaining about that. Okay, the previous godmothers had gone rogue, but it didn't take two of the top Guards to protect one small woman.

He snorted. *Small* was the wrong word to describe Stormy. That *small* woman created a hurricane whenever she tried magic. Except that once.

Wipe that ridiculous smile off your face, Hunter.

Nevertheless watching Stormy and keeping her safe was easy, and that was exactly what made it hard. Not exactly hard. Stormy constantly surprised him and, he had to admit, entertained him. He paused. When had the assignment gone from an annoyance to something he looked forward to?

Which created a second problem. He was getting too close to her. Their assignment held no challenges, but the lady herself was proving to be a huge one.

She made an interesting character study. Her ability to fool Sophronia Petros, to handle Ian, and to charm Luc LeRoy proved she was more of a chameleon than her demeanor indicated.

At that thought, all hints of boredom fled. Luc was an enigma, and enigmas could be dangerous in his profession. Stormy was the asset, his responsibility. She deserved to be safe from the godmothers, from this Luc, hell, from Ian, if it came down to it. She was savvy, but she was out of her league here. Despite her acting skills, she was naive. She could be surprised too easily. Witness her exuberance when he had shown her how to control her magic. He could still feel her in his arms if he tried. He could sense her warmth, her smell . . .

Enough. Feelings interfered with the job.

He pulled the black T-shirt that was part of the Guard uniform over his head. As soon as the wand and sword insignia on the sleeve hit the skin, it signaled. Tank needed him.

He grabbed his wand from his pocket and transported. He reappeared on the grass outside the studio. He found Tank and Ian waiting for him.

"Where were you?" Ian's superior tone left no doubt of his anger.

Hunter ignored him. "What's happened?"

"She's gone." No trace of Tank's casual air remained in his face. A lethal fire glowed in his eyes. The predator was in its place.

The change was instantaneous. Training honed into instinct took control of Hunter's head. A cold, logical commitment to their asset. He would find her. Cool determination flowed through Hunter's veins.

And something else. To his annoyance and surprise, a small hint of fear tainted his response. Fear for Stormy.

His reaction worried him. He had no time for wayward emotions. They distracted from the job. He ignored his thoughts and concentrated on the issue. "How?"

"If we knew how, we wouldn't be wasting time here with you," Ian said.

"Let us do our job." Hunter faced Tank.

Ian forced himself between them. "If you had done your job, she wouldn't be missing. I'm taking over." With a note of triumph, Ian lifted his chin in an attempt to strike an arrogant pose.

The putz was determined to hinder the search. Exchanging a knowing glance with Tank, Hunter nodded. "Fine. What do we do first?"

Ian floundered for a moment. "What?"

"You're in charge. What do we do first?" Hunter aimed his gaze at the shorter man.

"I . . . uh, well, I think she isn't here, right?"

"Brilliant, Sherlock." Tank stepped around him. "The shielding spell is still intact."

"Right. And there's no back door to the studio . . ." Hunter's voice trailed off just as Tank's head snapped up. "A back door."

They bolted into the studio and started their search.

Ian followed. "What are you looking for?"

"A back door," Hunter said without looking at him.

Ian glanced at the back wall. "There is no back door. Only the one—"

"Not a real one." Tank's hissed words revealed his barely controlled patience. "If you want to play with us, catch up."

"Play? I'm not—"

"Would you shut up and let us work?" Hunter shoved Ian to the side and touched the loom with his wand. Not here.

Red faced, Ian adjusted his coat. "Now see here—"

Tank whirled on him. "No, you see here. You're in the fucking way. Move."

Ian opened and closed his mouth like a carp. Hunter paid him no more heed. He reached out with his senses. Magic left a footprint. It always did. Where was the mark? It wouldn't be near the door—too close, too easy to detect there, so in the back . . .

He turned toward the back wall. Making sure his path was clear, he closed his eyes and stepped forward. Another step, and another. And found the evidence. "Got it."

Tank joined him immediately, closed his eyes, and nodded. They moved together toward the source. The footprint was stronger as they moved forward. Whoever made this back door had a sophisticated grasp of magic. Not everyone had the skills to cast this spell. It would require someone like a Guard or a godmother.

"Damn it. How stupid can we be?" Tank said, and

Hunter knew Tank had reached the same conclusion as he had.

"It's logical they put one in. They needed to talk to her." Anger at himself warred with fury at the women who had led Stormy—no, damn it, the asset—from them.

"Did you find her?" Ian asked, somewhat subdued.

"Not yet, but it won't be long now." Tank looked at Hunter.

"Now see here." Ian stepped in front of them. I think I should—"

"Stop trying to play hero and get out of our way," Hunter said. He pointed his wand at Ian.

Ian gulped and scampered to the side.

Tank swept the area. "There." His wand pointed to a spot in midair.

Hunter joined him. "If you want to make yourself useful, stay here in case she comes back."

Hunter didn't wait for Ian's response. He pulled a thin flask from one pocket and a sprig of sage from the other. He drizzled a few drops from the contents of the flask onto the plant, then held it to the tip of Tank's wand. Tank's wand glowed red for an instant, then flashed so white Hunter averted his gaze. When he turned back, the sage was smoking in thick curls of blue. The tendrils drifted lazily, then seemingly disappeared into nothingness in front of them. The back door.

"Ready?" Tank asked.

Hunter nodded.

"But how do you know where she went?" Ian asked before they could go through the portal.

"A door only opens onto one place," Hunter said and stepped through.

His vision went black. The familiar whooshing sensation of traveling through a portal gripped him and carried him through space. In less time than it took to take a breath, he finished his stride and landed behind a bakery. Tank landed beside him.

He hadn't expected to find Stormy standing at the other end. This was just the start of the search. He took in the surroundings. The smell of the sea was stronger here, and the fake English cottage facade of the buildings in the business district made identification easy. That and the bakery.

"Del Mar." Hunter cocked his head toward the bakery. "That was Regina Scott's place."

"Try there first," Tank said.

Hunter strode to the door and tested it. It was locked. He tapped the knob with his wand and heard the lock click open. No shields here.

He opened the door. A stairway led to the upper floor, and a door led, he assumed, to the bakery. He checked his watch. Nearly 4 P.M. The Star Bright Bakery closed at three. Knowing customers would be gone, he chose the door. He pointed to the upper floor. Tank nodded and took the stairs.

Hunter's heart pounded. If Stormy was in danger . . .

Where had his objectivity gone? He was on a mission, and he shouldn't be anxious to see her or worried about her.

Wand at the ready, he pushed the door open. The bakery was spotless, but not empty. Two people sat at one of the booths. They turned when they heard him. The young man had the soft, rounded features and bright eyes of Down syndrome. The woman had almond-shaped eyes and childlike features. She looked solemn, but interested. Hunter lowered his wand.

"You must be Hunter." The young man smiled at him.

The woman tugged on the man's shirt. "He could be Tank."

The man nodded. "You're right." He turned to Hunter. "Are you Hunter or Tank?"

He tried to relax his features. "I'm Hunter. And you are?"

"I'm Tommy." Tommy held out his hand. Hunter shook it. "And this is Joy. Reggie and Aunt Lily told us you'd be coming."

How did they know he was coming?

"It was Stormy who told us the names." Joy pursed her lips at Tommy.

Hunter didn't know how to react. "Stormy was here?"

Tommy nodded. "Yep. She's the next godmother, you know, just like Reggie. The bakery is closed, but Stormy said we could give you some coffee. We made it fresh." Tommy crossed to the coffeemaker and poured a cup. "She said you'd be mad, but not to worry because . . ."

Joy slipped a sheet of paper from her pocket. She handed the note to Hunter.

He opened the folded sheet. Hell, Stormy's writing even looked like an artist's.

Dear Tank and Hunter,

I know you're looking for me, but I'm safe. Sit down, have a cup of coffee. I promise I'll be back in a few minutes, and I'll return home peacefully. Try not to be too angry.

Stormy

Tommy's forehead wrinkled in concern. "You look mad."

"I am, but not with you." Hunter managed a smile.

Joy eyed Tommy with a look that clearly sent a message.

"Yes, go get it. Reggie said to treat them like guests," Tommy said with a hint of impatience.

Joy went to the counter and returned with a tray of pastries, breads, and cake slices. She placed these on the table. Then she looked at Tommy again.

Tommy sighed. "Okay, I'll tell him. Reggie said you should help yourself. They'll be back soon. You can wait for them here." He leaned closer to Hunter. "Joy is shy sometimes, especially with strangers, but she's a really good baker."

Joy smiled and then dropped her gaze.

Hunter looked at Tommy's friendly and open face and then at the food on the table. "Thank you for all this, but I really have to find Stormy—"

From the stairwell came a roar. "What do ye mean your partner is downstairs already? If he's done anything to Tommy or Joy . . ."

The door burst open, and a one-armed gnome with long silver hair and a matching beard charged into the room. Hunter's brows arched. The one-armed man didn't reach higher than his hips. Tank followed the gnome, rubbing his stomach.

"Step away from them, ye cur," the gnome snarled in a thick Scottish accent. "They're innocents. How dare ye come in here and—"

"That's Alfred," Tommy said, his smile never disappearing. "He likes to grumble."

The gnome glared at Hunter, and then turned to Joy. The gnome's face transformed. A caring, loving expression replaced the harsh lines of just moments ago. He reached up and stroked her cheek. "Are ye okay, my pretty one?"

Joy nodded. "I brought out the food just like Reggie said."

"Ye're such a dependable girl." The gnome gave her a wink and a thumbs-up, then started muttering again when he turned away. "I don't care if she is a godmother, I will give that girl such a talking to—"

Hunter interrupted. "Uh, Alf? Tell us where Stormy is, and we'll leave—"

The gnome held up a finger. "Alfred. Only me friends can call me Alf, and ye're definitely no' me friends." A second finger. "Ye have no business storming in here and terrorizing innocent folk." A third finger joined the first two. "If ye've scared Tommy or Joy, ye'll answer to me. Dinnae think I can't protect them. Just ask your boy-o there." He jerked his thumb toward Tank.

Tank shook his head. "He punched me in the stomach and hasn't shut up since I found him in one of the apartments upstairs."

"Darn right, I haven't stopped. Ye think ye can bust in here and frighten innocent—"

Hunter had to stop the verbal deluge somehow. "Tommy, are you frightened?"

Tommy shook his head. "Alf likes to worry."

"Och, Tommy, ye're a brave one." Once again the transformation of Alfred's face was almost magical. His voice was mellow and approving. Then he faced Hunter again, and the scowl returned. "Ye'd best respect them."

Shock jolted through him. "I wouldn't dream of doing anything else."

But the gnome was not appeased. "I know yer kind. The Guards, the Council." He nearly spat the last word. "We've dealt with yer kind before."

What had they experienced? He knew the Guard had been summoned to this bakery several times before Regina Scott had gone rogue, but what had they done? He exchanged a look with Tank, who appeared as perplexed as Hunter felt. "I don't know what's happened in the past, but we don't operate that way."

"Harrumph." Alfred's noise expressed his doubt.

Tank said, "Look, if you tell us where Stormy is, we'll leave."

Alfred lifted a finger again. "We dinnae know where she is. They brought her here then left." A second finger rose. "They told us to keep ye here because they were bringing her back when they finished." The third finger came up. "And finally, it isn't our place to help ye."

Hunter didn't know whether to laugh or yell. He chose neither.

"Och, ye may as well sit down and enjoy Joy's creations. Ye'll not have tasted the like before."

Hunter didn't like it, but short of browbeating the two bakers, which he wouldn't do, he had little choice. Of course, he could enjoy browbeating the gnome. In tacit agreement, he and Tank took seats at the café table.

"Finally ye're being sensible." Alfred nodded. "Tommy, I wouldn't mind a cup o' yer fine coffee meself."

THE TREE-LINED streets of Del Mar were cool as they always were this close to the ocean. Blue sky sparkled above Stormy's head, and in front of her diamonds glinted off the sea. No one watched them, this group of three elderly women and three young ones. As on most Southern California streets, pedestrians barely dotted the concrete, and those tourists and locals who occupied the sidewalks were too busy glancing into the high-end boutiques and lively eateries. Good thing too, because if their conversation would have been overheard, eyebrows would have risen. Or maybe not.

Talk of frustrations, hard work, and being misunderstood really weren't so different in any culture. Except the godmothers also threw in a few words about spells, wands, and magic.

"The thing is, I can understand what Lucas is saying," Kristin said. "There is an attraction to declaring Arcani freedom."

"Couched in those terms, he makes his ideas sound noble," Lily said.

" 'Freedom' is one of those words tossed around as if everyone understood its meaning, but they don't." Reggie frowned. "He makes Arcani secrecy sound shameful."

Stormy understood the issue of secrecy. Her fathers explained while she was still very young that none of her school friends could know about their magic powers. They weren't ashamed of being Arcani, but tolerance wasn't something Groundlings were known for. Not just Groundlings. Plenty of Arcani were intolerant as well. Being different bred hatred and fear.

"His supporters seem to think he's right. That hiding is somehow wrong. That it's time for the Arcani to take their rightful place in the world."

"His supporters never heard him offer to make me queen in the new order." Kristin chuffed out a breath of air.

A jolt of shock lashed through Stormy. This was the first she'd heard of Lucas wanting to start some sort of monarchy.

"I still don't understand why people don't see that Lucas is leading them toward a path of conflict and dictatorship," Hyacinth said.

"Because he's clever," Reggie said. "When I heard him, he never said anything overt. He introduced a topic and let others say what was on their minds."

"Manipulative," Hyacinth said.

"Meanwhile we're hunted ones." Rose sighed. "Really, the unfairness of it all."

"Grousing is getting us nowhere," Hyacinth said. "Stormy has to know about tomorrow."

Stormy blinked. "Tomorrow?"

Lily took her hand and patted it. "Stormy, dear, I know we told you we'd give you time, but the perfect opportunity has come up, and we need your help."

"My parents are throwing a dinner party tomorrow night, and you're invited," Reggie said.

"Me?" Surprise sobered her for a moment. "Why?"

"They've invited Lucas as well. We need to know what he's doing," Reggie said.

"No, I can't. Ian's taking me to some dinner." Stormy didn't want to disappoint them; she wanted to help. Heck, *she* wanted to know more about Lucas Reynard. Even Hunter seemed interested.

"Wait. Ian? Ian Talbott?" Reggie asked.

"Yes. He's my arbiter." Stormy looked at Reggie and remembered what Hunter had told him about Ian. "Oooh. That's right. He was supposed to be your brother-in-law."

"You poor thing. I feel sorry for you," Reggie said. "He's a real jerk."

She felt a kinship with Reggie. "So I've noticed. Although with me he's mostly pompous."

"Then he hasn't changed," Reggie said.

"Even Hunter and Tank don't like him," Stormy said.

"Who are Hunter and Tank?" Kristin asked. She had missed Reggie's instructions to Tommy and Joy.

"My baby-sitters." Stormy rubbed her forehead. "The Guards assigned to me."

"Oooo, you must be someone important. Like a godmother." A hint of a smile teased at Kristin's lips.

Reggie said, "Ian's not a problem. My parents invited him. That must be the dinner he's taking you to."

"Why would your parents invite Ian?" Stormy asked.

"They're proving to the world that they don't blame Ian for their daughters' indiscretion. It's brilliant actually." Reggie shook her head. "My mother is getting scary."

"Then we ruined the back door for nothing." Lily seemed displeased. A small frown curved her lips.

"What do you mean?" Stormy asked.

Lily said, "We used it to bring you here. The Guard will find it and dismantle it."

From the corner of her eye, Stormy saw a golden glint. She turned her head to see what had flashed into her vision and saw a mother leading her two kids toward the beach. Mom carried a cooler and a bag overflowing with towels and sand toys. The little girl wore a blue princess cover-up with flower flip-flops, and the boy wore bathing trunks with a Spider-Man towel tied around his neck.

Then she noticed that all the godmothers' heads were turned.

"Aww, how sweet," Rose said.

What was sweet?

"That's the worst part of this whole fiasco." Lily gazed after the children. "We just aren't around children anymore."

"I haven't granted a wish in two weeks." Reggie's shoulders slumped.

Stormy held up her hand. "Wait. You all saw something, right?"

They all stared at her.

"You've never seen a wish, have you?" Kristin said.

"How do you see a wish?"

"Watch the children." Lily pointed her back toward the family.

And a moment later she saw it. A golden crown floating over the little girl's head. Her head whipped back to the women. "You all see that?"

"Yes, dear. Those are wishes." Rose beamed at her.

Stormy looked back at the girl, but the crown had disappeared. "Now what?"

"Now what, what?" asked Reggie.

"Well, what was her wish?" Stormy pointed at the girl.

"You have to listen," Kristin said with a smile.

Stormy gave her a dubious look. "How am I supposed to listen from here? And it's not like she said anything."

"Just listen. Trust us." Reggie turned her toward the child.

The small family group had continued down the street, but the ladies had kept pace. A moment later a crown appeared over the little boy's head.

"I wish I catch a whale." He shook the small plastic bucket as he thought it.

Stormy's mouth dropped. "I heard that." Excitement bubbled though her. "I heard that."

"Of course you did. That's your job," Lily said.

"Well, it would be if we didn't have Lucas to deal with first," muttered Hyacinth.

"Don't spoil it for her," Rose chided.

Stormy didn't care. "Okay, so I heard his wish. But what happens next? It's not like you can use magic to let him catch a whale."

They had reached the coast. Seagrove Park overlooked the ocean. The family made its way to the incline that led to the water.

"Of course we can't give him a whale. That would be impractical," Lily said. "So we change it slightly." Shielding herself behind Rose and Hyacinth, Lily took out her wand, swished it, and said, "*Cetum voco.*"

That sounded like Latin. Stormy waited, although she didn't know what for. And then it happened. Like a ripple through the people walking along the paths in the park and playing on the sand by the water, voices began to cry out. People stopped whatever they were doing, pointed out to sea, and shouted.

Stormy followed their gazes. Just off the coast, swimming placidly close to the beach, was a minke whale. Nearby a pod of dolphins surfed in the waves.

"Mommy, look!" The boy yanked on his mother's arm and pointed.

The moment was sublime. Not only was the child excited, but the entire beach watched in awe as the magnificent creature all but paraded itself for viewing. The dolphins added comic relief with their antics.

A few minutes later the whale disappeared and the dolphins moved on, but the beach was still buzzing with animated voices, laughter, and eager shouts.

"That was amazing," Stormy said.

Seagrove Park had a playground. Stormy looked at the children playing and spotted more crowns. She concentrated.

"I wish my sister would stop bugging me."

"I wish we could see sharks next."

"I wish I could go to Disneyland instead of Grandma's."

Stormy smiled at the childish requests.

"I wish Daddy didn't drink so much."

Her breath caught in her throat. She turned to the others.

Lily nodded. "Not all wishes are happy."

Rose eyed the children with an expression of fondness and sorrow. "We can't grant all wishes, and some shouldn't be granted."

"I am not calling sharks to the beach," Hyacinth said.

They all laughed at that.

"But we try our best to help," Lily said.

Kristin hid behind Reggie and lifted her wand slightly. "She needs a friend."

The child whose wish had broken Stormy's heart a little walked toward her mother. The woman looked tired and worn. She carried a couple of shopping bags. Suddenly, a hank of doll's hair stuck out from the top of one of the bags.

"She'll find it when they get home and think someone placed it there by accident or that the store made a mistake," Kristin said. "A doll won't solve anything, but the girl has someone to talk to now."

Everything in Stormy cried out to grant a wish, but she didn't dare. She'd try to give a kid an ice-cream cone and cause a blizzard in August. In San Diego.

"As lovely as this has been, we have other worries right now. We can assume the back door is gone. How can we communicate with you?" Lily asked.

"Bubbles are too slow and unreliable." Hyacinth added her frown to Lily's.

"And we can't use cell phones. They can trace us through them." Rose wrinkled her brow, but couldn't quite frown."

"What about Twitter?" Stormy said.

Reggie and Kristin looked at her, then each other and smiled. Kristin nodded. "That would work."

"As long as we don't turn on the location app," Stormy said.

Kristin was beginning to sound excited. "They already know we're in San Diego."

"I like it," Reggie said. "We could set up decoy accounts."

Rose reached across and patted Stormy's hand. "Aren't you clever to think of the idea?"

Stormy shrugged. "I used to live on my computer." She twisted her mouth to the side.

Kristin chuckled. "It's pretty amazing how quickly you can lose touch with the Groundling world. Which is why I think the Council won't think of it."

Finding an empty bench, the aunts sat down, and Stormy and Reggie formed a screen. Kristin summoned her iPad. For the next hour, they set up accounts for themselves, after giving lengthy explanations to the aunts.

"Can we really get away with this?" asked Lily.

"We can if we're careful," Kristin said.

"Right. And since we're using aliases, we should be able to arrange meetings and communicate. Not with a code exactly, but with cleverness," Reggie said. "It's not foolproof, but it should work."

"Only use it when absolutely necessary," Lily said.

"No kidding," Hyacinth said. "And speaking of when absolutely necessary, don't you think it's time we returned Stormy?"

Kristin glanced at the top of her display, and Lily looked at her watch. They both gasped.

"Oh, we should have gotten you back already." Kristin shut the iPad and tapped it with her wand. It vanished.

"I'll take her back," Reggie said. "I want to see Tommy and Joy."

"Good idea, dear." Rose stood. "Send them my love."

Hyacinth waved. "Take care, Stormy."

Lily blew her a kiss.

Kristin hugged her. "See you later, Stormy. Be careful, okay? Try not to believe everything you're going to hear tomorrow."

"I won't," Stormy said.

Reggie led her to a hidden corner. "Ready?" Reggie held out her hand.

Stormy clasped it, and a moment later blackness obscured her vision, and the air squeezed out of her lungs. Before she needed to draw her next breath, they appeared behind the bakery.

Reggie released her hand and drew several audible gulps of air. She had closed her eyes. "I still hate traveling that way. I get so dizzy." She shook herself. "You'll have to go in by yourself. The Guards are still there."

"How do you know?" Stormy asked.

Reggie pointed to a square light above the door. It was glowing red. "That's Alfred's sign to me that the coast isn't clear. When it's safe, it's green. That's how I visit Tommy and Joy."

"Makes sense." Stormy wasn't sure if she could ever think in terms of such secrecy and stealth. She supposed she had better start if she didn't want the godmothers caught.

Reggie scrutinized her for a moment. "I wish we could just get to know each other without all this craziness."

"Me too." She didn't know Reggie or Kristin at all well, but had felt an immediate comfort with them. "I . . ." But she didn't know what to say.

"I know. It's awkward and forced, but it feels right too. Take care." Reggie smiled. "Now go."

Stormy passed through the door alone and entered

the bakery. At once all five gazes shot to her. Tommy, Joy, and Alfred smiled, and Hunter and Tank jumped to their feet.

She waved. "Hi, guys. I'm back."

8

JUSTIN'S GUIDE FOR THE ARTIST

•

A misstep is just an opportunity to learn.

STORMY SAT IN the kitchen, hands folded on her lap, gaze toward the floor, as Ian stomped up and down the tile floor. She thought it best to present a picture of contrition, even if she didn't feel it.

". . . irresponsible, incompetent . . ."

She tuned out again, which wasn't easy considering how loud Ian was.

Hunter and Tank stood at attention beside the wall. Her fathers flanked her at the kitchen table. They were having difficulty keeping straight faces, which wasn't helping her maintain composure. Ian's voice once again broke into her thoughts.

". . . let her out of your sight." Ian snorted. "You, Merrick, at least tracked her down, but Mr. Bryant here allowed her to slip away in the first place. The Council has relieved him of duty effective immediately."

Tank growled. "That's a load of—"

Ian raised his hand. "Take it up with your commander. The Council no longer needs your services."

Fired? Tank was fired because of her? "Tank shouldn't be punished for what I did. He didn't do anything," she said.

Ian pointed his finger at her. "Exactly. He didn't do anything. If he had, you wouldn't have been able to escape."

Escape? So now she was a prisoner? "I came back."

Ian sniffed. "Irrelevant. He's been relieved of duty."

Tank glared at him. "This is a two-man job. Who's my replacement? Hunter can't stay awake twenty-four/seven. Someone needs to spell him."

"We won't be needing him twenty-four/seven. Stormy's moving to the Council Hall."

Stormy's surprise was mirrored in her parents' reaction. They dropped all signs of amusement. "What do you mean she's moving?" Justin boomed.

"Exactly that. The Council feels the only way to protect Stormy is to keep her near. The rogue godmothers cannot be trusted. They will try to influence her and lead her astray."

Lead her astray? Who spoke this way?

"So the Council is setting up rooms for Stormy in the Council Hall. Hunter will only be needed on occasion. Like for the dinner tomorrow night." Ian gave a dismissive wave of his hand.

"You can't make her move. She has rights," Ken said. He grabbed her hand. "Honey, you don't have to go."

"Of course she doesn't, but the Council would view her lack of cooperation as suspicious," Ian said, glaring at Ken.

"This is her home," Justin said, his voice even louder.

"Don't I have a say in any of this?" Stormy said.

The men fell silent. Stormy couldn't help feeling a hint of amusement.

"Of course you do, baby," Ken said, patting her hand.

She faced Ian. "First, you can't fire Tank over this. I sneaked away. I tricked him. He shouldn't have to pay for my actions. It was my fault."

Tank shook his head. "It's not your fault. I screwed up. I should have watched you better. Besides, I'm not fired, just taken off this assignment." But there was a hint of tightness around his eyes, and he never smiled.

"That's the Council's decision, not yours." Ian pursed his lips, but she saw triumph flash in his eyes.

She tried to catch Tank's gaze to convey an apology, but he stared straight ahead without showing any emotion on his face. She felt awful. Letting her shoulders droop, she sighed. "Second, I'll move to the Council Hall."

That announcement brought all five gazes to her face.

"But this is your home," Ken said. He looked like a lost puppy.

"And it always will be, Dad, but we all knew living here was temporary until I found another place."

"I just thought, since you haven't been making a huge effort . . ." Ken drew his mouth into a pout. Justin placed his hand on Ken's shoulder.

"You were hoping I'd stay." She kissed his forehead. "I love you, Dad, but I can't live here forever."

"Why not?" Ken asked with a little laugh. "You're still my little girl."

"It sounds like she's made her decision." Justin winked at her. "You always were a heartbreaker."

Ian clapped his hands together. "Excellent. Then let's get you packed and moved. Merrick, you can help."

Hunter's gaze narrowed a fraction. "Do I look like a moving company?"

"Well, you don't expect me to do it." Ian stared down his nose at Hunter. Actually he stared up his nose, because he had to tilt his head back to glare at him.

"I can do it myself, guys," Stormy said. She pushed back from the table and fled the room. Maybe the guilt she felt would stay in the kitchen.

She knew her announcement had caused surprise and, from her dads, some sadness, but she had made the right decision. She needed to find out more about Lucas and decide which side she backed. No, in her heart she already knew her sympathies lay with the godmothers. And how better to help them than be close to the source of their trouble? The Council Hall surely held answers. Maybe she could find evidence to clear the aunts. The ultimatum Ian had delivered proved the Council's high-handedness. She wondered what the Council had done in the past to Kristin and Reggie?

As she grabbed a suitcase from the closet and unzipped it, Hunter walked in.

"What, no knock?" she said, turning to the dresser.

"Don't push it." Hunter opened the closet.

"Hey." She dropped the armful of clothes she had picked up back into the drawer. "I thought you weren't helping me move."

He faced her. "I said don't push it." He looked into the closet. "To hell with it." He pulled out his wand. "*Convenite.*"

The contents of her closet flew out and landed, neatly folded, in the suitcase.

"What if I didn't want all of those?" she asked, irritated.

"Take them anyway." His voice was cold and flat.

She placed her hands on her hips. "What is wrong with you?"

He barely twisted his head to look at her. "You have no idea what you've done, do you? Tank had a faultless record until your little game cost him his reputation."

"Game? I'm sorry, but—"

"You're sorry? Really? That's all you've got?" He faced her then and gave her a look that caused her to recoil. "It's one thing if he had really screwed up, but you did this to him. He, hell, *we* weren't expecting you to pull something this stupid. Didn't you understand that we were protecting you from attack? But you decided you're too important to listen."

"That's entirely unfair." Bile swirled in her stomach until it collected in a burning ball.

"No, what's unfair is that he has to suffer the consequences of your selfishness and recklessness." Hunter turned from her as if he couldn't bear to look at her any longer.

"If that's how you feel, maybe you should quit."

"I can't quit. I'm still under orders. And I follow orders." He looked at her as if she were trash.

She sucked in her breath at the pain. She had thought . . . She had hoped . . . No, she had just been stupid. "Well, maybe if you did more than follow orders, you might understand that I'm doing what I have to do." She picked up a T-shirt and threw it at him.

He whirled around and caught the T-shirt before it hit him. "Oh, you have a noble purpose?"

"I don't know. I may have. But I don't know. This whole situation is new to me. I'm acting blind here."

"So you trust them more than the Council?"

"What has the Council done to prove they're trustworthy? They're locking me up, aren't they?"

"They're protecting you from the godmothers."

"You can't be that dense. You can't actually believe the godmothers have turned their backs on me or the Arcani." Why did anger have to appear as tears? She swiped her cheeks.

"You have proof otherwise?"

"No, but some things you take on faith."

They stared at each other.

Hunter spoke first. "I took a pledge to protect and uphold the laws of the Council. I took the Oath of Allegiance."

"And I have no desire to overturn the Council," she said. "But what if the Council is wrong?"

He didn't answer.

Her anger drained from her. She felt empty, sad, and scared. She was alone. "Did it ever occur to you that I have things to learn, things I can only learn from the godmothers? Would you have willingly accompanied me to see them?"

"No." His voice was sure, but quiet.

"Then I had to sneak away."

"You'll do it again, won't you?" His gaze trapped hers.

She could lie, but there was no point. They would both know she was lying. "Yes."

He didn't move or speak.

"Would it help if I promise to do it when you're not on duty?"

He let out a mirthless chuckle laced with derision. "No."

They were at an impasse she knew couldn't be broken. She picked up a shirt from the drawer and folded it. "I'll need another suitcase." She knelt down and reached under her bed.

"You should use magic."

"Right, and have everything explode around me.

No, thanks." She pulled the suitcase out and tossed it onto the bed.

"You'll never learn control without practice."

"I know." She sighed. "But now is not the time. Ian is waiting."

"I'll leave you to this then." He gave a mocking bow. "Do you need me to do anything else?"

Oooo, that made her burn. "Yes. Fetch my computer from the studio." She'd need it anyway to keep in touch with the godmothers, but the regal tone was childish.

"As you wish." He paused in the doorway and drew his hand down his face. He inhaled deeply and exhaled loudly. "Look, I'm sorry I lost my temper with you. It wasn't professional."

His words made her sad. Of course all he cared about was his professional demeanor. But she would accept the apology. "And I am sorry about Tank. Whether you believe it or not, I didn't want to hurt either of you."

"That's what happens when you let emotions in." Then a sly glint appeared in his eyes. "But thanks for the warning about your plans. You won't find it as easy to get away from me." He left without another glance at her.

Yeah, she figured she had made a mistake there.

"WELL, WHAT DO you think?" Ian indicated her quarters with a sweep of his arm.

The rooms at the Council Hall were huge, if a little sterile. Too bad her looms weren't exactly portable. There was plenty of room here. As Stormy walked around taking it all in, her footsteps echoed on the marble floor. The walls likewise were marble and, although not a Parian white, light enough to make her wish for a few cans of paint and brushes. She almost wished she could re-create the fairy mural her fathers had made her. The floor was cold too. It seeped through her soles.

"It's lovely." It was probably best she not express how impersonal she found the place. The furniture—a large bed with diaphanous curtains, a dresser, and an enormous desk—looked like it belonged in some medieval castle. *Homey* was not a word that could describe the room. If this was how the Council lived, they were seriously out of touch with reality. "Um, where do I cook?"

"You don't. The kitchens are fully stocked. You can summon just about anything, but on the off chance they don't have it, just let the staff know. There's someone on duty twenty-four hours a day." Ian's voice held a note of boasting.

While she understood the need for an official body to be imposing, she was beginning to think that the Council was going far beyond trying to impress people. "How do I do that?"

Ian walked to the wall, pulled out his wand, and tapped a bas-relief of a Greek god reclining on a couch with a beautiful servant feeding him grapes. The carved servant turned to Ian. "What may I get for you, Miss Jones-Smythe?"

"This is Ian Talbott. Please send us a pot of lavender green tea and some appropriate food. I'll leave the assortment to you."

"Very good, sir." The servant froze back in position in the carving. A moment later the tea, cups, and a three-tiered plate rack appeared on a table near the window. The wide panes gave a view of the ocean from the top of a cliff. The sight stopped her for a moment. If she had to guess, she would say she was in . . . How odd. She knew she knew a place with a view like this, but she couldn't name it. She had no idea where the Council Hall was. They had placed some kind of spell on her, which left her completely confused about her location.

Ian sat in the chair at the end of the table and eyed the variety of savory tidbits in front of him. "Let's talk." He poured a cup of the tea for her, then himself, added sugar and cream, and loaded a small plate with food. He took a bite. "Outstanding as usual. You should eat something. The pastries are beautiful."

"Thanks, but I don't eat sugar." Stormy took a place on the couch that ran along the length of the table.

"Then have a cucumber sandwich. You won't regret it."

To appease him, she picked one of the small finger sandwiches. She had the feeling she'd lose any hint of an appetite after she heard what Ian had to say.

He sipped his tea, then placed plate and cup on the table. "The Council is willing to overlook the lapse in your judgment this one time, especially since you were so willing to make the move to these quarters."

Her heart started racing. How would he react if he knew the real reason behind her cooperation?

"We understand how confused you must be, how alone you must feel." He patted her knee, and it required all her discipline not to shrink away from his touch. "We want you to understand that we are here to guide you, to teach you what you need to know. We Arcani have a special role in this world. The Council isn't your enemy despite what some people would have you think."

Ian acted as if he were sixty years old instead of close to her own age. If he were any more patronizing, she would puke.

"You don't know enough about our world to judge these things for yourself. I'd hate to see you make bad decisions based on wrongful information. The Council worries about you."

She nodded to hide the shiver that went up her spine. Why did every sentence make her more wary? She masked her trepidation with earnestness. "I appreciate that."

"You'll see. The Council takes its responsibilities toward the godmothers seriously, which is why their betrayal hurts us all so deeply."

"I understand."

Ian stood. "Good. I'll leave you to your unpacking. You might want to use this chance to practice your magic. You can't hurt much here."

"An excellent idea," she said brightly.

"Good. I'll see you tomorrow then. If you need anything, just ask." He pointed to the bas-relief.

"I'm sure I'll be fine."

"Until tomorrow." He walked to the door. "Just in case you think you can transport out of here, you can't. The Council Hall is shielded. Besides, you're not allowed to leave your room without an escort."

She swallowed the shock his words produced. Before she could ask why she being locked up, Ian left.

Brilliant. As she glanced around the room, she wondered if her strategy was sound. Living in the Council Hall might prove more a prison than an opportunity to investigate.

But both Ian and Hunter were right about one thing: she had to practice magic. If she was going to be any help at all, she had to learn to control her powers.

She pulled out her wand and walked to the bed. Her suitcases and several additional boxes stood beside the bed. She looked at the first one.

There were no set words, just the feeling, just the flow of the magic. She'd succeeded once. Magic was about control and not letting it control you. Concentrating on one suitcase, she pointed her wand and said, "Places."

The zippers slashed open on both suitcases, and the tops of the boxes sprung open. Her belongings flew into the air.

For an instant, dismay flooded her, but then determination gripped her. She swished her wand and shouted, "No!"

Everything froze in midair. She lifted her hand. The magic warmed her palm. She motioned the first drawer open. It slid quietly out.

"Now." She flicked her wand, and the articles streamed to the drawer and dropped inside.

She grinned. Okay, the drawer was overflowing and several items had spilled to the floor, but it was a start. She'd work on folding next time.

9

JUSTIN'S GUIDE FOR THE ARTIST

•

Art requires muscles.

STORMY ROLLED HER shoulders as she sat on the edge of the bed. She was bored. She had practiced magic that afternoon—simple things, like summoning small objects and making things float. Controlling her magic was becoming easier; she had visualized it as pouring water through a tiny funnel instead of letting it gush out, but even so, she had spent a lot of her time either ducking or picking up the items that had crashed to the floor. The practice had left her arms with the strength of mashed potatoes. Even a few hours later, twinges ran down from her shoulders, and her neck gave out a few loud pops.

Maybe she *could* get her loom delivered to the room. Then she wouldn't be so bored. TV did not excite her, and she'd forgotten to bring her book, and while the Hall probably had a library, she couldn't open her door to explore. It was locked.

Another loud pop from her spine startled her. She felt tired and achy. Despite the vague pains, she set up her yoga mat. Nothing like a good stretch to remove any kinks. Five minutes of the sun salutation should suffice.

She stretched and breathed, stretched again, and meditated. Ah, that was better. Her body, used to such movement, relaxed, but the underlying weariness didn't abate. Still, she breathed in, then stood. Better. Definitely better. She took a step and gasped again. Her hip joints popped, and her back cramped for an instant. Two points just under her shoulder blades started to burn.

Magic took energy, but she hadn't expected so much pain. Maybe a bath would relax her. A bathing chamber, also decked out in marble flooring and walls, opened off the room. It had a tub that could easily seat two, and instead of spigots, water entered via a rock waterfall. She had to admit it was the most amazing tub she had ever seen. They were probably trying to impress her with the luxury.

A little experimentation with her wand—touch a rock here, the tub there—started the water flowing. Before disrobing, she grabbed a couple of ibuprofen from her desk and swallowed them. That should take care of the soreness. She laughed at herself. Yoga daily for years, running on occasion. She had thought she was in good shape. Who knew magic required such strength?

She reached to pull the hem of her shirt over her head and froze. Her tank top should have been tight against her body, but if flopped loosely against her skin. Come to think of it, her shorts were also loose. Something was wrong.

Glancing around the bathroom, she realized that the tub seemed bigger than when she had first seen it, and the handle of the door was higher.

No, it wasn't. She was smaller.

Her heart raced, and her ears buzzed as she tried to understand what was happening. Her breath whooshed out of her, and she panted until she could draw another. Black spots filled her vision as yet another tremor shook her body and racked her limbs with torture.

She screamed.

"Are you in need of service?" came a voice from a frieze in the bathroom. Artemis and her nymphs frolicked in a river surrounded by lush vegetation. Behind one of the trees, Actaeon peeked out at them. It was really kind of a creepy painting for a bathroom. "Are you in need of service?" one of the nymphs said again.

"Yes, I—" but the nymph had already nodded and frozen back into place.

Stormy wasn't sure if help would arrive. Her bones cracked again, doubling her over in pain. She needed help now. Perhaps she could call her father . . .

The door burst open, and Hunter ran in, wand drawn. He blocked the bathroom doorway with his body, facing out toward the threat. If she hadn't been so scared she would have laughed, but another shudder gripped her, and she groaned.

Hunter searched the room. "What is it? What's attacking you?"

"I don't know." Her words were choppy. "I'm smaller. Owww." Her legs creaked as they contracted.

Hunter's stance still shouted his alertness, but he examined her. His gaze didn't reassure her.

She looked down at herself. Her tank top flapped against her chest, and her legs stuck out of her shorts like chicken legs. A moment later, her shorts fell to the floor.

"You're shrinking," Hunter said.

"I'm what?"

"Shrinking. It was bound to happen. You need to be able to change." Hunter lowered his wand.

"Change? What do you mean 'change'?"

Hunter looked at her for a moment as if he didn't understand what she meant. Then he nodded. "That's right. You don't know. All Arcani have the power to transform themselves, so when we're children, the Magic changes us into something. I changed into a fox. I think the Magic was poking fun at my name."

"But I'm not a child."

"Clearly. I imagine most Arcani change as children because children are more flexible."

She grimaced as another series of pops issued from her body. "It hurts."

"Of course it hurts. You don't think you can just change your entire being without some sort of consequence."

"Thanks for the sympathy." She bit back another groan.

"That's why most Arcani don't like transformation. The pain never goes away, although once you become adept, it takes less time." Hunter shrugged. "It's one of the requirements of being a Guard. The ability to execute a quick transformation. You never know what might work best."

"You guys are masochists, I think." She clutched her top to her as it threatened to gap away from her chest. "What kind of animal am I becoming?"

He looked at her again. Perhaps a moment too long, because she grew uncomfortable under his scrutiny. His silence stretched, and her worry increased.

Just as she was about to panic again, his face relaxed. "You're a fairy godmother."

"Yes. So?" She was ready to throttle him.

He moved to her back, just as the skin in those two

burning spots exploded in pain as if a knife had sliced them. She grabbed the edge of the tub, which now was at waist level.

"Oooo, that had to hurt," he said.

Between clenched teeth she said, "What had to hurt?"

"Your wings just burst through your skin," Hunter said.

"Wings? I'm turning into a bird?"

"No, you're turning into a fairy." Hunter spoke from behind her. "They are beautiful. I'd guess they're purple, but these shiny white streaks shimmer through them."

She was turning into a fairy? Suddenly the pain seemed to recede as excitement bubbled through her. "I'll be able to fly?"

Hunter walked back around so she could see him. "I guess so. I've never been a fairy. Except for the godmothers, Arcani can't turn into other magical folk. We can transform into animals, but not fairies or trolls or whatever." He paused. "It could be useful to turn into a troll."

Stormy didn't come higher than Hunter's waist now. "So what do I do?"

"Nothing." Hunter shrugged. "This will happen naturally. You don't have to do anything. Although I'd take a couple of ibuprofen to lessen the pain."

"I've already done that."

"Then you're ahead of the game." Hunter looked down at her. "Okay, If you don't need me, I'll be going now."

"Why did you come if you were just going to leave?"

He didn't reply for a moment. "It's my job."

So he hadn't forgiven her. Not the she had expected him to. Nevertheless disappointment ripped through her. No, more. She didn't want to go through this alone. As excited as she was about flying, she didn't need one more thing to worry about right now. Tears welled up in her eyes. She looked up at him. "Please. I'm scared. Don't go."

God, she'd played the emotion card. Hunter looked down at her and saw the real fear in her eyes. This whole process was all new to her, and she didn't have anybody else, did she? He could call Ian, but he wouldn't wish that on his worst enemy.

Which she wasn't.

She was merely someone trying to make sense of a lot of new information at once. He did believe she hadn't meant to get Tank fired. If he were honest and fair, he'd have to place some of the blame on Tank as well.

"You may want to start thinking about what you're going to wear," Hunter said.

"What do you mean?"

"You've probably noticed your clothes don't grow with you. Unless you have something tucked away somewhere I can't see, you're going to be naked pretty soon."

She looked down and let out a squeak. Her tank top looked more like a very long and loose dress. Stormy closed her eyes as another spasm squeezed her.

"Get out."

"I thought you wanted me to stay."

"I do. I just . . . Turn around."

"What?"

"Just turn around."

He did. The next thing he knew she was shoving her tank top into his hand.

"Uh, Stormy?" He started to turn his head.

"No, don't look. Take that out there, find a pair of scissors, and make me something to wear."

"Me? I can't—"

"Just do it," she shouted. Her voice sounded two

octaves higher. "A sarong. I just need a longish rectangle. For my size." She gave him a push toward the door, which felt more like a pat.

Hunter left the bathroom. "Stormy?"

"Yeah?" came the squeak through the door.

"Where can I find scissors?"

"In the desk. I hope."

Hunter crossed to the desk and saw Stormy's laptop open. He nudged the touch pad, and Angry Birds covered the screen. Really? She had nothing better to do than play Angry Birds?

He found scissors in the second drawer. He held out the tank top first one way, then another.

"Are you sure you want me to cut this?" His voice sounded anxious.

"Yes." Her voice was getting harder to hear.

"A rectangle, huh?" Hunter placed the scissors to the hem. *Okay.* He cut a length, turned it ninety degrees, cut again, turned it, and finished the rectangle. Holding it up, he squinted. Maybe he should take a refresher course in geometry.

Well, the shirt was ruined anyway. He cut another one, and then another. None of them looked straight and they were each different sizes, but surely one of them would work. He knocked on the bathroom door.

"Don't come in here."

"I'm not. I just want to give you, uh, these." He flipped the material in his hand.

"I can't open the door."

He pushed the door open a crack.

"Don't peek."

He stuck his hand through and dropped the material. "I'm not peeking." And then as if the words had prompted him, his mind started to wander, to picture her as she looked at this moment. Without clothes. It wasn't too hard. Her usual wardrobe left plenty of skin to work with. Lots of skin. And now she would be showing more.

Oh, hell.

He wiped his palms against his pants. This totally went against the rules. He was on a job. His job was to protect her, not fantasize about her.

Speaking of protection . . . "Stormy? Stormy, are you okay?"

From behind the door, a tiny fairy zipped into the room. She flew with grace, speed, and joy. She swooped and dove and zoomed. She rose into the air, circled his head twice, twirled in the air in front of him, then hovered.

Her antics tugged a reluctant smile from him. "Nice outfit." She had twisted and wrapped one of the fabric pieces around herself, tying the ends around her neck. A bit togalike, but a workable dress.

"Ha-ha." Her grin belied her size. "Isn't this amazing?"

"Yeah, it really is." He drew his brows together.

She fluttered closer to him. "What's your problem?"

"Why are you so good at this?" Hunter squinted at her. "No offense, but your magic sucks—uh, hasn't gone so smoothly, but you fly like you've been doing it for years."

Her mouth twisted to the side. Clearly his words rankled. "Maybe it's because I've had years of yoga and it's given me an awareness of my muscles that most people lack. Maybe it's because my dads paid for years of dance lessons. Maybe it's just my gift."

She zipped away from him and flew through the room. At least she had the space to really give her wings a workout.

"I can't believe I'm a fairy."

"Technically you're not." Hunter crossed his arms over his chest. "You're as small as one, but you're still human like the rest of us."

"You really are a stickler, aren't you?"

"Somebody has to be. We have enough rule benders around here."

"Well, I may not be a fairy, but I am a fairy godmother." She gave a toss to her head as if she could give a fig about his opinion and flew to the desk. With a graceful arabesque she landed beside her computer. She glanced up and down at the screen, jumped on a few of the keys, and laughed when she prematurely exploded a couple of birds from her game. "I have a whole new respect for computers from this angle."

Her delight was contagious. Her earlier fear had seemed to vanish and if he wasn't careful he would be sucked into her enthusiasm.

She placed her fists on her hips. "So any bright ideas about how I change back?"

"Your wand," Hunter said.

"Right." She pointed at her wand, which lay upon the desk. It was several times her size. "And just how am I supposed to use it?"

"Would I lie to you? Just summon it." Hunter's voice held a hint of exasperation, as if her doubt annoyed him.

She focused on her wand and opened her palm without saying a word. The wand rose. As it flew through the air, it contracted until it was in perfect proportion to her diminutive size. She caught it in her hand. "That was so cool."

"Yeah, but it's time to change back. I don't want to spend my night here." No, he didn't. Despite the images that those words brought to his imagination.

"Fine. I'll just go back into the bathroom—Oh my God. The water!" She darted back into the bathroom.

The panic in her voice alarmed him and he followed.

The tub was near to overflowing. A few more seconds would have seen a lake forming. Stormy waved her wand.

"Stormy, what are you doing?" Hunter's voice stopped her actions.

"I need to turn off the water."

"You'd better let me." He pulled out his wand.

"No. I can do this. I practiced today, and look how good I was at flying. Besides, I turned the water on." She pointed her wand. The water lapped at the rim of the tub."

"I don't think that's a good idea." Hunter backed away from her.

"I'm small. How much damage can I do?"

She waved her wand.

Hunter ducked. A blast from her wand shot a stream of water high into the air and drenched everything in the bathroom. Stormy yelped. Her wings wet, she toppled to the floor and landed in the clump of now soggy shorts. Water sloshed out of the tub, while the waterfall continued to spill into the tub at an alarming rate.

Wiping the water from his eyes, Hunter stood and aimed his wand at the waterfall. It stopped. His shirt stuck to him and his pants were soaked. He glared at her.

She glanced up at him, her tiny eyes wide, her hair plastered to her head, and her wings drooping and dripping with water.

"I'd say your magic works just as well when you're small."

10

JUSTIN'S GUIDE FOR THE ARTIST

•

Applying logic without emotion can lead to grave errors, but following emotion without logic can be just as dangerous.

HUNTER STOOD AT Stormy's door at seven thirty. She'd been ensconced in the Council Hall for a day now, and he'd been off duty since she'd soaked him the evening before. His wet appearance in the barracks had caused rife speculation, but he hadn't shared the origin of his drenching. He'd received enough grief for this assignment. Tank was conspicuously absent. He had been given leave until further notice.

A flash of residual anger passed through him. He hadn't forgiven her yet for her disappearing act, but he had to admit he'd laughed about the water episode when he'd had a private moment in the barracks. He just wished he could think of her without any emotional reactions. So she was still his assignment, and as she was going out tonight, his presence was required.

When the door opened, he forced his face to remain impassive. She wore a red dress that revealed nothing, yet stirred the viewer's imagination to what lay beneath.

There was that fascination with her clothes again. And her nonclothes. His wayward thoughts were out of control.

"I'm surprised to see you here," she said. "I would have thought you'd try to get yourself reassigned after last night."

He remembered to breathe. "No such luck."

In a fleeting gesture, she pulled at her lower lip with her teeth, then released it. He might not have noticed it at all, except for the hurt that bloomed in her eyes. He steeled himself. He refused to acknowledge her reaction.

She pulled out her wand. He flinched.

She noted his response with a cool stare. "*Veni.*"

He flinched. A small, black, beaded purse flew into her hand. She opened the purse and put her wand inside as if she did it every day. He looked at her.

"I practiced some more." She stepped out of the room. "Is Ian coming for me too?" she asked as if nothing had happened.

"No. He thought it best I take you. He will meet us there."

"See? I told you it wasn't a date."

Her words immediately brought forth the memory of the last time she had said them and how much the thought of her date with Ian had upset him. He ignored the awareness curling in his belly. "I'm to take you to the Scott house and stay for your protection. Although several Council members will be present, the house was once the home of Regina Scott, and they don't want to take any chances."

"Lovely woman, Reggie. She's quite the threat, I'm sure." Stormy's voice rang with sarcasm. She looked up and down the hallway. "Can we transport from here?"

"No, we have to go to the station." He stepped aside to let her pass.

She didn't move. "You'll have to lead the way. I may live here now, but they don't let me explore."

That surprised him. "You haven't been outside your room?"

"No. I've got my own little dominion, and they want to keep me there. I think your knock unlocks my door."

She hadn't mentioned being locked in yesterday. Of course, she'd had other priorities then. He'd had no trouble getting in last night, but the door could be enchanted to recognize him. Why wouldn't the Council allow Stormy out of her room? She wasn't a criminal.

Troubled by his unanswered question, he led her down the marble halls, then up to the next level where the anteroom that the Guards called the station was. It was the one place where the Arcani could transport into and out of the Council Hall.

Her gaze took in the view of this second hallway. "I see the Council doesn't believe in varying the theme."

"What?"

"The marble. Everywhere. A little ostentatious, wouldn't you say? I mean, I know the Council is a government body, but this isn't Olympus."

"I hadn't thought about it."

"I wonder what this place looks like from the outside."

"Like a house."

She glanced at him.

He shrugged. "I've been on duty outside. It looks like a normal house for this neighborhood. The Hall extends beneath the decoy for several levels."

Outside the anteroom, they paused by a wall inscribed with names. "What's this?" she asked.

"A list of the Guards. Our names go up here, similar to the scroll of godmothers in the Council Chamber." He pointed to his name.

"Impressive," she said, her tone giving lie to her word.

He led her into the station. "Did you practice transporting?"

She gave him a look as if he'd said something stupid. "I was sequestered. I don't think I could have practiced if I wanted to."

Right. He held out his hand. "Then you'll have to travel with me."

She hesitated only a moment, but he felt her reluctance like a bucket of cold water. Still, when she placed her hand in his, he couldn't help but feel the fit.

Stop it.

He concentrated and transported them both to the front entrance of the Scotts' house.

Scaffolding covered at least half of the facade.

"What happened?" Stormy asked.

"We had to break the wall down to try to capture Regina Scott."

She gasped. "*You* did this?"

"Not me personally, but I was here."

"But you failed."

"We did." He wouldn't say anything else. That failure had cost the Guard much in the way of confidence and morale. He wasn't willing to talk about it. "The party will be in back. Talbott said he'd meet us out here."

She didn't press him. For which he was grateful.

They stood silently waiting for Ian to show up. She didn't speak to him, and he would also say she avoided looking at him. Luckily, they didn't have to stand the awkward silence for long. Ian arrived a minute later.

"Good to see you're already here." Ian wore a black suit with an ostentatious lapel pin. In the shape of a wand on top of a crest, it looked as if diamonds encrusted the hideous thing. She stared at it.

"I see you admiring my pin. It was a gift from Luc."

Stormy's eyes widened. Hunter wanted to meet her gaze in mutual horror, but remembered at the last moment it wasn't appropriate behavior.

"I think you'll enjoy this evening. Let's go in." Talbott took Stormy's arm.

Hunter maneuvered himself in front of them and was about to ring the doorbell, when Talbott said, "What are you doing?"

"My job. I need to check if the location is clear." Hunter swallowed the flash of annoyance that Talbott's question elicited.

"That's not necessary. She's with me. You can bring up the rear. And try to be unobtrusive. This is a dinner party, not a gangster war." Talbott rang the doorbell, and didn't so much as glance at him again.

Anger flamed in Hunter, but he simply clenched his teeth and reminded himself of his training. Talbott was an arrogant slug, but Hunter's focus was supposed to be on Stormy.

The asset. Remember that.

A uniformed maid opened the door and led them through to the stone patio at the rear of the house. From the backyard the house displayed no visible damage. A marquee had been erected over a parquet floor on the lawn. A bar complete with bartender stood at one edge, and guests milled around.

An elegant woman saw them and came to greet

them. She took Talbott's hands and kissed his cheeks. "Ian, it's been too long. I'm so happy to have you here."

Talbott nodded his head in acknowledgment of her graciousness. "Cordelia, you're looking lovely as usual. I'm so happy you harbor no ill will toward me."

She waved her hand. "As if I could. It wasn't your fault that my daughters made poor choices." She turned to Stormy.

Ian said, "May I introduce Stormy Jones-Smythe? Stormy, this is Cordelia Scott."

Cordelia took Stormy's hand in hers. "You are as lovely as they said you were."

"Thank you for having me, Mrs. Scott."

"None of that now. It's Cordelia. Come, let me introduce you to the others."

It didn't surprise Hunter that she had overlooked him. His uniform marked his position. He wasn't on the guest list. He was here on a job.

He scanned the yard for possible threats. Nothing jumped out at him, although the extensive garden could provide too many hiding places. He'd have to keep an eye on that area. Next he assessed the guests. He recognized more than a few Council members. From the way the guests were dressed, he guessed that this was a party for the elite. And, what do you know, Luc LeRoy was here. Hunter watched him greet Stormy like an old friend. Ian simpered beside her.

If Luc was here, then . . . Hunter glanced along the periphery. Sure enough, there, in the shadows against the wall of the house, stood Luc's servant, Dmitri. Hunter's instincts started buzzing. He was looking forward to renewing their acquaintanceship.

He sidled over to Dmitri, then clapped him on the back and in a jovial voice said, "Hey, buddy."

The look the Russian sent him would have shriveled him if the wizard had such powers. "You are buffoon."

"C'mon, Dmitri. Don't be so harsh with a fellow bodyguard."

"I am not bodyguard."

"Servant, then." Hunter crossed his arms and leaned back in an attitude of camaraderie. "So what's it like working for the old guy?"

Dmitri didn't answer. He kept his gaze on the gathering.

"You can tell me. Like, what does he pay you? It's gotta be good to buy this kind of silence."

"You are an idiot." Dmitri's gaze never left the party.

"No, seriously, you have to have a good gig. He's some sort of hotshot, right? Tell him if he's ever ready to move up to a real professional, I'm available."

Dmitri's muscles twitched in his jaw.

"Right. Well, see ya, Dmitri." Hunter pushed away from the wall. He didn't look back, but he would wager Dmitri was glaring at him. Instinct told him goading the man was the right course of action. He wasn't sure why, but he wanted to keep Dmitri off balance.

Now, however, his duty required checking on the asset. He took a position closer to the parquet, but remained distinctly apart from the party. Stormy was speaking to Luc, or rather, Luc was doing the talking and Stormy was beside him, listening raptly to every word. In fact, most of the guests were listening to his words. Hunter stepped into the shadow of a tree. He pulled out his wand and touched his ear. "*Audi.*"

Instantly the voices from the party were amplified. He didn't like to use this spell because the mishmash of voices often caused a headache, but sometimes it was useful. In this case Luc was doing most of the talking, so the drone wasn't too bad.

"We live in modern times now. Merlin wrote the laws a thousand years ago," Luc was saying.

"But our laws have served us well over these centuries," a somber-looking man said.

Luc lifted a finger. "Ah, but have they? We lost track of the *Lagabóc* hundreds of years ago. It follows that the Arcani laws have changed with those centuries since we didn't have the book to guide us. Look at the Americans and their Constitution. They *have* the document, yet the interpretation of those laws changes constantly. Do you really think the founders of this nation could have foretold the technological and societal advances made by the Groundlings? Of course not. Neither could Merlin."

The conversation level dropped for a moment as the guests considered this argument.

"But does that make the *Lagabóc* any less valid?" someone asked.

Luc shook his head. "We don't know. Tennyson Ritter discovered the book only recently. The scholars haven't finished studying it yet. We don't know yet what it actually contains."

A buzz grew after that statement. Hunter shook his head as if to chase away an annoying insect. This was why he didn't like this spell.

". . . spells and laws . . ."

". . . scholars, not real people . . ."

". . . reorganization of society. The chaos . . ."

"Friends." Luc lifted his hands, and his voice rose above the many conversations. "We've all heard the legends and tales of the *Lagabóc*—that it contains great spells, that it tells the history of our people, that it provides the guidelines for our lives. But we cannot *know* until the Head Council releases its studies."

"And a translation. I heard it's written in Latin and

Old English. I don't know about you, but I have trouble enough with new English," said a woman at the table.

A ripple of laughter sifted through the group.

Luc chuckled the loudest, but it didn't sound sincere. "Indeed, madame, there is that. And even the translations will have the input of the translator. I believe it may be time not to discard the *Lagabóc* perhaps, but to question its value and examine our position in the world."

Again conversations erupted at that statement.

". . . makes a valid point . . ."

". . . heard that they don't want to release . . ."

". . . dangerous magic in its pages . . ."

". . . *Lagabóc* . . ."

"What exactly is this *Lagabóc*?" he heard Stormy ask.

Luc smiled at her like a benevolent lord. "That's right, you don't know. Merlin's book of rules. His rules for our coexistence with the Groundlings. For years we believed it only a legend because it vanished. It was supposed to contain great wisdom and even greater magic."

"Sounds impressive. And we live by those rules?"

"Not exactly. Because the book was lost for centuries, we turned to the Councils for our laws." Luc eyed her. "Surely the other godmothers have told you."

"Why would they tell me?"

"Tennyson Ritter found it."

Stormy looked at Luc with wide eyes. "They didn't tell me."

"So you *have* seen the godmothers."

She nodded. "I suppose it isn't a secret."

Luc shrugged. "I know of your new living arrangements. The Council was very angry, *n'est-ce pas*?"

She sighed. "They were, but they also realized I

might be able to help them, that I can report back to them, even if I couldn't tell them where the aunts are. They used some sort of spell on me." She twisted her mouth to the side as if she were confused.

"You offered to do that?"

She hadn't, at least not as far as Hunter had heard. In fact, she had practically told him her allegiance lay with the godmothers. What game was she playing?

She shrugged. "Sometimes I think I'm just a pawn in this whole mess."

Noise from the others drowned out what Luc said next, but Stormy listened intently. Hunter took out his wand again and removed the listening spell. The ambient noise would effectively bar him from hearing the rest of their conversation. Besides, he noticed Cordelia waving the guests to their places at the table. Dinner was about to be served.

Waiters appeared carrying trays covered with plates. Hunter raised an eyebrow. This was some fancy meal.

Conversation became a hum as the guests tucked in. From his vantage point, he had a clear view of Stormy on the other side of the table. She sat between Ian and an elderly Council member who would be stepping down in this Time of Transition. The old man was questioning Stormy, and her replies elicited chuckles from him.

And then he felt a footprint. Oh, the low-level hum had been there all along, but this was an increase in activity. A minute directed burst. Someone had just done magic in a very focused and specialized way. He doubted anyone but a Guard would have noticed. Although Hunter could see the table, he was too far to pinpoint the source of the footprint.

Just as he was about to edge closer to the marquee, he saw movement out of the corner of his eye. Dmitri edged along the wall and was slinking away from the party. Suspicion told Hunter to follow Dmitri, but his training told him to move closer to Stormy. His first duty was to guard her.

The footprint had grown slightly above the low-level tingle of an Arcani house, but not enough to arouse suspicion. The closer he came to the table, the more unease he felt. Something was off. As he took up a position behind Stormy, he scrutinized the guests. They were chatting and eating; no one seemed watchful or preoccupied . . .

Except Luc. His smile held a hint of something—anticipation? amusement?—that didn't quite fit with the earnest expression the woman beside him wore. And then Luc's gaze flitted to the centerpiece in front of Stormy.

Hunter examined the decoration. It was a sculpture of a pixie looking at her reflection in a mirror pond. Real flowers and grasses surrounded the piece to give it a more natural appearance. As he looked at it, the mirror started to glow and the footprint increased.

Hunter whipped out his wand and dove for Stormy. As he reached her, the table exploded in front of him. He threw his arm around her, swung her around, and transported, the boom and her scream ringing in his ears.

He landed, rolling onto his back, still clasping her to him. His arms braced her against injury, but he wasn't sure he had succeeded until he heard her gasp for air. Relief punched through him. She was alive, but what shape was she in? Gently, he released her, then quickly took in the surroundings. He hadn't been sure where he had transported to, but saw the familiar beige walls of his condo. Made sense. His sanctuary. He pushed to his knees beside her.

Blood trickled down her face, and she stared at him with panic in her eyes. She pushed up on her arms. "What just happened?"

"Sit still. You're bleeding." He pushed her hair aside to search for the wound.

Then she gasped again. "So are you."

He looked down. Blood dripped down his right hand. His forearm had a long laceration. "It's nothing."

"You have a cut on your cheek." She wriggled her head from his hands, looked around, and started to push to her feet.

"Don't get up—"

She stood.

"—so fast." He shoved his wand into his pocket.

"I'm fine." She walked into the kitchen and grabbed a paper towel. After wetting it, she returned to him and dabbed at his cheek. "This might need stitches."

"No." He turned his head away from her ministrations.

"Hold still."

"No, you hold still." He dodged her efforts to hold him, slipped from her reach, and likewise went to the kitchen. He pulled out a clean kitchen towel, dampened it, then returned to her. He wiped the blood from her face.

She sent him a look of exasperation. "If you didn't have so much blood on your face, this would almost be funny." She pressed the paper towel against his cheek as he cleansed her face. "You should have brought another towel. This paper's too rough."

"Don't worry about me. Head wounds look worse than they are. What about the rest of you?" He parted her hair with his fingers to find the source of the bleeding. A thin gash oozed fresh blood. He placed the cloth against it.

"Ouch." She jerked back. "I'm fine, except for your pushing on my head."

"No pain anywhere else?" He reached for the cut again.

"No." She jerked back from the pressure and tried to wipe more of his face.

"Stop that. Let me see your head."

"Stop squirming."

"I'm not squirming."

She wadded up the now-pink paper towel. "This is not working."

"Fine. Let me take care of you, and then I'll worry about me." He pressed the cloth to her head.

"Ugh." She pulled back again. "How about this? I'll hold that against my head, and you take care of yourself."

She had to be feeling okay if she was this irascible. He placed the cloth on the spot and lifted her hand on top of it. "Here."

He pulled out his wand again and aimed it at the counter. A large box of first-aid supplies materialized. He flipped the lid and grabbed a large pad. Ripping it from its wrapping, he brought it to her. "Use this instead."

She nodded and handed him the towel splotched with bright red. A moment later, her hand began to shake and color drained from her face. Just as he expected. The adrenaline had stopped working.

He draped his arm around her shoulder and led her to the couch. "Sit. Stay." She nodded. He summoned a blanket and wrapped it around her.

Returning to the supplies, he bound up his arm in little time, then grabbed a mirror from the kit and checked out his face. It looked gruesome because of the blood, but the cut was clean and would probably heal without much of a scar. He leaned over the sink, washed the blood away, and taped a clean pad against his cheek. In a few minutes he could apply a couple of butterfly strips. But first he had to check on Stormy.

Her gaze followed his every move. Red discolored her blond hair, and her face was still pale, but she seemed otherwise okay. Distress about the situation had settled in, and he saw tears in her eyes. He sat down beside her and replaced the hand on her head with his free one. He checked beneath the gauze on her scalp. Already the blood had slowed. He applied pressure again, but this time she didn't pull away.

"What happened?" Her voice was thready.

"It was an explosion. The centerpiece had a mirror."

She gave him a blank expression. "So?"

That's right; she wouldn't know. "Mirrors can hold magic. That's why so many spells use mirrors as a conduit."

"But why . . . who . . . ?"

He wasn't ready to share his thoughts or suspicions with her. "I don't know. Yet."

In a sudden burst of activity, she flung the blanket from her and tried to rise. "We have to go back. We have to see if anyone else needs help."

With gentle pressure he pushed her down again. "No, what you need is a warm bath."

"I can't just—"

"My job is to protect you. I'm not about to let you return to the scene of the explosion. You have to trust that help is already on the way." He lifted the gauze again and was pleased to see the blood had coagulated. "I can take you back to your quarters, so they don't waste energy looking for you. There's a medical office at the Hall. We'll have them take a look at you."

"And you."

"I'm fine."

"And you," she said, glaring at him.

"And me." He sighed and looked down at himself. He really should change, but getting her back was more important. "Don't move." His voice was stern.

She nodded again.

He went back to the medical kit and removed the pad from his cheek. The cut could use a few more minutes of pressure, but it would stop eventually. He placed two butterfly strips across the edges, drawing them together, and then returned to Stormy. He held out his hand. "Let's go."

11

JUSTIN'S GUIDE FOR THE ARTIST

•

If you encounter a problem, try looking at it from a different perspective.

THE MEDICAL TEAM swiftly cleaned Stormy's wound and checked her for further injuries (there weren't any, which she could have told them), and then redressed Hunter's arm and cheek. He walked her back to her quarters. She couldn't have found them on her own anyway.

Hunter opened the door and let her enter. "You should rest." He moved to close the door.

"Don't go." She braced the door open with her palm. "I mean, please stay. I don't want to be alone just yet."

He looked at her for a moment. "They'll want to question us soon anyway." He stepped inside.

For whatever reason, when he entered, the room seemed smaller. Stormy tried not to stare.

"What?"

Okay, she had failed. "Your shirt's bloody."

"So are you." He flicked his wand and a black shirt

and jeans appeared in his hand. "Why don't you change first?"

She nodded, grabbed some clothes, and ran into the bathroom.

The great tub greeted her view. Room for two. No, she wouldn't think of that.

Discarding the red dress refreshed her. So did a quick shower, although the water on her scalp stung. Clean shorts and a tank, and she could breathe again.

"Your turn," she said as she stepped out.

"Thanks." He disappeared into the bathroom.

She looked around. A quick flip through the channels told her the TV showed only Groundling programs. She wanted news about the explosion. Did the Arcani even have a news station?

She moved to her computer instead. She logged in to Twitter. As expected, one message waited for her. From @Beastlover858, Reggie's user name.

Beastlover858 @TextileTyphoon Hey, girl. Heard you had an exciting evening. How did it turn out?

She recognized the plea for information in the innocuous words. Reggie's parents had thrown the party. She must have heard about the explosion. She wanted news about her parents.

Stormy contemplated her words carefully, then wrote:

TextileTyphoon @Beastlover858 It was a blast, but I had to leave early, so I missed the end. I'll let you know how it was soon.

That should convey her lack of knowledge. She hit send.

"What are you doing?" Hunter asked.

She started and whirled around in the chair.

He had stepped from the bathroom and was toweling off his hair. He hadn't pulled on his shirt yet.

Her breath stalled in her throat.

Still damp from his shower, his skin shone in the light of the room. Ridges defined his muscles, and his ribs tapered into his waist. The top of his jeans slung low over his hips. A thin line of hair ran from his navel and disappeared into the waistband, drawing the eye down, down . . .

She gulped in an attempt to moisten her mouth. "I . . . uh . . . computer. I was just checking Twitter."

He looked confused. Well, sure. Arcani didn't use Twitter, right?

"Have you heard anything yet?" He pulled the clean black T-shirt over his head.

"I wouldn't know where to look for it."

A knock came at the door.

Hunter drew his wand and indicated for her to stand behind him. He opened the door. Ian came into the room.

"Good work, Merrick. I received word as soon as you returned to the Council Hall," Ian said as he sauntered in. His arm was in a sling. "She isn't injured, I assume."

Hunter stowed his wand. "A slight cut on her scalp. I got her before the explosion completed."

"At least you've turned out competent." Ian sniffed.

Clearly he didn't notice the tightening of Hunter's lips at his pronouncement. Stormy thought she should run interference. "What happened to you?"

"This?" Ian said, indicating his arm. "I wrenched my shoulder when the percussion forced me back."

"More likely when you dove, you chickenshit," muttered Hunter.

Stormy pressed her lips together to prevent laughing. When she trusted herself to speak, she asked, "Was anyone else hurt?"

"Council Member Gardener was killed."

"Oh my God." All desire to laugh vanished. That nice old man she had sat next to was gone. Shock slammed into her. If Hunter hadn't been there, if he hadn't grabbed her, she might have . . . Her stomach threatened to rebel.

"He was set to be replaced anyway this Time of Transition, but still, the death of a Council member is not a light matter."

She stared at Ian. Would the death of any other guest have mattered less to him? And then she remembered Reggie's plea for information. "What of our hosts?"

"The explosion happened in the middle of the table. They sat on either end. A few scratches, but they're fine."

A wave of relief filled her. She could relate that information to Reggie in a few minutes. She would be happy for the news. Stormy shook off a feeling of dread. Reggie's parents were playing a dangerous charade. They had thrown the party for Luc. Her gaze found Ian. "What about Luc?"

Ian clicked his tongue. "A few scratches. He is so brave. Going out meeting his supporters, all the while knowing the godmothers are trying to kill him. Which brings me to the reason for my visit." Ian turned to Hunter. "We need to know what you saw. You reacted to the threat almost before it happened."

Hunter's eyes narrowed. "Are you asking if I had anything to do with the attack?"

"Don't get excited." Ian flapped the hand of his uninjured arm. "We aren't questioning your loyalty. You carried out your job admirably. But you had to have noticed something to react that quickly."

"No."

Stormy wrinkled her brow. That response was too quick. She looked at him.

Hunter didn't react to her pointed glance. "I mean I sensed the magic and got Stormy out of there."

Ian huffed out his breath. "That's all? We need to know."

Hunter shrugged. "Can't help you."

Now she did have questions. Hunter wasn't flippant. Ever.

Ian examined him, then nodded. "Disappointing, but I'm sure you wouldn't withhold any information."

The muscles in Hunter's jaws clenched as if he were in pain. He was probably annoyed with the doubt of his abilities. "Do you have any theories?" Hunter's tone was too precise.

Ian nodded. "We think it was an attempt on Luc's life. By the godmothers. He's a barrier to their plan to rule the Arcani."

This news stunned Stormy. "What?"

"Luc's plans to free the Arcani to take their rightful place in the world threatens the godmothers."

"How?" she asked.

"The godmothers have special gifts that make them unique. They enjoy an elevated status among the Arcani. Even among the Groundlings. Consider the many stories about them." Ian adjusted the fabric of his sling. "If the Arcani live openly, their role is unnecessary. They will lose all their prestige and celebrity."

Ian truly believed that the godmothers would threaten society for fame? Stormy could barely breathe from indignation.

"The godmothers know their influence has diminished. With technology and computers and such, the Groundlings don't need them, and if the Groundlings don't need them, and we take our place in the world, as Luc suggests, we don't need them either. So they're trying to cling to their power by taking over and preventing progress."

Unbelievable. Stormy didn't know how to begin a rebuttal. Anyone who knew the godmothers knew power didn't interest them. It didn't interest her.

"So they found evidence that the godmothers are behind the explosion tonight," Hunter said.

"Nothing tangible, but they're not through with the investigation." Ian faced Stormy. "Luc was devastated he couldn't spend more time with you. He has nothing against godmothers, only those who wish to kill him." He let out a false laugh. "He'd like to tell you his ideas and get to know you better. He's invited us to dinner tomorrow night."

"He made plans for tomorrow night? What if she had been injured?" Hunter asked.

Ian shot him a withering glare. "But she wasn't."

Hunter stepped back. Now Stormy was sure something was off. Knowing how Hunter felt about Ian, Stormy was sure he would never back down from Ian's stare, not unless he had a reason.

Ian said, "I shall see you tomorrow, Stormy. The Council has allowed us use of a chamber to practice your magic."

"I'm looking forward to it." She smiled. Hunter wasn't the only one who could act.

Ian gave a short nod of his head and left. As soon as the door closed, she whirled to Hunter. "What was that about?"

"I don't know what you're talking about."

"Cut it out. You would never have let Ian intimidate you." She placed her fists on her hips. "Spill it."

He shook his head. "You're already leaning toward rebellion. I don't need to encourage you."

"Me?" She was surprised.

"Your sympathies are with the godmothers."

"Because I can't believe they're dangerous? If that's what you mean, then yeah." She clicked her tongue in exasperation.

"See? You admit it."

"Then why haven't you turned me in?"

He hesitated.

Her instincts were right. He was holding something back. "Don't you think I'd be safer if I knew everything?"

"That's my job. As long as I'm here, you'll be safe."

"Look, mister, I don't need rescuing. I can take care of myself."

"Yeah, you probably can," he said. "This goes against my better instincts."

"No, it goes against your training. Your instincts tell you I need to know." She waited.

He let out a deep breath as if he had reached a weighty decision. "Did you know Luc has a bodyguard?"

She shook her head. "No. But if he believes he's in danger from the godmothers, it isn't surprising."

"Maybe, but Dmitri isn't your normal bodyguard. There's an arrogance about him, a smugness that doesn't fit. I don't think he's protecting Luc as much as carrying out orders."

"What do you mean?"

"He disappeared before the explosion tonight like he knew it was coming. In fact, I think he did it."

"You think *he's* trying to kill Lucas?"

"No, I think he's working with him."

She fell silent at that. Then she asked, "Why would Lucas attack himself?"

"That's what I've been asking myself all night."

"But Ian—"

"Ian is an idiot who would believe anything Luc told him. Haven't you noticed how Ian acts in front of Luc? Like he loves him."

"I thought I was the only one who thought that." She let out a puff of air that lifted her bangs for an instant. Then another thought struck her. "If this is what you think, then you have to be sympathizing with the godmothers too."

"Now you're just jumping to conclusions. Just because I don't trust Luc LeRoy doesn't mean the Council doesn't have reasons to doubt the allegiance of the godmothers. The Council hasn't shared their reasons with me, but that doesn't mean they're wrong."

She grew serious. "A man died tonight. If Lucas did create the explosion, then he's dangerous."

An odd expression flitted across his face, but he hid it just as fast as it appeared.

But she had seen it. "Now what?"

"Nothing."

"Stop it. If you know something—"

"I have no proof—"

She held up her hand. "Or you think something. Either way, I'll be safer if you tell me."

She could sense his reluctance, see the conflict in his thoughts. Finally he nodded. "I don't think Luc intended to kill the Council member."

"Why would he? He probably lost an ally."

"But I think he did intend to kill someone tonight."

That quieted her. She stared into his eyes.

"I think he wanted to kill you."

Her breath stopped in a most painful way, and then her heart beat timpani in her ear. Cold seized her gut. She swallowed past the rock in her throat. "Why?" The word came out a whisper.

Hunter dashed to her and placed her on the sofa. "Put your head between your legs."

"I'm not going to faint."

But he pushed her head down anyway. "You're as pale as a frog's underbelly."

"Those are words every girl wants to hear." She pushed against his hand and straightened up. Denial and disbelief raged within her. "Why would Lucas want to kill me?"

"How much do you know about the first two godmothers?"

"Reggie and Kristin? I've met them, and frankly they don't seem like outlaws."

"Exactly. You can't be partial." Hunter leaned back. "The new godmothers defied the Council and the old ones have refused to cooperate. The Council has had no choice but to condemn all of them."

"I understand that, but how does that explain why Lucas would want to kill me?"

"It would prove how ruthless the godmothers are if they killed one of their own."

She jumped on those words. "But they wouldn't. Even you think it's Lucas."

"Is it? I've done some research on the guy and he comes up clean. There's nothing in his background that's suspicious."

"Come on. He's evil-go-lucky."

He looked blank. "What?"

"Evil-go-lucky. You know, the opposite of 'happy-go-lucky.' Everything has gone his way."

"What proof do you have?"

"I—" She stopped. She really had no proof. "Then why do you believe he's the bad guy?"

"I don't."

She opened her mouth to protest, but he held up his hand. "I'm suspicious. That's all. I haven't finished digging yet, but so far I can't find anything. Chances are the Council hasn't either."

She shrank within herself. "The aunts told me—"

"Exactly. *The aunts* told you. The godmothers are the only ones with this information on Luc. *They* are the ones spreading the rumors of takeovers and coups."

Could the godmothers be wrong about Lucas? But why would the godmothers want to take over? Was Ian's nonsense right? The aunts just didn't seem the type. She knew better than to judge someone on outward appearances, but how could three old women and two magic newbies hope to succeed in a plot that would shake the Arcani world to its foundations? Wait. She raised her gaze to his eyes. "If you really believe the godmothers are trying to take over, why are you investigating Lucas?"

"Because my gut says not to trust him, and I listen to my gut." He ran his hand over his hair. "I said there's nothing in his background that makes me suspicious."

"So?"

"Well. That's just it. There's nothing. No records. Nothing. Like he doesn't exist. Like he made himself up."

"Do the Arcani have a witness protection program?"

"A what?"

"Never mind." She shook her head. "Then you have to believe the godmothers."

"No, I'm just saying I don't trust Luc." He expelled a breath. "Look, I work for the Council. I've given my oath to protect them and the Arcani world. I can't just toss that aside."

She nodded. "But you're willing to do more research?"

"Yes. I may have taken an oath to the Council, but I'm capable of thinking for myself."

She hid a smile. Clearly he didn't like being thought of as a mindless flunky. "So how does all this lead to Lucas trying to kill me?"

"First, because the explosion was set right in front of you. Luc sat farther down the table. If someone was really trying to kill him, they would have placed the explosion closer to him. This way, knowing he'd be safe, he can sport another eye patch and garner more sympathy.

"Second, it would explain Dmitri's weird behavior."

"He acted weird?"

"He left the area before the explosion, as if he knew something was about to happen."

"Okay, suppose I buy that. That still doesn't lead to Lucas wanting me dead."

He gave her a look of sympathetic patience. "The godmothers are the only ones spreading the story that Luc is behind the unrest. You're one of them, and thus, his enemy. He kills you, he's got one less enemy. He kills you and pins it on the godmothers, their credibility is shot."

"But I'm here. At the Council Hall. I'm cooperating. I don't even get to see the godmothers."

"You've already escaped your Guard once. Who can guarantee you won't again?"

She could, but she wouldn't because she *did* plan to see them again. She just didn't know when.

"The last two godmothers defected rather than submit themselves to the Council's will. You're the third. Luc has to know they will influence you. If, and this is a big if, the godmothers are right about Luc, then you're a threat."

"Why aren't you calling him Lucas? Lucas Reynard. That's his name."

"Not until I have proof."

If you believe he's trying to kill me, then you must believe the godmothers."

"I've been listening, but I haven't said I believe."

Frustration and helplessness washed over her. She could do nothing more about it today. "I guess we'll find out more tomorrow at dinner."

"You're not going."

"Of course I am."

"If he is the bad guy, it wouldn't be safe to see him."

"No, that's precisely why I have to meet with him. I have to learn more about him."

"And risk your life?"

She fell silent. Her thoughts turned to Mr. Gardener, the Council member who was killed tonight. He hadn't deserved to be sucked into whatever was going on and yet he had paid with his life. She hadn't asked for her role either, but she had accepted it. How much more sorrow and tragedy would occur because of her? For the first time she was glad she was at the Council Hall rather than at home. If anything happened to her fathers, she'd . . .

A short gasp burst from her throat. Her eyes welled up with tears. She whipped her gaze to Hunter. "My dads. They need protection."

"Already done. I asked to have Guards assigned to your parents."

"And you. You have to ask for reassignment. Hell, I'll ask for you."

"Hang on, where did that come from?"

"If you're right, you're in danger. You can't be around me."

He stared at her. His brows drew together, but not in anger. His face wavered through the sheen of tears that rose in her eyes. She blinked, and two drops spilled from beneath her lashes.

"Hey, easy." He placed his hands on the sides of her head and brushed the tears with his thumbs. "I'm not going anywhere. I'll keep you safe."

"But who will keep you safe?"

"That's my job."

"But I don't want you to have the job. No one should have to have a job like that. You're fired."

He let out a soft chuckle. "You don't have the power to fire me."

"Then . . . then, I'll run away again and get you fired."

He looked at her. "Really? You'd have to keep running then. Because that's the only way you'd be able to get rid of me. Besides, that would give Luc the advantage, and you'd never turn your back on this situation."

He was right. If she ran away, Lucas would be free to do as he pleased. She couldn't run away. Her breath hitched. "I can't let anyone else get hurt because of me." Hot tears spilled down her cheeks.

12

JUSTIN'S GUIDE FOR THE ARTIST

You have to love what you're doing;
if you don't, it'll show.

"HEY." OH SHIT. This was way more than just a couple of tears. She was seriously crying. Hunter glanced around for a tissue or something to comfort her. How was he supposed to console her? She hadn't packed her stuffed animals, and she was past the age when they could have brought her comfort anyway. His every instinct urged him to take her into his arms and hold her. That would be a mistake. He couldn't trust himself to just hold her. But a moment later, he couldn't stop himself. He pulled her into his arms. "None of this is your fault."

She smelled of lilacs and lavender. Her heat melted into him. When her arms twined around him, she melded against him. She fit.

He was in so much trouble.

"I'm putting people in danger. People have been hurt."

"No one got hurt because of you."

She lifted her watery gaze to him. Her pain emanated from her eyes. "How can you say that? Mr. Gardener is dead."

"You didn't kill him." He tightened his grip on her. "You don't deserve the guilt. You haven't done anything."

"But—"

"Uh-uh. You did not do this. If you're right, and we don't know if you are, then Luc's the bad guy."

"It's the same thing."

"No, it isn't. Would you ask a president to step aside because some people might want him assassinated? Would you ask a king to abdicate because anarchists want him gone?" He stroked her hair. "As much as you may not like it, you were chosen for an important position by the Magic. You've been given power and prestige, and terrible things can accompany that."

"But it hurts." The innocence and betrayal in her voice sounded almost like that of a child who has just realized the world is unfair.

"You can only do your best." He wanted to kiss the top of her head. Correction. He wanted to start at the top of her head and move downward from there. He wanted to touch her, taste her, inhale her. He wanted to see if those insubstantial scraps of material she called clothes would hold up under the onslaught of his attention.

Damn it, where the hell were his thoughts leading him?

"But I'm putting you in danger."

He let out a low laugh. "Honey, for the first time since I got this assignment, I feel useful. This is what I train for."

"You sound like you're enjoying yourself." A note of censure sounded in her voice.

"No, you're wrong. I don't enjoy violence, but I'm good at what I do, and it's important. There's a difference."

She didn't respond right away. Her tears stopped, but her eyes still held a sorrow that hadn't been present earlier. She made no move to pull away from him. "You're a complex man, Hunter Merrick." She turned her face so her cheek pressed against his chest. A deep breath tightened his arms around her. "Thank you."

"You're welcome." And without thinking he dropped a kiss on the top of her head.

Her gaze rose to his. For an interminable instant, she didn't move. And then she placed her hands on either side of his head and pulled him down to her.

Her lips invited him in. He was as powerless to stop himself from kissing her as he was to still his heart's beat. He had dreamed about this without even knowing it. Her lips pillowed his. Cool and smooth, they urged him to take more, push more, feel more.

Reason made one last attempt to stop him. He shouldn't be kissing her. He was on duty. She was his asset. Guard rules strictly forbade . . .

Reason be damned.

His mouth feasted on hers. He traced her lips with his tongue until they opened and he could explore the warmth and taste of her. His fingers delved into her hair, holding her exactly where he wanted.

Her hands slipped to his buttocks. Her fingers splayed, and she hooked into the flesh that filled his jeans. Her hips bumped his, and in reaction, his cock hardened, growing as she rubbed herself against him.

A low guttural moan sounded in his throat. She roused him as no other woman had. And she was so wrong for him. "We can't—"

"Don't go. Please." Her eyes pleaded with him. "I want . . . comfort . . . you. Tonight. Please."

It was wrong. Against the rules. Complicated. A bad idea.

He didn't care.

He scooped her into his arms, and a smile erupted on her face.

A few steps took him to the bed. He deposited her on the mattress, then sucked in his breath as she peeled off her tank top. A thin-strapped camisole still covered her, but clung to her like a sheen of water, showing the plump curves of her breasts and the pointed pebbles of her nipples. His penis stirred at the sight.

She hooked her fingers into the waistband of his jeans and tugged. He braced himself on one knee and bent over her. She lay back with a smile that promised diversions he rarely let himself think about. He was no monk, but he didn't often have time to indulge in sheer pleasure.

Stormy arched up and licked the indent at the base of his neck and then traced his Adam's apple with her tongue. "You're too far." She moved her tongue to his dimple.

A low hum vibrated in his throat. Hand on one of her shoulders, he pressed her back onto the pillows, then allowed his hand to slide over her cami to explore the fullness of her breasts. She wore no bra. Impatient now, he reached under the shirt to touch the skin. He pushed the material up to give him better access.

Her hands dove under his T-shirt and stroked his ribs and chest. Her touch burned a trail across his skin, and he nearly drew back at the excess of sensation when she rolled his nipples between her fingers. In response he bent his head and, without any warning, sucked the tip of her breast into his mouth. He gently pulled the hardened point between his teeth. Stormy gasped beneath him.

He buried his face between her breasts and inhaled her clean, spicy, and distinctly Stormy aroma. She reminded him of soap, rain, and spring all at once.

Stormy grabbed the bottom of his shirt and pulled it over his head.

"My turn," he said. But instead of removing the camisole, he flicked open the button of her shorts and eased the zipper down. She rippled beneath him. He slid his hand into the wisp of cloth she wore under her shorts. There was definitely something to be said for thongs. He pushed the thin barrier aside and let his fingers explore. When he brushed against her clitoris, her hips rose from the bed. His finger circled around it, and she let out an inarticulate purr. She was slick and wet.

"Too slow," she said with more breath than volume. Her wand appeared in her hand a moment later. "I want you naked."

His clothes vanished. Despite his surprise, he laughed.

"I told you I've been practicing."

"Glad you did." He summoned his wand and a moment later a slender packet lay on the bed beside him. He balanced himself on his knees and opened the condom.

"Magic isn't enough?" she asked.

"I could cast a spell, but summoning a condom is easier. I'd rather save my energy for you." He placed the condom at the end of his penis, and then found her hands replacing his to roll the sheath down his length. A tremor shook his legs at her touch and electricity unfurled in his belly.

She wriggled out of her shorts and wound her legs around his.

He could hardly prevent himself from plunging into her. Her exquisiteness called to him as surely as the sun called to the lark. Sucking in a deep breath to aid his control, he nibbled at her breasts again, kissing them, kneading them where his mouth couldn't give her attention.

She lifted her hips and rubbed against him. "Hunter, please."

Her hand reached between them, but he caught it and lifted it above her head. "Not yet."

She let out a small noise as if in pain, but her expression spoke of delicious frustration. Her head lolled back. Her eyes closed.

He straightened his arms for a moment and from above looked at her. Her lithe body, tan in places that showed she didn't wear a bikini when she lay out, rose and fell in tiny bursts of activity. She quivered as his gaze worked its way over her, and when he decided he needed another lick of her skin, a tiny tremor shook her. His tongue flicked over her nipple, and he heard the sharp intake of breath that hissed through her teeth.

She spread her legs, settling his length against her moist warmth, and then brought her legs together. Cheeky minx. She rocked her hips, cradling him in the juncture of her thighs.

He couldn't take much more. Propped on his elbows, he again thrust his fingers into her hair and held her head. He kissed her, deeply, hungrily, frantically. Now. He needed to be in her now.

Her hand, freed now, slipped between them. Her fingers closed over him and guided him to her inner heat. He pushed forward slowly, oh so slowly, feeling her body take him in, envelop him, embrace him. His breath left him like a sigh.

He moved in and out, unhurried, deliberate, feeling

the friction build with each repetition. She joined him, tilting her hips to match his movement. The pace increased, faster, harder, as the delicious pressure coiled deep inside his belly. Stormy quivered beneath him. The constriction wound tighter and tighter, until it sprang free through his body, sending jolts of energy arcing through him. Before the exhilaration left him, Stormy sang out a sound he understood at a cellular level. He felt Stormy's body squeeze around him, each spasm bringing added pleasure to the ebbing sensations.

For several minutes he couldn't speak. He rolled from her, his arm pillowing his head, staring at the ceiling seeing nothing. Now he *knew* he was in trouble. His body had hummed in tune with hers. Already, as he thought about what had happened between them, parts showed signs of rebirth. So to speak.

He didn't want to think about the number of rules he had broken. He had crossed the line, and why? For corporal gratification. Damn fine gratification, but he was supposed to be disciplined. What was it about her that made him forget his training?

She curled into his side. Her breathing came as a soft warm breeze over his skin. "Thank you for staying."

" 'You're welcome' somehow seems inadequate." The hell of it was he wasn't sure he wouldn't toss his principles aside again if she showed the slightest inclination. He found himself rolling toward her before he could stop himself. Disappointment in himself ate at him. Then he realized she had said something. "I'm sorry?"

"You are?"

"No . . . I mean, yes, uh, no. I didn't hear what you said." Blathering idiot.

"I said you were more than adequate." She lifted her hand and drew circles on his chest. "Maybe this whole bodyguard thing will work out after all."

He froze. No, no, no. He had a job, a duty. "You can't think this will happen again."

"Why not?"

Because I'm a Guard. Your Guard. We can't do this."

"We just did."

"Look, we both went through a trauma tonight. Maybe we weren't hurt, but we weren't ourselves either. This was a release. Thank-God-we're-alive sex." That had to be the only explanation. The tension had been too much. She had been available. That had to be it. Only he knew he lied to himself.

Her smile disappeared. She scooted away from him and covered herself with the corner of the blanket. "We're both grown-ups. We're allowed to have sex."

She didn't have to know how much she affected him. "No, we're not. I'm not allowed to have sex with you. You can have sex with anyone you want, but it can't be me." Only, the thought of her with someone else made his blood curdle.

She jerked back. For an instant those blue eyes widened, and pink stole into her cheeks. Then she lifted her chin and gazed directly at him. "That's good to know, because I wouldn't want to inconvenience you again. I'll look for pity sex elsewhere."

Pity sex? "No, that's not what I—"

"You've already apologized once. You don't need to do it again." She swung her legs from the bed and tried to stand as she wrapped the blanket around her. She fell back. "Do you mind getting up? You're on top of the blanket."

The coldness of her tone pierced him. He had fucked up. Grabbing a tissue from the nightstand, he cleaned himself as he stood. She whipped the blanket around herself.

He could salvage this. "Stormy, I didn't mean—"

"You've made yourself perfectly clear. We got lost in the moment. It isn't the first time this has happened. You're right. It was a great way to release tension. I feel better." Except her voice was sharper than a blade.

"You don't understand." Now a different type of panic was setting in.

"Of course I do. You're my Guard, and we broke the rules. Don't worry, I won't report you. Haven't you ever bent the rules before?" She paused. "Could you please put some clothes on? It's getting a little awkward talking to you while you're naked." She turned her back to him.

He summoned his wand, and with a flick of his wrist, sweats appeared. He pulled them on, but as soon as he finished tying the string, they disappeared. "What the hell?"

She turned around, then covered her eyes. "Now you're just making fun of me."

"No, I'm not." He summoned another pair, but as soon as he donned them, they vanished as well. He faced her. "Are you doing this?"

"No," she said, frowning. "I don't want to see you naked anymore."

Naked. He cringed. Damn it. "This is your spell."

"What?"

"You used magic on me. You said, 'I want you naked.' Now I can't keep clothes on."

Her mouth opened for a moment, and then she started laughing.

"It's not funny," he said through clenched teeth.

She caught her breath. "Yes, yes, it really is." And she started laughing again.

"You have to undo this. I can't go back to the barracks nude." He tore the sheet from the bed and twisted it around his hips. The second the end was tucked in, the sheet disappeared, which sent her into fresh gales of laughter.

She sucked in a breath. "I'm sorry. You're right. It isn't funny," she said between gasps. "Not wearing clothes might limit your efficacy. Not to mention giving people the wrong idea about us if they found you here." She snickered, but drew her wand and looked at it. "I don't know what to do."

"You said you've been practicing. So, do magic."

"But I don't know what I did in the first place."

"You used your instincts. Do that again." He resisted the inclination to cover himself. He refused to give in to some misguided idea of propriety when he wasn't at fault. Maybe she'd try harder if she was uncomfortable.

She focused on him, and a smile twitched at her lips.

"Concentrate." He almost growled.

She nodded. Her smile evaporated as she looked at him again. A slight narrowing of her eyes, a minute change in the set of her lips stole all traces of hilarity from her. The anger and hurt returned to her face, and as the silence stretched, she looked ready to cry.

Guilt weighed upon him. His words had been brutish and clumsy. He hadn't explained himself well. Once he had clothes again he would fix things.

"I take it back. I don't want to see him naked." Her voice broke, but she swished the wand in front of her.

Without waiting another instant, Hunter summoned a pair of pants. He pulled them on, fastened the zipper and button, and held his breath. They remained on him. He let out the breath he had been holding.

She turned away from him. "You can go home now." Her tone was flat.

"Stormy, I want to—"

"Go home, Hunter. If you're still my Guard tomorrow, I'll see you when we go to Lucas's house." She walked into the bathroom.

The silence of the room sounded like an accusation. He summoned a shirt, pulled it on, and walked to the bathroom. He lifted his hand to knock, but stopped. She didn't want to see him now. Maybe if he gave her some time . . .

As he turned to leave, his gaze fell on the bed. Thinking of what had happened there sent shivers through him even now. His stomach clenched. Damn it. He had really screwed up. She had no idea how much his emotions were tangled up in her.

And damn it, he had lost two of his favorite pairs of sweats.

13

JUSTIN'S GUIDE FOR THE ARTIST

•

Restraint is not a weakness.

STORMY STUMBLED TOWARD the bathroom, mopping her forehead with a towel. Ian's workout had been brutal, but nothing compared to the way she had pushed herself. Every breath seemed a major effort. She blinked several times because tiny black dots floated in her vision. That morning, Ian had put her through magical exercises, but he had left before lunch to start getting ready for their dinner. Could he be more of a toady? Her fathers were gay and they didn't primp as much as Ian did for Luc. Since she couldn't leave her room, she had continued practicing on her own.

She almost fell as her sole caught on the highly polished marble floor. *Really, Stormy, lift your feet.*

Her arms felt rubbery. She must have pushed herself too hard. Not reckless by nature, she knew she was taking a risk, but her lack of competent magic skills bothered her more. She never wanted to face an unwanted naked man again. Besides, she had two hours before Ian came to get her for dinner, and she wouldn't have to do magic tonight. Something to drink, a little snack, and a power nap would revive her.

Just before she pushed the door open to the bathroom, someone knocked. "Come in, since I can't open the door for you."

Hunter stepped inside.

Her stomach dropped, and she grimaced. No, no, no, no, no. Why the hell did he have to be here? Hadn't he caused her enough pain last night?

"Go away," she said as she braced herself on the wall to keep from folding to the floor.

"I thought we could talk—" He broke off and stared at her.

"Not now. I'm not up to it."

"What happened?" He hurried to her. "You never left the Hall. I checked. Who did this to you?"

"Nobody did anything to me." She saw the bed and imagined it calling to her. *I'm coming.*

"You're ill." He picked her up.

She was too tired to protest. And frankly it felt good not to walk. "I'm fine. I was just practicing."

"How long?"

"I don't know. Three hours? And Ian was here this morning—"

"You little idiot. You overdid it." He laid her gently on the bed.

In her exhaustion, she thought about the last time he had carried her here. Last night, in fact. That had been nice. Except afterward. Maybe they could try again and do it better this time.

Hunter dashed to the bas-relief and touched it with his wand. The slave carving sprang to life. "How may I—?"

"I need some type of sports drink, something with lots of sugar and vitamins. Also pasta, uh, spaghetti carbonara, and don't scrimp on the bacon."

"No, Hunter." She tried to sit up, but could barely lift her head. "I'm going to dinner in a little bit. I can't eat ahead of time."

"And send up some cookies right now. Any kind."

"Fruit would be healthier," Stormy said.

He strode back to the bed. "I don't care about healthy. You're about to crash."

"What?"

The fruity drink materialized along with a plate of oatmeal raisin cookies. He grabbed them. "Perfect."

Propping up her head, he placed the edge of the glass to her lips. "Drink."

"I don't like sweet stuff. Can't I just have water?"

"No. Drink." He tilted the glass.

She shuddered as the sugary stuff hit her tongue, but when it slid down her throat into her stomach, she felt a little refreshing tingle. "That wasn't so bad."

"Now eat this." He shoved a cookie at her.

"It'll spoil my appetite. Besides, I don't eat sugar."

"You do now." He pushed the cookie into her mouth.

She didn't have the strength to fight. The cookie was the most delicious thing she'd ever had. Maybe she should rethink this no-sugar thing.

A minute later the spaghetti appeared. She closed her eyes and inhaled. Cheese, bacon, and garlic. The aroma alone was scandalously fattening. Hunter was already twirling a mouthful on a fork. He held it out to her, and before even thinking about the calories, she curled her lips around the fork and let the blend of flavors play on her tongue. Oh my God, it was worth ruining her appetite to eat like this. "Mmm, that is so good."

He fed her another bite. "I know. That's why I ordered it."

She felt guilty that she was making him work so hard. "You don't have to feed me."

"Yes, I do. You're not strong enough right now." He fed her another bite.

"No. I'm good. Let me show you what I learned." She summoned her wand and was about to make another cookie fly to her, when Hunter grabbed her wand from her hand.

The wand sparked. Hunter jerked back, but he didn't drop it. "No magic. Not now." He placed the wand on the bedside table and shook his hand.

"Are you hurt?"

"Nothing I couldn't handle." But he looked at the wand with a curious expression on his face. "Drink some more."

She swallowed more of the sports drink, but then pushed it away. "Does this have alcohol in it? It feels like I'm drunk."

"You're not drunk, but you are dangerously low on energy." He made her eat another bite. "One more. Then you need to sleep."

"I can't sleep. I'm going to dinner, so just a nap."

"I'll stay here and wake you for the party. How much time do you need?"

Sleep sounded so good. "An hour."

He moved the dishes away from her and covered her with the comforter. "You'll feel better after you sleep a little."

"Okay." She snuggled into the pillows. It was comfortable. "Wait." Her voice sounded weak to her ears. "Why are you here so early?"

"Never mind. It can wait." He tucked the blanket around her. "Now sleep."

He may have said something else, but she missed it because the moment she closed her eyes she was out.

"STORMY."

His voice echoed in the ballroom. Everyone was watching the two of them, but they had eyes only for each other.

"Stormy."

Her name sounded like a caress from his lips. They met in the middle of the dance floor. He lifted his hands, but instead of putting them around her to dance, he shook her shoulder.

"Stormy."

That wasn't right. Her eyes flew open. Hunter was here, but they weren't in a ballroom. They were in her room, and he *was* shaking her shoulder.

"It's time to get up. Ian's coming in half an hour."

The dream faded and reality returned. Her confusion left as she remembered where she was and who she was. She nodded. "Got it."

She swung her legs off the bed, and Hunter helped her stand. "How are you feeling?"

She took inventory. "Better, I think. The drunken feeling is gone."

"Good, but you can't push it. No magic tonight."

"I wasn't planning on it, Dad." Sarcasm dripped from her words.

He gave her a flat stare.

"Sorry. Have you been here the whole time?"

He nodded.

Chagrin replaced the annoyance she felt with him. She hadn't expected him to play nursemaid. What kind of man willingly took that much time for a woman he didn't want to sleep with? And acted as an alarm clock too? "You didn't have to do that."

"Yeah, I did. You were pretty out of it."

"I was pretty loopy, wasn't I?"

"You could call it loopy. I'd call it stupid." He gave her a look that dared her to contradict him.

"Maybe, but I needed to work on my magic."

"Not to the point of collapse. It will come with time."

I don't think I have much time. But she didn't say those words aloud. "I need to get dressed now. You're coming too, right? I mean tonight, not while I get dressed." Smooth.

"Yes, but not as a guest. You're still my assignment." He was wearing the black jeans and black T-shirt of the Guards, his uniform. She hadn't noticed earlier.

"Then you can keep an eye on me and make sure I don't do anything else stupid tonight." She crossed to her closet, grabbed the dress she would wear, and walked to the bathroom. "I won't be long."

"Uh, Stormy."

She turned around. "What?"

He pointed. Her wand was bobbing in the air beside her. "Oh. I forgot to stow it." She grabbed it and said, "Sanctum." The wand vanished and she ducked into the bathroom.

Thirty-five minutes later, makeup and hair done, dress donned, she stepped out. The room was empty. Disappointment fizzled in her stomach, but she chided herself. Who was she making an entrance for anyway?

A moment later, she heard a knock at the door. "Come in."

Once again the door seemed to unlock for someone other than herself. Ian marched into the room. Hunter followed behind him. He must have taken up a post outside while she showered.

Ian wore that same extravagant lapel pin he had the other night. "Good. You're finally ready. We're late."

"Late? The dinner is at seven. It's only six thirty-five now."

"Yes, but it will take us forty minutes to get there." Ian glanced at his watch in annoyance.

She wanted so badly to meet Hunter's gaze behind Ian's back, but she no longer felt comfortable enough to share the moment of exasperation at Ian with him. "We could always pop over there."

"Luc's house is shielded. We have to drive. Although if you want to try, we have to transport to the car anyway."

"No." Hunter stepped forward. "She can't transport. I'll take her to the car."

"Suit yourself. But let's get going." Ian spun on his heel and exited the room.

Eager wasn't he? She wanted to share those words with Hunter too, but didn't.

The drive took forty-five minutes, made especially unbearable with Ian expressing his impatience every thirty seconds or so.

Lucas's house was in Rancho Santa Fe. The beautiful Spanish-style house glowed a warm brown in the setting sun. Stormy looked at the facade as they pulled into the circular driveway. This place was huge. Luc wasn't hurting for money.

The man himself greeted them as they pulled up. He opened the door for Stormy and helped her from the car.

"My dear, Stormy. I am so happy to see you weren't injured last night. Such a tragedy." He kissed her hand.

The man had charm, she had to give him that. Which reminded her. Ian had lost his sling since yesterday. Apparently his injury hadn't been as serious as he thought. "You weren't hurt?"

"A scratch. Nothing really. Of course I have suffered

worse recently." He touched the patch that covered his eye. "I'm sure you've heard the story. I don't blame you, of course, but I am happy to hear you're limiting your contact with the godmothers."

He hooked her arm with his and led her into the house. "You know, I was thinking about the abysmal situation in which you find yourself."

Ian joined them. "It really is tragic, isn't it?"

Lucas spared him no attention. "You need guidance. Clearly you can't rely on the godmothers to give you any. I'd like to offer my knowledge and expertise."

As if she would trust anything he'd say. Especially after he tried to kill her. But she smiled. "No, I couldn't impose. You're a busy man."

"I can think of nothing I'd rather do," Lucas said.

"An outstanding idea, Luc." Ian nearly bounced with excitement.

"But this evening isn't about the difficulties you face." Luc guided her to the bar that stood at one end of a long living room. "Wine?"

"Please." She could use a drink. She glanced around. The room was well proportioned and tastefully decorated. "You have a lovely house."

Luc clicked his tongue. "It's adequate. Unfortunately my home was destroyed. This is temporary until I can find the right place to rebuild." He handed her glass.

"Rebuild?"

"You didn't hear?"

"No."

Ian spoke in an almost eager tone. "The godmothers destroyed Luc's house."

She hoped her face betrayed none of her thoughts. She'd have to ask the aunts the next time she saw them. "That's awful."

"He was lucky to escape with his life." Ian's earnest

expression nearly brought out an inappropriate response. Like laughter.

Lucas lifted his hand. "But none of that now. Tonight we shall celebrate our escape from danger."

Stormy glanced around the room. "Is it just us?"

"Yes. I thought we'd have a more intimate gathering tonight. Other people would just distract us. I am eager to get to know you."

"Especially since you will be working so closely together," Ian said.

"What a delightful idea." She smiled at Lucas. Inside she was anxious. Did he really expect her to spend more time with him? Apparently Ian expected her to, and he had too much say over what she did. Lucas was dangerous. He hid behind a great deal of charm, but the danger was there. And if he was ready to step in as an ally, he must believe he was powerful enough to convince her. His plans must be further along than they thought.

Don't get ahead of yourself, Stormy.

Hunter took a position against the wall. Despite the awkwardness between them, she was glad to have him here.

Lucas steered the conversation onto innocuous subjects. Ian basked in the attention, even though most of Lucas's focus was on her. She found it hard not to laugh at or mock Ian, especially when he pointed out that he wore his lapel pin in Lucas's honor. It had taken all her strength not to burst out in guffaws. Nevertheless, she maintained her facade of interest while trying to glean insight into Lucas's aims and goals. But he was smart. He wasn't revealing anything about his agenda. Yet.

Dinner was casual even with Dmitri serving them. Good food, banal conversation, pleasant, but not intriguing. She tried to observe Dmitri, but spotted nothing unusual about the servant except that he was creepier than Ian in his attitude toward Lucas. She was beginning to wonder if she'd learn anything worthwhile. Hunter moved only when they did, and then only to a different position on the wall.

When dinner ended, Lucas pushed back. "I understand your father is Justin Jones. I admire his work. In fact, I believe I own one of his pieces."

He believed? "I'm sure Daddy would be thrilled to know."

Ian said, "Stormy weaves."

Lucas nodded. "Yes, I understand you're also an artist of a sort."

She didn't allow the "of a sort" remark to dim her smile.

Lucas rose from his chair. "Come. Perhaps you'll let me show you my collection."

She stifled a snort. That sounded like a bad pickup line. "I'd love to see it." She took his arm.

Ian padded along behind them. "You're going to love this."

Lucas led them through the hallway to a recessed door. "I keep my treasures in here." He pushed the door open to a room with soft, museum-quality lighting.

Whoa. She stepped into the room almost reverently. She had grown up with art and knew how to appreciate it.

Hunter followed them into the room and leaned against an empty spot.

"I'd prefer you didn't touch the walls," Lucas said.

Hunter lifted his hands in apology and stood away from the wall, hands clasped behind his back.

She barely noticed the exchange. The art filled her, and she took the time to gaze over the whole room as one before examining the pieces individually.

Lucas stood beside her. "Works that reflect our world."

She said nothing, preferring to study art in silence. She stopped in front of a brilliant Renaissance painting that depicted a witch burning. Brilliant, but disturbing.

"I see you're admiring my Caravaggio."

"Mmm." She didn't want to speak yet.

"Such a tragic scene, but quite accurate. We've suffered much at the hands of the Groundlings."

Her attention shifted focus. Here was the agenda she was waiting for. "I hadn't heard about that. I don't know Arcani history."

"Ah, yes, the years you spent as a Groundling. There's so much you need to learn."

It was time to let him think he was winning her over. "You know, I feel my lack of knowledge is such a burden." She sighed and moved to the next painting, but out of the corner of her eye she spied a tapestry. It captured her attention. A pang hit her as she realized how long she'd gone without sitting at the loom. This weaving brought her a feeling almost of homecoming.

She stood in front of the tapestry. It was ancient, beautiful, the threads still vibrant, the weave tight. The scene depicted a wizard holding a staff, handing a red orb to a woman.

"You found the masterpiece in my collection." Lucas stroked a finger down the length of the woman's cloak. She heard the soft swish of his finger against the wool. "This piece was found by Mother in a castle in Prague. She hid it during the war."

"How lucky she saved it."

"Yes. She could save very little else." He gazed at the image and a slight frown appeared on his lips. "It has an interesting history. Perhaps I shall have the honor to tell you someday."

"I would love to hear it, but you should write it

down, just in case." She took a step toward the painting beside the weaving, but took one last glance at it.

She froze. Her heart pounded. Not trusting her vision, she stepped back in front of the tapestry and leaned in closer.

"What do you see?" Lucas asked.

Trying to act as if nothing were out of the ordinary, she smiled up at Lucas. "Nothing. I'm simply admiring the craftsmanship. Do you see the detail in the wizard's hands? I could only aspire to create something like this in my lifetime." There were errors in the weaving. Too many errors. And the warp thread colors matched the weft as if to camouflage the mistakes. No piece of work this great should have so many mistakes.

"It is spectacular." He watched her, then looked at the fabric, then back at her. She moved on to the next piece.

Her heart hammered in her chest. She drew in slow, deep breaths to prevent her cheeks from burning. She stopped at the painting and pretended to examine it, but she didn't notice anything about it.

The tapestry had a hidden pattern. She could see it because she understood how the warp was laid out, but she could make no sense of it without further study. She doubted anyone else would notice it. Perhaps Lucas knew more about it—it was his tapestry after all—but somehow she didn't think she should ask him.

Dmitri appeared. "Coffee and dessert are ready."

"Thank you, Dmitri." Lucas turned to his guests. "Shall we?"

A welcome diversion to be sure. She nodded.

He ushered them back to the living room where Dmitri poured the coffee for them.

"There, isn't this nice?" Lucas asked. "A fine dinner, and beauty. And some art as well." He winked at her.

She let out a small laugh and took the seat beside Lucas.

"I'm concerned about you, my dear," Lucas said.

She could do without his concern. However, she gave him her best listening expression.

"I'm worried that you haven't been exposed enough to the crisis we Arcani face."

What crisis? She may have lived her life as a Groundling, but her home life had been normal . . . well, as normal as could be with fathers who had magic. They exposed her to no angst or crises except the normal teenage stuff. "I was raised as a Groundling. My fathers never told me about a crisis."

"Precisely. We are a hidden society."

"Um-hmm. But don't you think that's necessary?"

"With our power? We skulk about, yet we should be ruling. Magic is an integral part of this world, but we pretend it isn't. We've let the Groundlings take control."

"I've never thought of it that way." She felt Hunter's gaze on her, but she ignored it. "How do you propose to change that?"

"The Arcani must take their rightful place in the world." Lucas leaned in to her. "*We* need to take our rightful places, you as a godmother, I as a thinker."

Ian perked up. "As a great thinker *and* leader, Luc."

Lucas bowed his head. "I thank you for your faith in me."

His words cleared up a question she had. Although he had tried to kill her (if Hunter was right, which she didn't doubt), he had failed, so why go to the effort of getting to know her? Here was the answer. He wasn't above using her if he could.

"The Council is coming around to your thinking," Ian said.

"And it is gratifying to find like thinkers." Lucas

frowned. "But it is not enough. We must take action. The defection of the godmothers shows how strong this cancer is. They have chosen the Groundlings over their own kind."

Their own kind? They were all humans. Groundlings and Arcani. Lucas was wrong.

"We mustn't forget the godmothers stand against us. We were attacked yesterday." Lucas struck one fist into the other palm. "They must be stopped. They are holding us back."

Lucas's lies came so easily and with such passion. Stormy didn't dare look at Hunter. "Do you think they'll try again?"

Lucas nodded. "I believe so."

If she hadn't had more information, she'd absolutely believe him. His charm and vehemence combined to give his words veracity. He was a superior manipulator. A shiver that she didn't bother to hide ran down her spine. Lucas was frightening. Only now did the full extent of the danger she placed herself in hit her. And she used that fear to further obscure the true purpose of her visit. "You don't think the godmothers will try to hurt me too?"

His eyes filled with sadness, or at least widened in an attempt to portray sadness. "If you stand in their way."

Stormy gazed into Lucas's eyes and saw the hunger for power burn in them. Steely resolve flamed to life within her and replaced the fear. She was as good an actor as he. "I'm not afraid. I will do what's right."

14

JUSTIN'S GUIDE FOR THE ARTIST

•

You must be true to yourself to access your inner strength.

ENOUGH. HUNTER PUSHED himself from the wall. "Stormy needs to leave now."

Ian scowled. "You don't make the decisions here."

"I do when her safety is involved."

Ian looked affronted. "You think she's threatened here?"

"That's my job—to find the threat everywhere. But I'm more concerned with her energy levels. She did a lot of magic today. She needs to rest."

"Is this true, Stormy?" Luc asked.

She nodded sheepishly. "I was rather stupid today."

Good girl, Hunter thought. "Talbott, you coming or will you find your own way back?"

"You should accompany her, Ian," Luc said. "She is important."

Ian scurried to his feet. "Okay then. Shall I call you tomorrow?"

"That won't be necessary." Luc shared a look of amusement with Stormy.

Since when had they been able to communicate without talking? Hunter didn't like it.

"If I may . . ." Luc summoned his wand and held out his hand.

Hunter stepped forward, ready to respond to the magic.

A moment later a hinged jewelry box appeared in Luc's palm. He opened it and revealed a diamond brooch. "I would like to give this token of my esteem to you."

It looked like a feminine version of Ian's lapel pin. A graceful diamond wand lay across a crest inlaid with rubies and emeralds.

Stormy's eyes widened. "I couldn't accept that. It's too . . . beautiful." She reached out a finger to touch it. "Are those real?"

Luc laughed. "It wouldn't have much worth if it wasn't. I would be honored if you would wear it." Before she could protest, Luc took the pin from its bed and lifted it to her bodice. "May I?"

Stormy smiled and offered the silky black fabric to him.

Wrath uncurled in Hunter's insides, stretching its tentacles through his nerves like a slow working poison. When Luc's fingers slipped beneath the fabric and touched her skin, he wanted to grab Luc's hand and break each bone, one at a time, just to hear them snap. Somewhere in his head, reason was telling him it was an innocent gesture, but Hunter didn't want to listen. It required every trace of his training not to lapse out of sentry mode and smash his fist into Luc's smug expression.

"To remind you of your place in the Arcani world. May you wear it in great health." Luc bent over her hand and kissed it.

"Thank you," Stormy said. She touched the brooch. "It's lovely."

Luc smiled at her. "And now good night, *mon amie.* I am thrilled we had this chance to talk and become friends."

"Good night, Luc. It's been most enlightening," Stormy said.

In a few minutes they were seated in the car, Ian and Stormy in the back. Hunter's instincts hummed. That whole pin episode was off. Stormy had acted weird there toward the end. Not as weird as he had, but he was ignoring his own reactions. She had learned something this evening, but he'd watched her the entire time and didn't notice anything. He needed to question her without Ian around. He needed to get her alone.

Right. As if that was a good idea after last night. She wouldn't want to see him. He still hadn't explained himself or apologized for his behavior. Not that he'd had the chance.

But this was different. They had to talk about Luc.

No one spoke on the ride home. When he checked in the rearview, he saw Stormy sleeping, her head leaning against the side of the car. At least she wasn't using Ian as a pillow. He didn't think he could stand that.

When he parked the car, Stormy woke up. "Where are we?"

"The garage." Hunter climbed from the car, opened the door for her, and reached in a hand to help her out.

She brushed past him.

Ian waited a minute, but Hunter just glared at him. Ian pressed his lips together and clambered from the backseat. "A chauffeur is supposed to open the door for his clients."

"Yeah, well, I'm not a chauffeur, I'm a Guard, and you're not my client, she is."

Ian looked as if he was counting to ten as he climbed from the car. Facing Stormy, he said, "I'll leave you here then. Stormy, you should be honored that Luc has taken such a liking to you." He touched his lapel pin and nodded to her as if they were sharing a secret. Brandishing his wand, he vanished, leaving a slight shimmer in the space where he had stood.

"Ugh." She removed the pin and stuffed it into her purse.

"Don't you like your gift from Luc?" He hated the petulant tone in his voice.

She shot him a cold look. "Do you mind? I'm tired."

"Can you transport yet?"

"I couldn't earlier. What makes you think I learned at Lucas's?"

She was in a pissy mood. He decided not to ask, just grabbed her arm and popped into the Hall's anteroom.

"Hey," she said when they arrived. "A little warning."

"Why? You just would have argued."

She clamped her mouth shut, then nodded. "You're right."

"I'm right?" He drew back. "What do you mean I'm right?"

She shrugged. "I would have argued." She headed for her room.

Hunter fell in step behind her. "We need to talk."

"I know." She reached her room. "Come in."

He sighed and followed her directive.

With a slight shudder, she tossed the purse into a dresser drawer and faced him. "So talk."

He ran a hand over his hair. "Last night, it didn't end like I wanted."

"Oh, really?" She raised an eyebrow. "I thought we were going to talk about Lucas."

She wasn't going to make this easy for him. Hell, he

wasn't making it easy for himself. How did one apologize for having great sex? He drew himself upright. "Stormy, I was ham-fisted last night. Nothing came out right, and every time I tried to explain, I stepped in it further."

"I'm listening." He couldn't read her expression. She stared at him without revealing anything.

"That's why I was here earlier. To talk to you and apologize." He raised a finger. "Luckily as it turned out."

She cocked an eyebrow at him. "Now you're procrastinating."

This was going so badly. Again. Everything from his mouth sounded lame. "You're right, but I haven't ever had a conversation like this one."

"Are you asking me to cut you some slack?"

"No. I don't deserve slack after last night." Finally. That felt sincere.

She crossed her arms in a nonthreatening manner. "You know, you're kind of cute when you're contrite."

"Honestly, last night was wonderful, but I can't have a relationship with my asset."

"Is that what I am? An asset?"

He nodded, hating himself for doing so because he saw the hurt return to her eyes. "That doesn't mean I didn't . . . couldn't have feelings for you if I wasn't assigned to you."

"But you are."

"I am."

"And you won't ask for a transfer?"

"I have, and they didn't give me one."

She said nothing for a moment. Then on a sigh, she spoke. "I suppose it's for the best. I have so much going on right now the last thing I need is another complication." She squinted one eye and sent him a sideways glance. "No offense."

"None taken." There. It was settled. So why did the urge to take her in his arms rise so powerfully in him?

She said, "So about Lucas . . ."

Good. Safe subject. Sort of. "The guy's insane. He can't seriously think the Arcani can rule the world."

"I think he does. With him ruling them." She paused. "He has the charisma."

"That slimy, undetectable film that coats politicians and the like? Yeah, he does." Hunter's heart rate increased as her face softened in appreciation of his comment. "The Arcani don't have the numbers. If we expose ourselves, the Groundlings will try to take advantage of our magic and kill many of us."

"Not to mention Groundlings will be killed by zealous Arcani. Or the civil war that will erupt in the Arcani world between those who want to remain hidden and Lucas's side." She hesitated. "You don't think he's right, do you? That the Arcani are a hidden society and that we shouldn't be afraid to be in the open?" Her voice was unsure.

He faced her. "Look, I believe in freedom as much as the next guy, but freedom is a word that's tossed around without a lot of thinking about its meaning."

"Hunh. You know, Reggie said the almost the exact same thing."

Somehow that wasn't reassuring.

"So what does freedom mean to you?" she asked.

"It doesn't mean imposing one's will on someone else, or claiming superiority over someone. Or using it as a catchword to cover your own agenda."

"Sounds like you've picked a side."

"Not Lucas's. We aren't all-powerful beings who can ward off every danger to ourselves. If we could,

Lucas wouldn't be wearing that eye patch. Dead is dead." He shook his head. "And frankly, my faith in Groundlings is limited. Most of them are wonderful, but can you imagine what they would do to the gnomes and fairies and dragons?"

"Dragons? There are dragons?"

He laughed. "Aye, there be dragons. But even fewer of them than Arcani."

"So if Ian is right, and the Council decides to follow Lucas, what will you do?"

He thought for a moment. "Right now I have to believe they won't. I am a Guard, and my loyalties have to lie with the Council."

"And mine lie with the godmothers." Her gaze never wavered from his.

A piece of his heart broke. She had declared her defiance of the Council. She looked at him.

"Don't do this, Stormy." He had to touch her, to transfer some sense into her. He brushed his knuckles along the curve of her upper arm.

Her eyes welled up. "What would you have me do? Give up being a godmother? This is who I am. I have a duty too."

He couldn't stop himself. He leaned down and kissed her softly, gently, willing her to change her mind. To stay with him.

Her kiss was accepting and poignant. To him it spoke of what might have been if they had made different choices.

She broke it off first, but leaned her forehead against his. "We can't do this."

"No." He closed his eyes. For the first time in his life, he questioned his duty. He summoned his wand. "Stormy Jones-Smythe, I arrest you—"

"What?" She pushed back from him, but his fingers gripped her arm.

"—for treason, intent to subvert the rule of the Council, and create anarchy."

"Hunter, you can't do this." Her shock had drawn all the color from her face.

As his gaze bore into her, he followed the drill. He drew his wand. "Will you come peacefully?"

"You can't be serious." A note of panic colored her tone.

"Will you come peacefully?"

Her brows furrowed. "No." Her wand appeared in her hand.

He was prepared for that. They all tried that. But Guards knew all the tricks. Without releasing his hold on her, he lifted the wand in his other hand and said, "I command you—"

"You can't touch me." Her voice wavered as if she were fighting back tears.

The fingers that gripped her arm tingled, then burned. He jerked back, releasing her, then tried to grab her again. The pain flared in his hand and radiated into his arm as if a baseball bat had hit him. He let go. "What are you doing?"

"I don't know, but you can't touch me."

Touch. She'd done it again. No one had ever broken through the Guard's spell. Except her. "Damn it, Stormy, you can't do this."

She moved away from him. Tears spilled from her eyes. "I can't let you take me. I have to help the godmothers." She spun and tried to dash from the room.

He raced her to the door, and as she pulled it open, he slammed it shut. Without touching her. "You're under arrest. I can't let you go."

She faced him, conflict evident in her expression. Then she touched his arm.

He yelled. The pain was more intense this time.

"I'm sorry," she cried, sobbing, but still holding him. "But I can't let you stop me. I have to stop Lucas."

He collapsed to his knees, the agony obliterating all ability to stand. "Stormy."

"I didn't want to hurt you. I'm sorry." She pulled the door open. Then she let go and ran.

THANK GOD HUNTER had been there. The door only opened for her because he had unlocked it with his presence. Stormy knew she had to leave the Hall, but how? She ran to the anteroom, the only place where one could enter or exit. But now what?

It was late. The anteroom was empty except for the two Guards on duty. They straightened when they saw her. They knew she wasn't supposed to go anywhere without an escort.

Hunter lumbered into the opening and grabbed onto the archway to the chamber. His face looked drawn, and beneath his tan, his skin seemed pale. Her heart constricted at the evidence of the pain she had caused, but she was glad he was okay.

"Grab her. She's under arrest," he shouted, although his voice was weak.

The two Guards ran to either side of her and grabbed her. They both dropped their grip almost at once.

"What the hell?" one said and grabbed her again, only to drop to the floor a few seconds later. The other one pulled his wand and aimed it at her.

They were going to kill her. Stormy clutched her wand and closed her eyes.

"No," she heard Hunter say, but the sound faded.

Her breath squeezed out of her lungs. She felt the air swirl around her as if she were swept into a vortex. A moment later she could breathe normally.

She cracked her eyes open. How did she get on the beach?

She looked around. She didn't think she was dead and in heaven. Nope, the sand crunched under her feet, she could taste the salt in the air and hear the waves curling onto the shore. She had little light because the moon was a mere sliver, but she could see the cliffs that rose from the beach. No way. She had transported to Black's Beach?

Whoo-hoo! She had popped out of the Hall by herself.

The jubilation didn't last long. She sank to the sand and laid her head on her knees. She had hurt Hunter and the other Guards. Her soul ached, if such a thing was possible.

Ten minutes or so later, she declared an end to her self-pity. She stood, brushed the sand from her dress. Crap, her shorts were at the Hall. She gazed up at the cliff she now had to climb. In a dress. For a moment she wondered if she should try to zap herself up to the top, but after the earlier overuse of magic and then her escape tonight, she felt woozy enough. She hadn't enjoyed the drunken sensation that Hunter had helped her through.

Hunter.

She refused to think about him. He had wanted to arrest her. No, he had arrested her; she had just escaped.

Slipping her shoes off, she climbed. Half an hour later, she reached the road. Now what? Where could she go? She had no money, no clothes, and no idea where the aunts were. Home was about twenty miles away.

The lights of UC San Diego shone in the night, and

the road stretched long beyond the campus. With a sigh, she started up the highway, wishing she had worn tennis shoes instead of heels with the dress. As she walked, she tried to forget what she'd done to Hunter. Instead she focused on the tapestry. What had she seen in that image? What was its significance? And why had it affected her so deeply?

For an hour or more of dodging cars, rocks, students, bikes, and other debris, she hiked along Torrey Pines Road, as it curved down from the top of the bluff, past the golf course and state park, back down to the beach. The magic and the hike had depleted her energy levels, and her high heels had rubbed blisters on her feet. She didn't think she could go much farther. It was late, and hope of rescue was minimal. Until she spotted a couple walking back to their car from the beach and had a brainstorm.

"Excuse me."

The pair looked up in surprise. Wariness covered the man's features. "Yes?"

"I'm sorry, but could I use your phone?"

"Uh . . ."

She scrambled for a story. "I know this looks odd, but my date got angry with me and dumped me on the side of the road. He's got my phone. If I could just log on to Twitter . . ."

The woman's face became more sympathetic. The man still looked doubtful. "Why don't you just call someone?"

"As stupid as this sounds, I'm just visiting my aunt here, and I don't know her number. But I *do* know her Twitter address. She loves Twitter. It's always on. I can tell her to send a taxi." It sounded lame even to her ears. Great. As if she didn't feel guilty enough about Hunter, now she could add lying to the total.

"Here. I have a Twitter app," said the woman, handing Stormy the phone. Their fingers touched, and the woman jerked her hand back. "Hey, you shocked me."

Stormy let out a laugh that sounded brittle to her ears. "I think you shocked me." She had forgotten about the spell she had placed on herself. She shook the phone. "Thanks for this." She touched the screen, opened the app, and composed a rescue message of 140 characters or less.

Behind her the man was arguing. "How do you know she isn't calling her backup to come and rob us?"

"She's not calling anyone at all. Besides, did you see her dress? She was shoved out somewhere all right. Poor thing." The woman shook a finger in her escort's face. "You ever try that with me, I'll shoot you."

Tweet sent, Stormy handed the phone back, careful not to make contact with the woman. "Thank you again."

"We could drive you," said the woman.

The man whipped his head to her, but the woman just elbowed him in the side.

"No, really, that's okay. My aunt doesn't live far."

"We can't just leave you," the man said.

"Really, I'll be fine." She could only hope the aunts got the message soon and not leave her stranded all night at the beach. That prospect was not appealing.

A moment later Kristin and a man appeared in the parking lot. The couple stared. "Where the hell did they come from?"

"Damn." The man accompanying Kristin pulled out his wand and quickly said, "*Glacia.*"

The couple stiffened, frozen. Their eyes darted back and forth in a panic.

"What did you do?" asked Stormy. Her stomach flipped at the thought of bringing more pain to someone tonight.

"No time for intros." The wizard turned to the couple and said, "*Dediscite*."

The couples' eyes grew blank, and the wizard said, "You will forget this woman and us. In thirty seconds, you will go back to your car and carry on as if nothing had happened." He grabbed Stormy's hand, then dropped it. "What the—"

"Sorry." Stormy summoned her wand and touched her shoulder. "I'm done now." She felt energy flow from her as if something had rippled away.

"We have to go." He looked at Kristin as if telling her to hurry up.

Kristin grabbed Stormy's hand. "Ready."

Blackness enveloped Stormy, and the air rushed from her lungs, but a moment later she was in the center of a cheery room. The aunts beamed at her. Two other men were in the room in addition to the wizard who had just transported with her, and Reggie was here as well.

The wizard turned to her. "Sorry about the brusqueness. I'm Tennyson Ritter." He held out his hand.

15

JUSTIN'S GUIDE FOR THE ARTIST

•

Surround yourself with others who understand you; usually those are other artists.

THERE WERE MORE people here than Stormy expected. She looked into the tall, dark-haired man's eyes and saw sympathy. She took Tennyson's hand. "Hi, I'm Stormy."

Kristin led her to the other men. "This is Jonathan Bastion and Zack Glass."

Both men were blond, but Jonathan wore slacks and a button-down shirt, whereas Zack wore flip-flops, shorts, and a T-shirt. Jonathan shook her hand first and gave her a welcoming smile. "Such a pleasure to finally meet you, Stormy."

When she turned to Zack, he held out a fist and bumped it against hers. "One more beautiful babe. This is the wickedest army ever." His voice betrayed his love of surfing.

She had to smile at his enthusiasm.

"I think you know everyone else," Kristin said.

"Callie's going to hate missing you, but she's home with the spud." At her questioning look, he added, "My son, Jake." Zack's head bobbed as if contemplating some huge truth. "Sometimes I think that girl loves me only for my kid."

Rose came forward and took Stormy's hands. "Your twitching idea was so clever."

"Twitter," Hyacinth said.

"Whatever." Rose's smiled didn't fade an iota. "And it works so well."

"But how did you get the message so fast?" Stormy asked.

"We've have one computer running all the time with an alarm set to ding, just in case," Kristin said. "Zack set it up."

"It was easy." Zack dismissed his action with a wave of his hand.

"Well, I'm glad you did. I wasn't looking forward to spending the night on the beach." Stormy looked longingly at the couch. Her legs felt like rubber bands.

"Can't you people see she's tired? Sheesh." Hyacinth pushed through, put her arm around Stormy, and led her to the sofa. "Someone get her some water or something. She looks like hell."

Stormy laughed at that because she knew Hyacinth was right. Reggie summoned a glass of water while the others tried not to look at Stormy's ruined dress.

"So, you going to tell us what happened or do we have to wait for the movie?" Hyacinth took the glass from Reggie and pressed it into Stormy's hand.

Stormy nodded, but took a long swallow first. She hadn't realized just how thirsty she was. "I don't even know where to start."

"I recommend the beginning," Lily said, taking a position on her other side. "We knew you'd be joining us. We just didn't expect it so soon."

Stormy drank again and then drew in a deep breath. "I guess the beginning was dinner with Lucas."

The friendliness dropped out of Zack's face at the mention of the name. Tennyson and Kristin clasped hands, and at least one of the aunts clicked her tongue.

"How's the one-eyed bastard doing?" Jonathan asked.

She shot a glance at Jonathan. He was the one who'd taken out Lucas's eye. Funny. He didn't look like a beast. "Too well, I'm afraid."

Stormy told how Lucas tried to convince her about the superiority of the Arcani, Ian's support and belief that the Council was beginning to back Lucas, then about her attempted arrest and her escape. When she explained about the spell she had cast that caused whoever touched her to feel pain, Tennyson nodded in understanding. Except for the gasps from Rose, and a few inarticulate grunts of anger from the men, nobody interrupted her story.

Reggie spoke first after Stormy finished. "Don't worry. We'll get you settled in here tonight and worry about everything else tomorrow."

"Right now you need some sleep," Rose said.

Stormy looked down at her dress.

"I don't think we can summon your things from the Hall." Tennyson stroked his chin. "The Guards have probably placed a trace on your clothes. We shouldn't risk it."

Stormy looked at Reggie, who was shorter than she, and Kristin who was taller. "Maybe I could borrow a T-shirt to sleep in?"

"We'll find you something. Don't fret," Lily said. "I'll go make up a bed for you." She left the room.

"Where are we by the way?" Stormy asked.

"A house in Oceanside," Zack said.

"Zack owns it," Tennyson said. "We move around a lot, and the Council hasn't realized we have a Groundling to do our transactions."

"Between Zack and Jonathan we have quite a few places to hide," Reggie said, slipping her hand into Jonathan's. He dropped a kiss on her head.

Their tenderness triggered the memory of Hunter's kiss, a good-bye before they even had a chance to start a hello. "I guess I'm really in it then." Stormy didn't know when she had felt so tired. She tried to look optimistic, but couldn't summon the energy to smile. Another thought struck her. "Can I call my dads? They'll be so worried."

"The Guards are probably already monitoring the house," Jonathan said.

"They are. Hunter arranged protection for them." Stormy felt a knot form in her stomach. Her dads would be frantic when they heard the news. She knew she was doing the right thing, but she hadn't realized just how much pain her actions would cause. Wait. "I could call my birth mother. She'll take a message to them."

"Now you're thinking like a rebel," Hyacinth said. "Phone's in the kitchen."

"And then you need a shower and bed. I can scrounge up a toothbrush and a few more things." Kristin pulled out her wand.

Ten minutes later, Stormy headed for the bedroom. She had spoken to Barbara, who assured her that they were on her side. Two Guards patrolled outside her fathers' house. Barbara agreed to tell Justin and Ken that Stormy was fine. After promising to contact her later, Stormy was ready to crash. A quick shower, a large T-shirt as a nightgown, and she was ready for sleep.

She didn't think she had ever been so happy to crawl between sheets.

WHEN SHE OPENED her eyes, Stormy felt refreshed until she remembered the circumstances that had brought her to this strange bedroom. She rolled from the bed and saw the ruined black dress on the floor. At least the T-shirt reached her knees. The men here were big.

She padded down the hallway toward the voices she heard and pushed the spring door open to the kitchen. The three aunts bustled, laughing, chatting, fixing breakfast.

Lily looked up. "Stormy, good morning. How are you feeling?"

"Better, thanks. Uh, what should I do about clothes?"

"We took care of that last night." Rose walked to the sofa and picked up a pile of clothes. "We all donated something."

"It may not fit the best, but it's better than running around naked. At least in this company," Hyacinth said. "When the stores open we'll pop over and do some shopping."

"Thanks." She took the items from Rose. "I'll get dressed now."

"Good idea. The others will be here in a moment." Lily said.

As Stormy passed the counter, she took a sausage from a pile on a plate. "How many people are we expecting?"

"Everyone." Rose added another slice to a plate already stacked tall with French toast. "Men eat a lot."

Five minutes later Stormy was dressed and back in the kitchen. The table held so many plates and so much food that Stormy wondered where they would all sit.

Slowly the rest of the household wandered in. Zack

had gone home, so they were eight for breakfast. They ate, they talked, they avoided the seriousness of the previous night until the meal was over. Then, the dishes put away, Stormy became the center of attention.

Reggie spoke first. "How did my parents seem?"

A sudden rush of compassion filled Stormy. "I bet the explosion didn't help their state of mind, but if you hadn't told me they're helping you, I never would have guessed."

Reggie smiled and nodded. "I know. It's like they were born to be spies. Thanks for the update, by the way. I can't believe someone was killed."

Kristin frowned. "I can't believe they think we would do something like that."

"Hunter and I think Lucas planned the explosion." Stormy ignored the pang the thought of him brought. "Hunter thinks he was trying to kill me."

"Who is Hunter?" Jonathan asked.

"My Guard. I mean, he was my Guard, but now he's just after me. I mean he wanted to arrest me after I declared my allegiance to you." She tamped down the jolt of regret that accompanied that thought. "He doesn't trust Lucas either, though."

"But you went to dinner at his house," Lily said. "Why would you take such a risk?"

"I had to do something. I hoped I could find out what he has planned, but he only spouted his Arcani superiority crap. Besides, Hunter was there."

"You seem to trust this Hunter," Rose said.

Stormy couldn't hide the sadness that crept into her tone. "Not exactly. He made it clear that his first duty is to the Council. If I'm on your side, his job is to protect *them*." The aunts gazed at her with sympathy and understanding. She wished they weren't so perceptive.

"Lucas's actions seem to be escalating. If Ian believes

the Council is coming around to Lucas's plan, then we don't have a lot of time to stop him." Lily frowned.

"Yes, but Ian is a putz," Jonathan said. "He's so full of his own importance that he may be overeager."

At Jonathan's word choice Stormy had to smile to herself.

"Lucas has killed twice in the last month to further his cause. We have to stop him now." Kristin tapped her wand on her iPad in conjunction with her words.

"Won't Merlin's Gifts stop him?" Reggie asked.

"What are Merlin's Gifts?" Stormy looked around the table.

"They're three artifacts Merlin left for the godmothers. The three items give the godmothers greater power," Hyacinth said.

"According to the *Lagabóc,* they appear at time of great need," Tennyson said.

"And we have two of them," Kristin said.

Stormy didn't know whether to be intrigued by the story or amused that they were taking turns telling her a line at a time.

Looking for all the world like a professor, Tennyson continued. "The *Lagabóc* describes the three Gifts, tells us how the sphere and the staff work, and also says the three must be united before they can work together. It doesn't give any hint how."

"The staff increases one's strength," Reggie said. "It saved Jonathan and me from a tight spot."

"Yeah, but you zapped us away before I could take out Lucas's other eye. I would have liked that." Jonathan gave a beastlike smile.

"The ruby sphere adds energy to the user," Kristin said, "so you can perform magic longer."

Wait. A ruby sphere? Stormy remembered seeing one. Her mind raced in an attempt to make sense of what was tumbling through her thoughts. "What's the third artifact?"

"A tapestry," Tennyson said, but he shook his head. "We know where it is. We just don't know what it's for. The *Lagabóc* only says it exists."

"Lucas has it." Stormy's thoughts fell neatly into place.

They all looked at her. "You've seen it?" asked Kristin.

Stormy nodded. "He showed me his art treasury. The tapestry depicts a wizard handing a woman a glowing red ball. That was the ruby sphere, wasn't it?"

Reggie and Jonathan looked at each other before Reggie affirmed her guess.

Jonathan had an almost feral look in his eyes. "He still has that room? We tore it up pretty well."

"If you did, he fixed it up nicely. The art is still there, and so is the tapestry." She drew in a deep breath. "And I know how to use it."

No one moved for a moment. Stormy was intensely aware of the disbelief and hope they projected onto her.

Tennyson spoke first. "Do you want to explain?"

"Maybe 'use' is the wrong word, but I know what it's for. I'm a weaver. Of course the tapestry held the most interest for me. As I was looking at it, I realized something was off." She gazed into one face after the other. "I don't think anyone but a weaver would notice it. It's worked into the design, but the tapestry contains some sort of pattern."

Tennyson looked stunned. "The *Lagabóc* doesn't explain the weapon because the tapestry does. Merlin was a freaking genius."

"Well, that's why he was Merlin," Hyacinth said dryly.

A quiet ripple of laughter greeted that pronouncement.

"So I guess this means we have to steal it," Reggie said.

That idea cast a pall over the group. Stormy watched the solemn expressions as they all mulled over the prospect of breaking yet another law.

"How are we going to do it?" Kristin asked.

"I could break down his door," Jonathan said.

Reggie turned to him. "Subtle. You know they can kill you even when you're Nate."

He pulled her into his lap. "And you'd hate that."

"Damn straight I would." Reggie cupped his face and kissed him.

Kristin sidled closer to Tennyson too. "It's going to be dangerous no matter what we do."

"And he'll know we have all three Gifts." Tennyson stroked Kristin's hair. "It might push him to act sooner. He might also tell the Council."

"What if he didn't know we had it?" A sudden inspiration hit Stormy. "What if we switched the tapestry for a fake? He might not notice for a while, and it could buy us some time."

"Where are we going to get a duplicate?" Tennyson said.

"I could make it."

LUCAS STARED AT the tapestry. What had Stormy seen in its image? There was nothing there.

He couldn't tell if he had swayed her. The brooch had failed him. Leave it to a common woman to discard an exquisite piece of jewelry so quickly. Like Ian's, the pin allowed him to hear and see what was happening around the wearer. Whatever she had done with it, she had effectively blinded and deafened his lens onto her world. It had been a long shot anyway. While he would have preferred to have her on his side, the brooch's lack of success hadn't changed anything. It had been a calculated risk, just as the attempt to kill her had been. Neither failure affected his plans. In fact, the death of the old man had proven to be a boon. More people were ready to listen to him based on this evidence of the godmothers' perfidy. Although Stormy's death would likely have achieved the same effect.

Dmitri entered the art room, holding a telephone. "Sir, Ian Talbott is on the phone for you."

Lucas scowled. "His cloying attention would be welcome if he had the brains to accompany his passion."

Dmitri lifted one corner of his mouth in amusement. "Shall I tell him you are occupied?"

"No, no. I'll speak with him." Lucas took the phone from Dmitri and released the hold button. "Ian, my friend, how are you today?"

"You are always so gracious. I wish I had good news to share with you. I'm calling because the Council is concerned for your safety."

Lucas raised an eyebrow. "My safety?"

"Yes. Stormy has joined the godmothers."

Lucas felt a slow burn in his stomach. Damn her. Damn the godmothers and their misplaced sensibilities. None of them had vision. Except his mother. She had seen through the worship of the weaker race and died to right the wrong of the centuries.

He calmed himself. "You say the Council is worried?"

"They believe that your house may not be as secure as you'd like. Regina, Bastion, and now Stormy have seen it. The Council is worried that they might have too much knowledge and contrive to get inside and finish the task they attempted the other night."

An eager spark lit in Lucas's breast. Perhaps this wasn't all bad. They *would* try to get inside—he was certain—but not to harm him. They wanted the tapestry. And if he was ready for the attempt, he could get it all—the Gifts and the women. "Thank you for the warning, my friend. I shall have Dmitri look into the security."

Ian hesitated. " Are you sure you want to stay there? I could convince the Council to provide a place for you."

"I shall stay where I am. If I go into hiding, then they've won a victory, haven't they?"

"But your safety—"

"No, Ian. I trust Dmitri's skill. But thank you for the offer. It is heartwarming to know I have friends like you."

"We're searching for them, Luc. We've increased the hunt. A platoon has been sent out."

"I wish them all the best."

Again Ian's hesitation came almost palpably across the connection. "You don't blame me for Stormy? That I couldn't control her?"

Idiot. It wasn't entirely Ian's fault, but a stronger man would not have let her slip through his fingers. "Of course not. How could it be your responsibility that her thinking is twisted? I'd sooner lay the blame on her parents. They probably filled her head with the wrong ideas."

Ian let out a nasty chuckle. "How could they not? She was raised in an artist's colony. They don't live like the rest of us."

Lucas allowed himself to give a comradely laugh. "On this we are in agreement. I shall see you soon, yes?"

"Indeed. In fact the Council would like to invite you to appear in front of them."

Lucas smiled. "Me? What wisdom can I impart to the Council?"

Ian nearly gushed through the phone. "They want to hear your ideas. I think they're ready."

"When do they want me to appear?"

"In two days. Will that work?"

"It is most opportune."

"I'll tell the Council." Eager excitement filled Ian's voice. "I'll meet you at the anteroom."

"See you then." Lucas pressed the button to disconnect and handed the phone back to Dmitri. "He can be useful."

Dmitri nodded in understanding. "Shall I bring your tea in here?"

"Give me a few more minutes and then I shall come out."

Dmitri bowed his head and left the room.

Lucas once again stood in front of the tapestry and stared at it. He had lost the first two Gifts. He wouldn't lose this one, this he swore, but the *Lagabóc* was strangely silent about the tapestry. His translation told only of a weapon the three Gifts would make when used together, but not how to combine them. Surely the omission of a description of the tapestry meant it was something extraordinary. And it was his.

He examined the tapestry more closely, then moved farther away. Still nothing.

What had she seen?

16

JUSTIN'S GUIDE FOR THE ARTIST

•

Understanding a problem is the first step to conquering it.

HUNTER GROWLED. LITERALLY. A rumble emanated from his throat in perfect accord with his mood, and if he could have, he would have raised the hackles on the back of his neck too. "I'm fine."

"That's for me to decide." The doctor picked up the chart and jotted down a note. She checked his pulse. "We've never seen magic like this before."

The white walls of the infirmary were as clinical as the doc's demeanor. Under strict orders not to leave his hospital bed, he was as upright as the angle of the bed allowed. Hunter looked down at his arm. Red still marked the outline of Stormy's hand where she had touched him. "How are the others?"

"Like you. You got the most of it, but I'm holding them too."

Hunter glared at her.

She chuckled. "If I could be intimidated by a stare, I

never would have made it through med school." She pulled out her wand. "Block me."

She sent a jet of energy toward him. He reflected it without drawing his wand. "There. Are you satisfied?"

"Not yet." She jotted down something else, then looked at him. "Take out your wand."

With a long-suffering sigh, Hunter summoned his wand.

"I want you to produce a glass of orange juice."

He pointed the wand at the bedside table and conjured a glass of orange juice.

"Good." The doctor marked something on the paper, and then said, "Now drink it. It says here you didn't eat breakfast."

"I can eat at home."

"Not as long as you're here."

"Come on, Doc. There's nothing wrong with me."

The doctor clutched his chart to her chest and calmly met his gaze. "I can release you at noon, but no sooner."

"I'll take it." He folded his hands over his chest and waited for her to leave. As soon as the doc left the room, he jumped out of bed and summoned clothes. Jeans and a T-shirt would cover him so much better than this flimsy gown that didn't close properly.

Stormy was so going to pay for this humiliation.

The door opened again, and he dove for the bed.

Tank strolled in. "I give you an eight point five."

"Suck it, Bryant." Hunter stood up and reached for his clothes.

"I thought you were on bed rest."

"You thought wrong." He reached for his jeans.

"But that gown suits you so well. Especially the peekaboo flap."

Oblivious to Tank's presence, Hunter pulled on his

clothes, then tossed the gown to his colleague. "You like it so much, it's yours."

"Think I may cry." Tank threw the hospital gown onto the rumpled bed. "And I didn't get you anything."

"Yes, you did. You're getting me out of here." Hunter strode to the door. "You coming?"

"Hell, yeah. I was hoping you were going to say that."

They walked down the hallway to a desk. The doctor was leaning over the counter. She looked up, wrote one more thing on the sheet in front of her, then handed Hunter the papers.

"What's this?" Hunter asked.

"Your discharge. You didn't think I believed you'd actually stay here, did you?"

Although taken aback by the doctor's perception, he grinned and stuffed the papers into his pocket. "You're okay, Doc. I'll recommend you to my friends."

"Because that's just what I need. A bunch of patients who don't listen to orders. Get the hell out of here."

Still grinning, Hunter walked from the Council Hall infirmary and straight to the anteroom. "How'd you get in?"

Tank kept pace with Hunter. "Hey, I'm just visiting a friend in the hospital."

"Uh-huh. What can you tell me, Tank?"

"They've sent a squad out after the godmothers. They can't ignore the situation anymore."

"Six godmothers who've defected. The Council has to be afraid. When Elenka left she was alone."

"And look at the trouble she caused." Tank shook his head. "Two Guards have been posted in Stormy's neighborhood in case she returns. Her dads have agreed to placing shields around the house, but I think it's just a show. No one else is helping."

"Of course."

"So, what do you want to do?"

"Track her down." Hunter pictured Stormy's blond hair and blue eyes in front of him and frowned.

"Don't you mean 'them'?"

"What? Yeah, sure." Hunter cursed at himself. Tank was right. He had to stop focusing on Stormy. But she would be the easiest to find. "Who do we talk to get assigned to the unit?"

Tank shook his head. "They've already made the assignments, and we're not on the team. I'm officially on leave, and you are too, as soon as you leave the infirmary, which was about one hundred yards ago." Tank handed him more paper.

Shit. He stopped. "Then we go on vacation."

A sly smile curved Tank's mouth. "I knew you wouldn't disappoint."

They had reached the anteroom. "My place?" Hunter asked. "So we can make vacation plans? I think we should go hunting."

Tank shot him a grin. "I'm right behind you."

Hunter and Tank vanished from the Council Hall.

PLANS, LISTS, STRATEGY. Within an hour, they had a course of action. Stormy focused on Barbara's house and with a little guidance from Kristin, they popped into Barbara's kitchen.

The moment Stormy appeared, Barbara embraced her. "We have been so worried about you."

Stormy gave the woman a big hug back. "How are my dads?"

"Frantic, as you can imagine. The Guard is here, and the Council sent some muckety-muck to warn us about how dangerous you were."

Kristin looked unsure. "Maybe this wasn't such a good idea, Stormy. Are you sure you trust everyone?"

Barbara drew herself up. "We are a family here. No one hurts any of us."

Stormy patted Barbara's hand. "Don't get mad. She doesn't understand about our life here. Barbara, this is Kristin Montgomery."

Barbara's mouth dropped open.

"Yes, one of the other godmothers, the one you read about in the paper." Stormy turned to Kristin. "I trust everyone in the enclave. Barbara's right. They're family."

Kristin lost her militant posture, but still didn't look quite relaxed.

Barbara looked at the younger woman with understanding. "I expect you don't have many people you can trust right now. It won't mean much, but the Council doesn't like us much either. We were always too free thinking out here. Artists, you know." Barbara winked.

Kristin nodded, and the atmosphere in the kitchen eased. "Thanks for your help."

"I'd do anything for Stormy. We all would." Barbara smiled. "Now, what's the plan?"

"I need to get into my studio and work for a while," Stormy said. "We'll need my dads' help."

"I'm on it." Barbara picked up the phone and dialed. "Hello, Ken? Conrad is out, and something is wrong with my garbage disposal. Could you and Justin come over and take a look at it?" A pause. "No, both of you. I made a fresh pot of coffee and a new cake you have to try." Another pause and a giggle. "No, I'm not trying to make you fat, but it is guaranteed to cheer you up. Just come over." She hung up. "They're on their way."

Nerves twisted in Stormy's stomach. She hadn't seen her dads in a while. How would they react to her? Would they forgive her?

She heard them before she saw them. Justin was talking—booming actually—as they arrived at the back door. Escorted by two Guards. Barbara poked her head out and looked pointedly at them. "You weren't invited."

The Guards didn't respond, but shot each other looks and took up positions outside the house.

"They are so annoying," Ken said, not bothering to hide his contempt for his escorts. "Now let's see about that garbage disposal." He brushed past them and entered the house. And froze for an instant.

Stormy lifted a finger to her lips.

"The *coffee* is on the dining room table," Barbara said. "I thought we'd chat first. You know the way." She pushed Ken further inside, then hustled Justin through the door. "Get inside before they spot her," she whispered.

As soon as they were clear of the window, Stormy ran into Ken's arms and couldn't stop a few tears from falling. Then she turned to Justin and gave him a fierce hug as well. Justin's arms enveloped her and nearly squeezed her too tightly. Just as they always had.

Ten minutes of greetings, introductions, and parental worryings and scoldings later, they all sat at the dining room table, away from prying eyes.

"The Guard are outside our house, expecting you to show up," Justin said. "They've placed an antitransport spell over the house and the studios too."

"We're 'cooperating.'" Ken made double hooks in the air with his fingers. "Was that the right thing to do? Because I'll kick them out if you want."

"No, they'll just get suspicious if you do that." Stormy frowned. "I really don't need to get into the house. I just need to work in my studio for a few hours."

"Won't they hear you?" Ken asked.

Justin's expression lit up. "No, they won't. I think it's time I work on an outdoor sculpture."

Ken's eyes brightened. "With jackhammers?"

"With jackhammers."

Stormy smiled. The noise of her childhood. Sculpting with a jackhammer would easily cover any sound her loom would make.

"And I know just how to get you inside the studio." Justin paused for effect. "Skunks."

Ken nearly bounced in his chair. "I love you when you're devious."

Although Kristin looked confused, the rest of them nodded in understanding. Skunks were prevalent in Southern California and had always lived around the compound. Yes, the occasional smelly accident happened, but for the most part, the skunks and the people lived in harmony. In fact, the female that lived in the open field beyond their neighborhood had twice brought her litter around to the delight of the compound residents.

An hour later, a huge rock sat in the backyard. Barbara's kitchen window provided a view of the proceedings. Justin wore slings and straps hung with chisels. Noise-canceling headphones hooked around his neck, and power cords led to an electric jackhammer that rested in a special pouch over his shoulder. With his wand he erected scaffolding surrounded the rock. When the rock first appeared, the two Guards had argued with him, probably over the way the rock blocked their view, but Justin's booming voice had carried over to them, saying he was an artist and sometimes a work had to be done outdoors.

She and Kristin waited for the next step of the plan. They didn't wait long. Ken appeared in the backyard. Ostensibly, he carried a snack out to Justin, but the instant he was behind the stone and out of the view of the Guards, he pulled out his wand. A moment later three baby skunks appeared in the bushes at the far end of the yard and the mama was at the other. Between them stood the rock, Justin, Ken, and the two Guards. The kits started their mewling, almost like a snarling whistle, and the mama perked up her ears.

"Look out, gentlemen," Justin called from his perch at the top of the scaffolding. "I wouldn't want to be between a mother skunk and her babies."

The mother skunk stamped her feet.

"She doesn't look too happy." Ken backed up toward the Guards as if he feared the animal.

Stormy could scarcely keep from laughing at the panicked expression on the Guards' faces. Beside her Kristin struggled to restrain her mirth as well.

"Aren't you worried that the skunk will spray?" Kristin asked.

"Not really. They're harmless creatures, and as long as they're not harassed, they won't attack. Of course, mama skunks have been known to go on the offense protecting their kits." Stormy watched the unfolding farce with a crooked grin.

"Which is why my husband, Conrad, created a spell many years ago to get rid of the smell," Barbara said. "We have a lot of skunks around here."

From their vantage point, Stormy saw the Guards eye the skunk. One of them raised his wand toward the animal, but the other pushed it out of the way. The babies waddled toward their mother, and mama walked toward them. The Guards, caught between the skunks, finally decided on a course of action. They stepped toward the kits, and mama skunk promptly turned and lifted her tail toward the two men. With a loud yelp, the two men vaulted over the babes and raced around the corner of the house. Funny, how even big, strong men could be afraid of skunks.

"Go," Kristin said.

Stormy threw the back door open and ran to her studio. Justin and Ken waved her in. Stormy entered her studio silently and shut the door. She peered through the glass. The skunk had lowered her tail and was back with her children, and the family group waddled off into the empty lot behind the property.

Justin called out. "It's okay. They've gone." The Guards came back and took up their positions, casting wary glances toward the field where the departing animals were still visible.

Stormy backed away from the window. Kristin had stayed in Barbara's kitchen to keep an eye on the events and summon help if needed.

In her studio, a sense of belonging filled her, and her tension meted away. It was comfortable and familiar and, even if it was an illusion, safe. Stormy pulled a piece of paper from her pocket and unfolded it. This was the picture she had to copy. Kristin had pulled the image from her memory and printed it out for her. Magic was so cool.

Ken's voice sounded through the wall. "Justin, if you need anything, just let me know. I'll be inside." Those were the words that let Stormy know she could start work.

Justin's jackhammer started drilling against the rock. Stormy drew her wand and concentrated. "*Citior.*"

A cool breeze enveloped her and wrapped around her like an aura. And then as she pulled her tapestry loom out of view of the window, she took stock of the wool she'd need to replicate the tapestry. She almost let out a shout of exuberance. If anyone saw her now, she knew that he'd see little more than a blur. Tennyson had showed her the seldom-used spell to speed herself up so she could get the tapestry done today. The spell was dangerous because it would shave time off of one's life. Stormy estimated that under normal circumstances the weaving would take three days, so she was sacrificing three days of her life. Tennyson had warned her that some wizards had used this spell so often, they died of old age at thirty-five.

The spell would also drain her of energy, which was why she needed Kristin's help to pop back to the god-mothers, but she'd be able to complete the copy.

Thank God the piece wasn't too large. Though she could see herself clearly, she still felt as if her fingers flew through the work. She loaded the frame with the warp, traced the design onto the threads, then began weaving the tapestry.

She didn't take as much care as she would have with one of her own pieces or even if she were making a true replica. Their goal was to fool the eye, not to make a forgery. Someone taking a quick glance would see a tapestry depicting a wizard handing a red orb to a cloaked woman. If Lucas was obsessed with the tapestry, the chances were he'd notice a fake, but perhaps not at once. Stormy knew she could match the colors. She had an eye for colors and design.

She didn't know how long she worked. Justin's jack-hammer was a mere buzz in her ears, but really she heard little because the work absorbed her. The sun had shifted the next time she took in her surroundings. The tapestry was about three quarters done, and she was feeling the toll of the spell. Taking a moment to drink some water and shove a Twix bar from the stash she kept in her desk into her mouth, she hunkered back down at the loom and let her fingers do their work.

The sun was even lower when she next looked up.

Her chest was rising and falling as if she had just finished a 5K, and her cheeks radiated heat. She pulled out her wand. "*Tardior.*"

She almost pitched forward as her movement slowed to normal. Bracing against the loom, she pulled herself upright and wiped her brow. The tapestry was finished. The final check she'd do at normal speed. She felt woozy, but she could power through.

The image was clear, but not as rich as the tapestry that hung in Lucas's house. It didn't matter. It would fool most observers. She hoped. She threaded several embroidery needles to fill in a few details and bent back over the work.

Justin's jackhammer stopped. She looked up. The skylight had grown gray. Even an Arcani sculptor needed daylight to create a statue outdoors. Yes, they could hook up artificial lights, but that never worked as well as natural light. Besides, she couldn't turn on the lights in her studio without giving herself away.

She finished up the last few stitches and examined the tapestry in the fading light. From outside she heard the sounds of tools being put away and Justin speaking to the Guards. His voice was especially loud, as though he was making sure she heard him. As if he needed amplification. God, how she loved him.

The strength of the emotions cramped her stomach. What had she done to her family? They loved her and were risking so much for her. She hated the deceit, and she hated the risk she placed on her family. Why was doing the right thing so hard?

Clenching her jaw until it hurt, she secured the edges of the tapestry and was about to lift it off the loom when the door to her studio opened.

She whirled around.

Hunter walked in. His gaze pinned her to the spot. He

was smiling, but the smile held no pleasure or amusement. One deliberate, slow step after another brought him closer to her. Confidence and anger exuded from his expression.

"Gotcha."

17

JUSTIN'S GUIDE FOR THE ARTIST

•

To forget love is to forget everything.

HIS VOICE WAS low and menacing. It was nothing compared to how he was feeling.

Stormy shivered. "How did you find me?"

"Did you really think I wouldn't?" His gaze narrowed. Anger warred with pain. She looked too lovely, too innocent. No, that look hid her treachery. *Focus on that, Hunter.* "You had to come back here. I know how you think. All I had to do was apply logic. And a little alarm."

"Your magic must be failing then because I've been here for hours."

"We weren't sure. Something was interfering, like you were here, but at the same time not."

"The *Citior* spell."

Disbelief shook him. "You used *Citior*? Stormy, that's insane. Do you know the dangers, the risk . . . ?"

"Yeah, well, desperate times and so on . . ." She

didn't show fear. She drew herself up and looked him straight in the eyes. "You're wrong about the godmothers. They want to prevent the war that Lucas is trying to start."

"Doesn't matter. I work for the Council, and they want you. You can tell them your story."

"The Council won't listen."

"Not my problem."

As if suddenly weighed down by a thousand pounds, her shoulders drooped, and her posture sunk into herself. All spark vanished from her eyes. She looked tired, but he couldn't trust her not to use magic. Her gaze pleaded with him. "Can't you just forget you saw me?"

"The Guards already know I'm in here talking to you. So do your parents."

"No hope then." Her eyes lost the life they'd had and seemed to deaden. "You won't hurt them? My dads?"

"No."

She held out her hands. "I'm ready."

He looked at her hands and raised a brow. She expected him to manacle her? "Uh, I don't have handcuffs."

Two red splotches appeared in her cheeks. "You don't have to laugh at me. Just arrest me, and then leave me alone. Call the other Guards. I'm sure they'll help you control me."

So she had a little life left in her, and it was his job to snuff it. He hated himself. "Stormy, I . . ."

"What are you waiting for? I won't hurt you again." Her voice hitched as if she were hanging on to the last vestiges of her control. Her voice dropped to a faint breath. "I couldn't."

He hesitated. "Don't make this harder than it already is. You made these choices. The Council—"

"Damn the Council. Do you really think the Council will believe me after everything that's happened?"

"No." He had no reason to feel guilty. She was the traitor. *Hang on to the anger, damn it.* She had destroyed Tank's career, attacked him and two other Guards, betrayed the Council . . . His thoughts trailed away as his gaze fell on the tapestry still on the loom. His brows drew together. "This is the piece from LeRoy's collection. You could barely look away from it. Why would you risk your freedom to make a copy?"

"Because I'm going to steal the one Lucas has."

That didn't make sense. Even if she was a traitor, she wasn't a thief. Right, because she would draw the line at breaking only some laws and not others. Even to himself the words sounded stupid. But she wasn't the type to be a thief. "Why?"

"The one Lucas has is one of Merlin's Gifts."

His gaze shot to her. Impossible. He searched her expression for any signs of lying, but saw none. But she was a good actress. With a slight tilt of his head and a narrowed gaze, he challenged her story. "Merlin's Gifts are a fairy tale."

A strangled laugh squeaked out of her. "Apparently not."

If that were true . . . if Merlin's Gifts were real . . . the threat to the Arcani and the Council grew bigger. Finally he looked straight at her. "Luc has Merlin's Gifts?"

Before she could answer, a ripple appeared in the back wall. Plaster and wood separated, leaving a gap. The magic was quiet and powerful. It would have to be to get through the barriers placed on the building by the Guards. He recognized the woman who ran in through the hole before she spoke. Kristin Montgomery.

"Stormy, we've got to go. The Guards know you're in—" Kristin stopped as she spotted him. "Oh."

"How did you get in?" Hunter asked.

"What's the point in being a Rare One if you can't do magic?" Kristin aimed her wand at him.

Stormy placed herself between Kristin's wand and him. "Kristin, don't do this."

"Stormy, move," Kristin said.

"No." Stormy faced Kristin.

"The Guards will know the room has been breached in a moment." Kristin tried to aim around her.

"Then you don't have a lot of time. Take the tapestry and go," Stormy said.

Hunter eyed Kristin. "If you're going to kill me, you should do it now." He pushed Stormy out of the way.

"Stop it." Stormy jumped between them again. She grabbed Hunter's hands. "Please, Hunter. Trust me. I swear, I swear . . . I don't know what I swear, but please, if you ever liked me—"

"Liked you? Hell, I thought I could love you." Hunter stared down at her.

Kristin lowered her wand. "Oh, damn." She looked like she was in pain.

He looked at the two women. They weren't very good at threats if they crumpled at the first sign of difficulty. God, he was so going to regret this. "Go." A stab of pain pierced his gut.

Stormy looked at him. He would have sworn hope bloomed in her eyes.

He placed a barrier on the door that would delay the entrance of the Guards. "Stun me first, then go."

Kristin grabbed Stormy's hand, then shot a stream of energy at him. Ropes bound his arms and legs, and he fell to the floor, twisting so at least he fell on his side and wouldn't break his nose. It still hurt. But not as much as the constriction attacking him from inside.

"Hunter." That was Tank's voice. The air filled with shouts from outside, and blasts of magic hit the door.

"Go," he hissed.

Stormy waved her wand at the tapestry, which flew into her hands, and looked at Kristin. "Okay."

They ran through the opening, which was beginning to close. Stormy looked back at him. She opened her mouth to say something, but Kristin grabbed her and they vanished.

The door broke open in the next moment. Glass shards from the spiderweb window tinkled as they hit the floor, and Arachne's face split in two. Tank ran to Hunter and slashed the bonds around him with a flick of his wand. Hunter rolled and leaped to his feet. He pointed. "There."

The Guards ran toward the opening in the wall, which closed in front of them. They pulled out their wands and blasted a hole through the back of the studio.

Tank looked at him and asked him a question without words.

He couldn't meet Tank's gaze. "Kristin Montgomery was with her. Apparently she's getting control of her powers as a Rare One." A lie of omission was still a lie. He clenched his teeth against the pain.

Tank looked stunned. "You're okay?"

"Yeah."

It was the second lie he had told in the past ten seconds.

"HE LET US go." Stormy's voice was quiet but filled with emotion. She still couldn't believe Hunter had let them escape. Encouraged them to escape. It didn't make sense. Stunned and unable to think clearly, she looked at the others in the room. "You don't know how big this is."

Reggie laid her arm around her.

"He sounds like a nice man," Rose said.

"Hmm," Jonathan said. "I'll reserve judgment."

"Be nice." Reggie shot a pointed look at Jonathan and then gave Stormy's shoulder a squeeze.

"He did take a risk letting us go." Kristin's gaze sought Tennyson. Stormy could see the questions in her eyes.

"If we ever see him again, I shall thank him," Lily said.

Stormy gulped. Lily was right. She might never see him again, this man who said he could have loved her. Her heart cramped at the thought. She needed something else to think about. She strode to the table and spread out the tapestry she had made today. With a critical eye, she saw the many flaws her speed had caused, the uneven sections, the missed stitches, but it would have to do.

Kristin joined her at the table. She compared the piece to the picture pulled from Stormy's memory. "I'm not an expert, but I'd say this copy is pretty good."

Tennyson performed the same examination as Kristin. "Art is not my thing."

"But it is mine," Stormy said. She pointed to the wizard's hands. "This doesn't come close to the vitality of the original. And this part here"—she pointed to another section of the tapestry—"is loose. The quality of the original shows how much care and work went into it."

"Looks the same to me," Hyacinth said.

"But will it be enough?" Lily asked.

Stormy shrugged. "I can't say. I see a huge gap between the piece I saw and this slapdash version."

Reggie shook her head. "That's only because you're

an expert. Okay, maybe yours isn't as good, but it will do."

Stormy sighed. "So what's next?"

"We have to get into Lucas's house and make the switch," Lily said.

"Any ideas?" Kristin grabbed a pad of paper for notes.

"You can't do magic in the art room," Reggie said. "Lucas has it enchanted."

"But you escaped," Kristin said.

"I had the staff. We can't count on doing magic in there."

"I think we'll still have to use magic for a good bit of our adventure," Hyacinth said.

"And for the rest, we'll just have to do it the Groundling way." Stormy looked at her friends. She tried to joke past the dejection she felt. "Anyone have any experience with breaking and entering?"

Reggie raised her hand. "I stole the *Lagabóc* from Tennyson's office, but I used magic."

A candle flared to life on the dining room table. "Mail," Reggie said, grabbing a piece of paper. She held the sheet over the flame and allowed the black smoke to curl over the surface.

"Special candles," Lily said. "A matched set and rather rare. You write something at one end, burn it in the flame, it comes out at the other end. It's how we communicate with Reggie's parents."

Reggie finished reading. "Lucas has been called to testify in front of the Council tomorrow morning."

"About what?"

"Us, I'd guess," Reggie said.

Hyacinth nodded. "That's our chance to do this thing."

Kristin looked at her sheet of paper. "Hyacinth's

right. He'll be out of the house tomorrow morning. It's the best opportunity we'll have."

"So how do we do this?" Rose asked.

The debates began. Stormy glanced over at Kristin's notes. Writing covered the page, each idea bigger than the last. The talk went back and forth, unproductive for the most part as one idea after another was discussed and scrapped. The despair that had plagued Stormy all evening grew. Their task seemed impossible.

And then it struck her.

"I think it's time to think smaller."

LUCAS WALKED INTO the round Council chamber. Twelve chairs stood in tiers above the floor behind a low wall, two of them empty—the chairs of the two dead Councilors. The arrangement amused him. He smiled to himself. The layout was intended to intimidate those who came in front of the Council. Any speaker would have to look up at the members, while the members had the superiority of position and gaze. Even the material of the chamber meant to make an impression—the black marble, the dark wood railings, the high-backed thronelike chairs of the Councilors. No chair existed for the speaker.

He didn't mind. He thought better on his feet.

As he gazed around the room, he saw the guest gallery, the area reserved for those who were witnessing the procedures. Ian was there. At the eager look on Ian's face, Lucas nodded, but did not otherwise acknowledge him. Ian was probably waiting to lead the others in a cheer.

A few other faces filled the guest area. He let his gaze drift over them until he came to the last one, that idiot Guard who had let Stormy go twice. How stupid did one have to be to let one like her elude him? She had no talent, no class, no intelligence. Not only had the godmother escaped under his watch, he had failed to capture her after finding her again. He must be here to report to the Council. What had he told them? That he was an imbecile?

Incompetence. Lucas almost snorted. When he ruled the Arcani, such behavior would be criminal.

He took his position in the center of the circular floor and gazed up at the Council members. He knew they expected him to bow before them, as was the tradition when speaking in the chamber. For a moment he maintained his erect posture, then conceded with a tilt of his head to them. "My esteemed colleagues."

He heard the quick ripple of surprise at the informal address, but he wasn't about to acknowledge their superiority to his. "You asked me to come before you today because of the situation with the godmothers."

"Yes," a sonorous voice spoke from the gallery. "And we thank you for acquiescing to our request. Can you tell us why the godmothers seem to have made you their target?"

"Because I am exposing the truth about them." He held his hands out in front of him in a gesture of bewilderment. "Perhaps because I am a newcomer to the area, a foreigner, or a successful sorcerer, I can see their motives more clearly. More likely it is because they know I abhor their agenda."

"What do you believe their agenda to be?" asked another voice.

"Is it not clear? They aren't happy with their role in our world. They know they are obsolete, but they wish to maintain their influence over Arcani and Groundling both."

"How do you mean?" another male voice asked.

"We bestow the godmothers power, but only because we are hidden. Ostensibly, they walk among the Groundlings, listen to them. *They* provide us with our knowledge of the Groundlings. *They* tell us if the Groundlings are dangerous. *They* claim the Groundlings have greater strength than us. Is this really so? How could a Groundling have more power than an Arcani? We control magic. Groundlings have nothing that can stop magic.

"If we lived openly, using our magic, we'd have no need for godmothers. The Groundlings wouldn't bother with wishes because they would know real magic exists. And they would pay us the proper respect because of our power.

"So the godmothers seek to take over the Council to prevent becoming obsolete. They are determined to prevent us from taking our rightful place in the world."

He bowed his head as if he were coy, but he knew he had their rapt attention. "Many of you have spoken with me and know my beliefs."

"And just what are your beliefs?" A female voice spoke from another position.

He sought out the speaker. There she was. Sophronia Petros. He had met her, but had failed to win her full support. In fact he didn't know how the woman thought. At all. She was a variable, an uncertain element. Perhaps it was time for another member of the Council to meet with an accident. "I believe the Arcani have renounced their claims long enough. I believe we have lived in fear long enough."

Ian jumped to his feet at those words, clapping fervently. A smattering of applause from some others also accompanied his statement.

He raised his hand for silence. Like a good puppy, Ian sat down, and once again Lucas felt the attention of the room on him. "The godmothers seek to take over before you are aware of their insignificance. They are trying to wrest control from the Council and place it in their own hands. As long as they can convince us of the need to remain hidden, we allow them to have power over us. The time has come for us to regain our place in the world. To live in the open."

Once again, Ian jumped to his feet, but this time a low murmur accompanied his enthusiasm. Lucas stood, his gaze raking the gallery, almost daring any Council member to contradict him.

18

JUSTIN'S GUIDE FOR THE ARTIST

•

Details matter; the smallest things sometimes hold the answers.

JONATHAN SAID, "I still don't like it."

"Neither do I," Tennyson said.

Hyacinth shook her head. "Gentlemen, we discussed this. Now go take your positions."

Stormy felt nearly as much trepidation as the men. No, probably more. Although any Arcani could transform into an animal, only godmothers could become true fairies, which allowed them to maintain their human logic and thinking capacities. A mouse might have been able to sneak into Lucas's house, but it required cleverness to steal the tapestry. Stormy, Reggie, and Kristin looked at each other, popped the ibuprofen into their mouths, and touched their wands to their heads.

"Déjà vu," said Kristin as she quickly dropped a kiss on Tennyson's cheek before it rose out of reach.

Reggie did the same to Jonathan.

Stormy tried not to think of Hunter as her bones

started to crack and pop. She would have liked to kiss someone too and have someone worry about her. Parents didn't count. Neither did Hyacinth, who had accompanied them.

The men stepped away and took up their positions as lookouts elsewhere on the street. The exclusive neighborhood offered many bushes and rock walls and topiary someone could hide behind. The houses were spaced well apart from one another, and not one skimped on landscaping. Lucas was still at the Council Hall, giving his testimony . . . as far as they knew.

Stormy glanced over at her partners in crime. Clearly, Reggie and Kristin had transformed more often because they were already significantly smaller than she was, but already her clothes flapped against her. In a matter of moments, Kirstin was naked in a pile of clothes, and Reggie joined her in that state soon thereafter. Hyacinth passed out two tiny dresses to them.

Although Stormy was shrinking faster this time, she still had a couple of feet to go before she was the size of a sprite. She winced as a particularly painful torsion of her bones took place. Despite the faster pace, the transformation still hurt. Still, she had to admit she was looking forward to flying again, even if she yelped as the wings popped through the skin of her back.

Just a few minutes later, she stood naked in the pile of her clothes.

Hyacinth handed her a tiny dress. "Since we haven't had time to fit you properly, we made you a sari-styled one. Just wrap it around yourself."

The material was light and gauzy and slipped through her fingers like water. She'd like this. She started from the front, twined the fabric around her waist, and as it passed in front again, she gave the ends a quick twist to form a halter top and tied it off at her neck.

"Crap, you look great." Reggie walked over to her. Gorgeous wings of aquamarine and green jutted from her back. "I tried that once and it looked like I'd tied a rag around me. Of course, I had, but you look elegant and natural."

"I borrowed my dress from a fairy." Kristin joined them. Her gold and black wings were striking. "Callie and I are the same size, almost." She tugged at the bodice of the dress where it gaped a little.

Stormy gently opened and closed her own purple and white wings.

"Oh, the white changes color in the light," Reggie said. "They're beautiful."

"No, we're beautiful," Kristin said.

"And you have a job to do," Hyacinth said. She placed three earphones on the ground. She waved her wand over them. "*Minuscula.*"

The pieces jerked and flipped over, but didn't change size. Hyacinth glared down at them. "Damn it. Not now."

"What's wrong?" Kristin asked.

"Our magic has been getting wonky as the Time of Transition goes on. Especially if it has to do with changing sizes."

A hint of unease went through Stormy. They had wanted the others to do the prep magic, so the three entering the house could save their energy for the tasks ahead. Hyacinth had volunteered to come despite the objections of Lily and Rose. And now the men had gone.

"It'll work this time." Hyacinth frowned slightly, stared at the earphones, and said again, "*Miniscula.*"

This time the headsets shrank down to their size. They each grabbed one and fitted it to their heads.

Stormy hooked hers around her ear. A tiny microphone came down over her cheek, pointing toward her mouth. An ear bud fitted into her ear canal, and the other components nestled in a slim section on the earpiece itself. She felt so Secret Servicey.

A crackle in her ear startled her, then Tennyson's voice came through as clearly as if she were standing next to him. "Kristin, are you there?"

Kristin touched the button on her earpiece. "Right here. Can you hear me?"

"Loud and clear. Have the others test theirs too."

Reggie pushed the button on hers. "I'm here. Jonathan?"

"Gotcha." Jonathan's voice sounded almost nervous. "Don't be a hero, Reggie. Get in and get out, okay?"

Reggie laughed. "Look who's talking."

Tennyson's voice came on again. "Stormy, now you."

"I'm here." She couldn't help but feel a little sorry for herself. They were working together, but she didn't have anyone waiting for her outside except Hyacinth, and Hyacinth was there for all of them.

"Good. You're all coming through really well," Tennyson said.

"What? I don't count here?" Hyacinth said in her own earpiece. She winked down at them.

Jonathan chuckled. "I keep telling you you're worth more than the others put together, but you still won't marry me."

"I can't marry you, Jonathan. You couldn't keep up with me," Hyacinth said.

They all laughed. Stormy had to admit the banter helped relieve her tension.

"Just one more thing." Hyacinth placed Stormy's tapestry on the grass beside them and once again said, *"Minusculum."*

Just when they thought Hyacinth's magic had failed again, the tapestry contracted into itself. Stormy picked it up and tucked it under her arm.

"We're good," Hyacinth said.

Tennyson came back on. "Okay, here we go. Silence will be the rule unless we see something or you need something." He paused. "Be careful in there."

Stormy looked at the other two fairies and then took off into the air. She loved this. Her magic might be iffy at times, but flying she was good at.

Kristin and Reggie followed her. Although the tapestry created more drag, Stormy felt the same exhilaration and grace she had the last time. They flew toward the top of the house. In their analysis of the break-in, they had agreed that Lucas probably had powerful spells over the house to detect any attempt at magical entry, no matter how small, especially after Kristin had used her fairy size to get into Lucas's last house. But even a sorcerer's house used water and electricity. Magic was not an efficient way to run a dishwasher.

The right vent or pipe would lead them inside, and in a unanimous decision, they decided the dryer vent was preferable to any effluvium pipes. As they approached the vent, Stormy felt the tingle of the shield, the footprint that defined the edge of the spell. She moved no farther and hovered in her spot. She looked at Kristin and Reggie, who likewise had stopped.

Kristin touched her finger to her earpiece. "Now."

They only had to wait a few seconds before a spot in the lawn began to bulge and bubble. A moment later a gnome popped his head through the grass. From the house one of Lucas's men dashed outside.

"It pays to have gnome friends," Jonathan said through the earpieces.

Stormy smiled to herself. Their plan had worked.

They knew Lucas wouldn't have left his house unguarded. The gnome had triggered the magic barrier. Thank God, Reggie had been able to convince Alfred, the gnome who ran her bakery, to help them. The gnome was in no danger from Lucas's Arcani sentry. Gnomes had magic of their own, and he would be safe. She could hear this one arguing with Lucas's man that he had been given the wrong directions and had popped up here by accident, and not to worry, he wasn't staying. Not waiting another moment, Stormy flew to the dryer vent. Reggie and Kirstin landed beside her.

Kristin drew her wand and sliced through the grill over the vent with magic. A moment of envy passed through Stormy at Kristin's control, but she didn't dwell on it longer than that because she flew into the vent. By the time she reached the dryer hose, a thick layer of fuzz had attached itself to every inch of her. Reggie and Kristin caught up a moment later, looking like they had bathed in cotton balls. Reggie stroked through the hose with her wand, and the three slipped through to the laundry room. There were always things to be grateful for—for instance, even sorcerers had laundry they needed to clean.

Reggie shook her hair and a cloud of lint flew off her. "I will never feel clean again," she whispered.

Stormy looked at her two companions. "You look like sheep." She bit her lip to keep from laughing. She unrolled the tapestry and shook it to release the dust.

"I wouldn't talk, Miss Q-Tip," Kristin whispered, her lips curving into a smile.

They spent a minute knocking off as much lint as possible, and then squeezed under the door to the house proper. Stormy took the lead, with Reggie behind her. Her nerves quivered with anxiety. Because they couldn't be sure no one was in the house, she approached every corner with caution, but she never saw anyone. Not that their luck helped her relax. She was not cut out for breaking and entering.

When they reached the art room, they saw no space to squeeze underneath. The door sealed the entrance completely. Stormy expected this. Fine art required precise temps and moisture control. Clearly Lucas's treasures had great value.

Reggie flew to the knob and tapped it with her wand. They heard the click of a lock sliding out of its bed. Then working in tandem, Reggie turned the knob and Kristin and Stormy pushed the door open a crack. They were in. Eager to finish their task, Stormy dashed inside. As soon as she stepped through, her bones began popping. The earpiece dropped from her head, now huge relative to her. She dropped the weaving, which returned to full size almost at once and might have covered her if she hadn't run from it.

"What's happening?" she asked.

"Damn it. We knew we couldn't do magic in here." Reggie stepped out of her dress. "Apparently we can't maintain magic either."

Already her sari felt tight. Stormy loosened the cloth, but it wouldn't last as a cover more than a few seconds longer. "Can we summon something?" She untied the knot at her neck and unwrapped the makeshift dress.

"No, I was only able to do magic here because I had the staff." Reggie searched the room for something to cover herself with.

"Of course. The staff. Reggie said it. Merlin's Gifts." Kristin concentrated and held out her hand. A glowing red orb appeared in her hand. "Lucas's rules don't apply to Merlin's Gifts."

Stormy watched in amazement. As if it recognized its like, the tapestry fluttered on the wall.

Kristin closed her eyes. *"Requiro."* In the next blink, she wore black Capris and a T-shirt. She then turned to them and waved her wand. *"Requiro."*

The orb glowed brighter, and Stormy felt herself covered by shorts and a T-shirt. They were loose, but she was still getting big.

Also clothed, Reggie looked impressed. "Glad one of us can think under pressure."

Kristin smiled and said, "Sanctum." The orb disappeared.

Reggie turned to Stormy. "Let's get to work."

Her bones were still creaking and aching, but they didn't have time to deal with the pain. Besides, the uneasiness Stormy felt was worse. She picked up her weaving and moved to the tapestry. She shook more fluff from the fake and looked at the original. Her stomach dropped. Hers was terrible and amateurish in comparison. "This won't work."

Reggie took the weaving from her and looked between the two. "It's better than you think. You're just an expert."

Stormy doubted it, but they really had no choice.

Reggie lifted the tapestry from the wall. For a moment Stormy expected alarms to sound as they would in a museum, then realized how ridiculous that would be. Lucas was a wizard and his house was protected with magic. He had no need of Groundling security measures. He probably wouldn't use them anyway.

Stormy slid the rod out of the tapestry's loops and slipped it though hers. When she hung the fake on the wall, she realized that the lint made her work appear older. It might help to hide the flaws. With great care she rolled up the ancient piece, apologizing to it in her head. This was no way to treat a work of art. "Ready."

Kristin was leaning against the wall. She pushed herself off and let out a sigh. "Let's get out of here."

Reggie picked up the fairy dresses and the earphones. Stormy looked around to see if they left any evidence. None, except for her tapestry.

Kristin stumbled slightly.

Reggie grabbed her arm. "Are you okay?"

"A little drained. Working against Lucas's magic took more out of me than I thought." Kristin shook herself.

Stormy was feeling tired herself. Transforming twice in a short amount of time hadn't been without cost. "We have to get out of here."

The earphones crackled. Reggie shoved one against her ear and a look of despair came across her expression. "Lucas is coming."

They looked at each other.

Kristin whispered, "Go. I'll cause a diversion. Run outside. You can transport once you leave the perimeter."

Stormy shook her head. "We're not leaving you."

"I shouldn't do any more magic right now. I'm stuck. Stopping Lucas is more important than I am."

"That's bull," Stormy said.

Reggie looked stricken. "Kristin, he nearly killed you once. He won't stop this time."

They heard the front door open.

"Go," whispered Kristin. She grabbed a vase and lifted it over her head, but before she could throw it, a new sound reached them.

"Hey, Lee Roy."

Stormy sucked in a breath. Hunter? Here?

Kristin replaced the vase and looked at her.

"Mr. Merrick?" Lucas's voice held surprise. "What can I do for you?"

Hunter *was* here. Oh, God. Kristin and Reggie signaled their concerns and questions with shrugs, but she ignored them. Without releasing the tapestry, she crept down the hallway to gain a vantage point. Lucas stood in the doorway facing outside. Dmitri had positioned himself between Hunter and Lucas.

"I heard what you said in the Council today. About the Arcani and Groundlings." His voice sounded at once familiar and foreign. Why was he here?

"Indeed?"

"It made a lot of sense."

That wasn't right. She had talked to Hunter about Lucas's ideas, and Hunter hadn't agreed with them.

"That's gratifying. Now if you will excuse me—"

"I've come to offer you my services."

Stormy nearly cried out. Her heart twisted painfully. Her feelings for him must have been stronger than she thought if his announcement caused her such pain.

Lucas chuckled. "How noble of you, but I have no need of your services. Dmitri—"

"Dmitri is fine, but I am a trained Guard."

"Who has let an insignificant woman out of his grasp twice." Lucas's voice was sharp. "Your record doesn't speak well for you. However, your eagerness is in your favor. Perhaps I can—"

A bell sounded. All three men looked up. After the first clang, the bell remained silent, but the alarm had been raised. Stormy could feel it. It rippled inside her. Lucas's security system. From the other side of the house the man they had seen earlier ran out.

"An intruder," Dmitri said, drawing his wand.

"Let me help." Hunter drew his as well.

"Go," Lucas said.

The three men ran out. Lucas drew his wand as well and turned toward the hallway.

Stormy ducked back. Reggie and Kristin waved her toward them, but she didn't have the time to make it down the hallway. She heard his steps come closer.

"I found her." Hunter's voice came from the doorway. Lucas returned to the door.

"It's one of the godmothers."

Hyacinth. A cold wave of fear crashed over her. Stormy looked back at the women. Reggie held her hand over her ear, and her eyes widened. She pointed to the earphones. She must have heard something from the men.

"Do you have her?" Lucas asked.

"Right here," Hunter said.

Lucas let out a shout. "Excellent."

Stormy heard the return of Dmitri and the other man.

"I can change her back, if you want me to. They teach us that in the Guards," Hunter said.

Stormy's gut seethed at his betrayal.

"Make sure she's covered up. I have no desire to see her naked," Lucas said.

Stormy felt a tingle of magic from the living room. Hunter must have cast his spell over Hyacinth. Fear for Hyacinth flooded and drowned her anger at Hunter. Reggie waved her fingers, indicating Stormy should join them, but how could she leave Hyacinth? She shook her head.

"Hello, Lucas," Hyacinth said. Her voice was strong and confident.

"What brings you here, Hyacinth?"

"Do you really have to ask?" Hyacinth sounded amused. "The tapestry, of course."

Lucas laughed. "So predictable. As you can see, you can't get past my safeguards."

"Not this time."

"Not ever. Your time has run out."

A hand clamped down on Stormy's arm. She whipped her head around and saw Kristin. Kristin tugged her toward the rear of the house.

Stormy pointed toward Hyacinth.

Trust me. Kristin mouthed the words.

With reluctance, Stormy allowed herself to be pulled back, the tapestry tucked securely under her arm.

When they reached the end of the hallway, they slipped outside through a back door. Stormy didn't believe they would trigger any alarms—after all, they were coming from inside. When they reached the edge of the property, she felt the curtain of magic flow from her as she passed beyond Lucas's shield.

Jonathan and Tennyson materialized in front of them. Kristin stumbled into Tennyson's arms, which closed around her.

"You pushed yourself." Tennyson's voice held on accusation.

"Lucas has Hyacinth," Stormy said.

"We know. It's part of the plan," Jonathan said.

"Plan?" Stormy looked at Reggie, who shot her an apologetic look.

Reggie tapped the earphones. "I couldn't tell you inside. They would have heard."

"So what happens now?"

As if on cue, they heard yelling from the front of the house, and the sound of wand blasts.

Jonathan grabbed Reggie and Stormy by the hand. "We leave."

19

JUSTIN'S GUIDE FOR THE ARTIST

•

Art often requires pain and sacrifice, both physical and emotional.

THE AIR SQUEEZED from her lungs, and blackness enveloped her vision. As usual, the sensation didn't last longer than a second before they appeared in the living room of the safe house.

Stormy jerked her hand from Jonathan's grasp. "What is going on?" She held the tapestry awkwardly, then placed it on a chair.

Before anyone could speak, the air shimmered and compressed. Hyacinth and Hunter popped into the room. All words left her. She couldn't think or breathe. Stormy stared at Hunter.

Wrapped in a sheet, Hyacinth stumbled to a chair and flopped into it. "I haven't had that much fun since the last time I went to Disneyland."

As if on a cosmic exhale, the tension eased in the room. Rose came from the kitchen, a large tray in her arms. "I figured you'd need nourishment after your adventures." She placed a variety of cookies, fruits, and sandwiches on the coffee table. "I'll be right back with drinks."

Kristin picked up a cookie and shoved it into her mouth with a look of ecstasy on her face. "God, I needed that."

Stormy took it all in, but only peripherally. She still stared at Hunter. Neither had moved. She didn't think she was capable of movement.

"You'd better eat something too," Hunter said. "You probably used a lot of energy back there."

"That's all you have to say to me?" She felt as if the dam that had been holding back her emotions had burst inside her and now all the feelings were crashing through her. "Eat something?" Her voice had risen to a pitch she didn't know she could hit.

Her legs filled with sudden power. She whirled away from him and stormed from the room.

He caught her arm before she could take more than three steps. "Your name really should be Tornado. Stormy is too calm for you. I could apply for federal disaster aid since you came into my life."

"You? You think my life has been calm since I met you? You're bossy, thick-headed, tunnel-visioned—"

"Oh, hell." He grabbed her other arm and pulled her to him.

Before she could even think about pulling back, he kissed her. And then she couldn't think at all. This was what she had wanted. This was what she had mourned for two days. Him. And now he was here, kissing her, and she wanted to crawl inside him.

"I told you we could trust him," Hyacinth said.

Applause broke out around them. Stormy blinked and looked around. She had completely forgotten they had an audience.

"Now will you eat?" Hunter asked. Then he leaned forward and whispered in her ear. "I didn't risk everything to have you collapse now. You have to promise me you'll take care of yourself."

His warm breath sent shivers up her spine, but he was right. She leaned her cheek against his for a moment, then pushed away. "Okay. I'll eat." She crossed to the table, grabbed an apple, and chomped into it. "Satisfied?" But she smiled while she chewed.

"Not at all, but it's a start." He drew in a quick breath and smiled at her.

Rose and Lily carried out more food, and Hunter grabbed a sandwich and fed her more than he ate himself. For a minute no one said anything of consequence.

Finally, after she noticed that the replenishing of energy had slowed down, Stormy asked, "Now can someone tell me what happened back there?"

"We have questions too," Jonathan said. "Like why weren't you wearing the earphones and where did you get those clothes?"

The story was told in pieces. How the art room had blocked even the magic they had performed before entering. How Kristin summoned the orb despite Lucas's spell and clothed them. How they got the tapestry.

"We saw Lucas arrive," Tennyson said. "We thought we'd have to attack or something. But then Hunter showed up and found us."

Stormy looked at Hunter. "Why—"

"I heard him speak at the Council." Hunter cleared his throat. "He's announced his agenda to them, and they're falling for it. So I followed him home to see if I could get into his inner circle. He's got to be stopped."

She bit back her cry of triumph.

Hunter turned to Jonathan and Tennyson. "No offense, guys. You're pretty good at avoiding the Guard, but you suck at missions. I spotted you as soon as I arrived. You're just lucky Lucas didn't see you."

Tennyson spread his hands. "Hey, I'm just a historian."

Hunter snorted. "Just." Then he pointed at Jonathan. "And don't tell me you're just a wand maker."

Stormy's curiosity was nearly bubbling over and the men were sitting there bonding. "So what happened?" she prodded.

"Hunter came up with a plan." Jonathan gave a grudging nod. "A fairly decent one."

"While he went in to distract Lucas from finding you three, I changed into a fairy." Hyacinth gave a contented smile.

"Oh no, Hyacinth, you didn't." Lily turned to her friend, her face a mask of concern.

"I volunteered. It made more sense than sending in one of the young men. Besides, I've done this sort of thing before." Hyacinth waved her hand. "I'm fine."

But Stormy looked closer. The plate in front of Hyacinth was clean. She hadn't eaten anything, and a shadow darkened the skin under her eyes.

"That was a long time ago," Rose said, her voice sharp with worry.

"Yeah, but it's good to know I haven't lost the touch." Hyacinth lounged against the cushioned back of the chair.

Stormy drew her brows together. Hyacinth wasn't leaning so much as using the chair as support. "Hyacinth, maybe you should—"

Hyacinth pointed a finger at her and grinned. "Young lady, I still outrank you. I wouldn't have missed this for the world."

Lily shook her head. Stormy heard her say under her breath, "Stubborn woman."

"She triggered Lucas's magic sensors while she was a fairy," Jonathan said with admiration in his voice.

"And I captured her. Of course it was easy since I knew exactly where she would be," Hunter said.

"Which explains my lovely outfit." Hyacinth swished a corner of the sheet she wore.

"So then while they had Lucas's attention, we told you to get out. Reggie had the headset on again, and there you are." Tennyson draped an arm around Kristin. "You used too much magic summoning the orb."

"I pushed it. A little. But I am a Rare One, right?" Kristin ate another cookie. "Nothing like magic to burn off calories."

Although their voices were cheerful, the undercurrent of fear and anxiety was evident in the room.

"Right. As comfortable as I find this outfit, I think I'll go change." Hyacinth left the room, but Stormy thought her steps were heavy and slow.

"And maybe we should look at the tapestry." Tennyson stood, his fingers staying on Kristin until the last possible second as if he were loath to let go. He moved to the dining room table and looked at Stormy.

She nodded and picked up the tapestry. The urge to put on conservators' gloves flooded her, but she ignored the impulse. She carried the weaving to the table and spread it out, trying to keep from touching the front. It was the least she could do.

Once again the vibrancy of the work took her breath away. The figures had a lifelike quality that she knew she hadn't achieved.

"Cut yourself some slack, girl." Reggie held her shoulders. "You did a great job."

"I didn't know mind reading came with this job," Stormy said.

"It doesn't, but sometimes it doesn't have to," Reggie said with a smile.

They gathered around the table and examined the tapestry. Although she had identified the errors in the weaving before, they were even clearer now. They jumped out at her. A tapestry of this quality wouldn't have this many dropped stitches, nor would the warp blend in so well at every spot.

Silence reigned as they bent over the weaving. Stormy glanced from one error to the next trying to detect a pattern.

"Uh, Stormy, what are we looking at?" Kristin said.

Stormy's gaze darted up from the table. They were all looking at her. She waved at the weaving. "Don't you see it?"

Kristin shook her head. "No."

One by one they all shook their heads. Stormy suppressed a giggle. "Sorry. I really thought it was obvious." She pointed to one of the mistakes. "See? The weaver left out a stitch here. That can happen."

"So there's a misplaced stitch in the picture," Hunter said.

"There isn't one. There're dozens." Stormy pointed to several all over the tapestry. "Too many for a tapestry of this quality. Unless it was deliberate.

"Where the stitch has been dropped, the warp shows through. Those are the support threads. But you can see the warp matches perfectly to the color of the design in that spot. It would require a warp of dozens of colors. No one weaves that way. The weaver who created this tapestry didn't want the errors to show, but she wanted the viewer to see the warp in those spots."

They looked back at the tapestry, then sent her questioning glances.

She tried again. "It's brilliant, really. You don't notice

the errors because they blend into the picture, but the weaver who created this image has too much skill to have made so many errors. They had to be on purpose."

Tennyson bent closer. "I see what you mean."

"Why would anyone do that?" Reggie asked.

"There has to be some kind of message here." She looked back at the cloth.

"What does it say?" Reggie asked.

"Now that I don't know."

"There doesn't seem to be a pattern to the skips," Tennyson said.

Stormy frowned. "I know. But this is the third of Merlin's Gifts, and I'm telling you, no master weaver would ever make so many errors unless it was on purpose." Her fingers brushed against the surface.

As if in answer to her touch, the dropped stitches lit up in a cascading flow as her finger moved down the cloth. She felt a surge of power flow into her arm as it lit up. She jerked her hand away. "How did I do that? I saw Lucas touch it and nothing happened."

"It's a gift for the godmothers," Rose said. "Lucas is not a godmother."

"Do it again," Lily said.

Stormy started at the top of the tapestry and slowly ran her finger down the weaving. As she hit each row, the warp lit up where it was exposed, sometimes one in a row sometimes two. At the bottom of the tapestry, an urge struck her to lay her palm on the cloth, so she did. Every exposed spot glowed.

"But what does it mean?" Kristin asked.

Stormy mentally connected the spots of light to see if they created an image. Nope, just a bunch of spots.

"Maybe it refers to a constellation," Reggie said.

"Unlikely," Tennyson said. "Arcani don't believe in the zodiac."

What if it's a map to another location?" Kristin said.

Tennyson lifted his shoulders. "It could be."

"We don't have time to travel," Jonathan said.

"What if it's a map, but not to a location exactly?" Hunter said. "Suppose the positions symbolized something." Hunter pointed to a spot near him. "Like five rows down eleven across could mean fifth page, eleventh word."

"Of the *Lagabóc*," Tennyson said. "That's the only thing it can be."

"You'd need the original to check," Hunter said.

"We have it," Reggie said.

Hunter looked at her.

"Not the *original* original, but a copy, a facsimile," Kristin said.

Hunter stared at them. "The Council never told us that."

"They probably didn't want you to be scared," Jonathan said. "There's some serious magic in there."

"What are you all talking about?" Stormy said. She removed her hand, and the tapestry stopped glowing.

"The *Lagabóc*. Merlin's book of rules and magic."

"The one Tennyson found?" Stormy said.

They all looked at her.

"Lucas told me about it," Stormy said. "He told me it was a book of Merlin's rules for the Arcani."

"It is, but it also talks about his magic, spells, and his Gifts," Tennyson said.

"Apparently Merlin's Gifts combine to form some sort of weapon, but the details weren't in the *Lagabóc*," Reggie said.

Kristin pointed to the tapestry. "Or they are, and we just didn't know how to find them until now."

"Stormy, may I take this and work on it?" Tennyson asked.

"Why are you asking *my* permission?" Stormy asked.

"Well, technically you found it. It's yours."

"I *stole* it."

"Doesn't matter. It recognized you," Tennyson said.

"You can't light it up?"

Tennyson ran his finger down the cloth. Nothing happened.

She struggled not to feel too much glee at the lack of magical response. This was her display of power and it felt good. "Of course you can take it."

Tennyson rolled up the tapestry. "I'll be careful with it. But I may need your help to illuminate it so I can check my numbers. And maybe to help me count since you're so familiar with weaving."

"You got it." She smiled. She finally felt useful in this group.

"What about him?" Jonathan asked, pointing to Hunter.

Stormy lifted her gaze to Hunter and found him already looking at her. Something in his expression, something in his eyes, made her uneasy, but he smiled at her.

"We could use his expertise," Kristin said.

As Hyacinth came back into the room, she shook her head. "No."

Stormy looked at her in confusion. She thought Hyacinth liked Hunter.

Hunter took Stormy's hand, but turned his gaze to Hyacinth. "If you know that much, then you also know that I don't have to say it."

"Say what?" Stormy asked.

"No, damn it. I won't let you." Hyacinth stood in front of them. "You can still go back."

"Too late. My mind is made up." Hunter's grip tightened on Stormy's hand.

"No, stop him! Don't let him join us!" Hyacinth shouted at Stormy. "Tell him you don't want him here."

Panic raced through Stormy. Jonathan and Reggie had pulled their wands and were pointing them at Hunter, and Tennyson stood in front of Kristin and shoved the tapestry behind him. Lily and Rose tried to hold Hyacinth back, but she shrugged them off.

Hunter ignored them all. He placed his palm on Stormy's cheek. "I've never met anyone like you. I would have liked to get to know you better."

She didn't understand. What was he talking about? Had he called the Guard down around them? He sounded as if she was about to die.

Then Hunter fell to one knee. He sucked in a loud breath, and his grip tightened even more. His other hand knotted into a fist so tight, his knuckles blazed white. He screwed his eyes shut.

"Damn it," Hyacinth pushed to Hunter's side. "I told you not to let him."

"Let him what?" Stormy's voice cracked. "What's happening?"

"It's the Oath of Allegiance. He's broken it." Hyacinth drew her wand. "And now he's dying."

Stormy looked down at his face. He was hiding it, but he was in pain. "No!" Confusion and fear challenged each other for the top spot. Fear won. Stormy dropped to her knees beside him. She cupped his face. "What can we do?"

Hyacinth muttered something, then touched him with her wand. His breathing eased for moment. He looked at Hyacinth. "How did you know?"

"I loved a Guard once," Hyacinth said, not looking at his face, but seeking another spot on his body. "He made the same choice."

Hunter winced and doubled over. Stormy sought help from the others and saw the horror in their faces.

"Help me lay him down." Hyacinth touched him again with her wand.

Dropping the tapestry onto the table, Tennyson ran forward and helped Hunter lie on his back. Reggie hugged Kristin, and both were crying. Stormy didn't have time for tears. Hunter couldn't be dying. She knelt by his head and stroked his cheek.

"Was it worth it?" Hunter asked Hyacinth.

Hyacinth passed her wand over him again. "Are you asking me if he should have done it? No. I wanted him alive. But he couldn't live the lie, and that would have destroyed him as surely as the Oath did."

Those words seemed to give Hunter peace. "Then you understand."

"No, I don't. Men and their honor." Hyacinth's voice broke and a tear slipped down her cheek. "Sometimes I think you're all stupid."

Hunter actually laughed for a second, but it ended in a gasp. "Stormy?"

"I'm here." She clasped his hand to her.

"You're worth it. Don't let anyone tell you otherwise."

"Save it for later, Hunter. You're not dead yet and you won't be for a while if I have anything to say about it." Hyacinth knelt beside him, placing one hand on his head and the one with her wand over his heart.

Flustered and nervous, Rose and Lily rushed over. "Hyacinth, you can't," Lily said.

Hyacinth looked up at them, grinned, and gave them a wink. "No, *you* can't, or rather you shouldn't. I can't think of anything I'd rather do . . . now."

Tears spilled from Rose's eyes. She swiped at them impatiently. "But we're not ready."

"Neither is he, but I am." Hyacinth eyes had tears as well. "I haven't felt this good in months."

Stormy looked between the three aunts. She didn't understand what they were talking about, but Hunter's chest jerked, and her focus shifted to him again. His breathing was shallow and sporadic. A pain-filled keen filled her soul. "Don't go," she whispered.

Then, where she clasped his hand, magic buzzed and sought entrance to her.

"Help me, Stormy. Make him let me in," Hyacinth said.

"No." Hunter's voice was little more than a rasp.

Stormy didn't know what was required of her, but she concentrated on the tingling, and let the magic in. It whooshed through her, lightening her spirit, circling, filling her, and returning to her hands, infusing her with a trail of power.

Her awareness didn't stop at her fingertips. Somehow she had entered Hunter, as if her being had merged into him.

"That's it." Hyacinth's voice was triumphant.

Stormy couldn't see any longer. No, that wasn't right. She was on a different level of awareness. The room, Reggie, Kristin, and the others had disappeared from sight, but they were still there. She felt them, but mostly she felt Hunter, as if they shared one soul, one life. And then she felt the presence of another soul. Hyacinth.

They spoke without speaking, the three life forces intermingling, twining, ribboning over, through, and around one another. Entwined in Hunter's essence, an angry vortex sucked energy from him. Hyacinth tried to weave tendrils of herself around him, which Hunter dodged.

"You're so stubborn, boy," Hyacinth said, but she didn't actually use words.

"I won't let you do this." That was Hunter.

Stormy moved between them, through them, in them, and then she saw it, felt it. The black canker in Hyacinth's life force.

"Hyacinth?" Sorrow swamped her.

"No sadness," Hyacinth said with great joy. "Don't you see? I want to do this. I can do this. Please, Hunter, let me do this."

He had seen the malignancy as well. "Oh, God."

"No. Oh, Life!" Hyacinth gamboled over them. "Now let me in, you silly, stubborn man, so you can live." She dove.

Hunter blocked himself, but Hyacinth disappeared into him. Stormy stroked and offered her strength to Hunter, who was still weak. Then she felt strength flowing back into him. The vortex was gone.

Hyacinth's life stream returned to them. Her ribbon had changed. Angry purple streaked with black twisted through the sunniness that she once was. As Hunter's spirit glowed brighter, Hyacinth's life force slowed.

Stormy felt love flow over both Hunter and herself from Hyacinth, and she returned it in kind.

"What's the point of being a godmother if you can't do great magic?" Hyacinth's ribbon had thinned to a thread. "I have it now. Now go, before you take some of it back with you."

Hyacinth's awareness disappeared. The magic was ebbing. Stormy felt herself being pulled back into her body. Grief struck her. A moment later, she looked up from the floor into Kristin's eyes. How had she landed on the floor? It didn't matter. She pushed herself upright. Hunter's head lay in Rose's lap, where her tears dropped on him, but she smiled at him through her sorrow. His eyes were opening, but his ordeal had been brutal, so he wasn't moving yet. Lily cradled Hyacinth.

Stormy crawled to Hyacinth and held her hand. She now knew what the black was. "Cancer?"

Hyacinth drew a shallow breath. "Some things even magic can't cure."

Lily stroked Hyacinth's hair. "You've always been reckless. And brave. What are we going to do without you?"

"You'll be just fine." Hyacinth's voice was no more than a whisper.

"I love you," Lily said.

Rose joined them, taking Hyacinth's other hand. Hunter was now sitting, propped up on the legs of a chair.

"You were always the strong one," Rose said.

Hyacinth shook her head. "Nah. I was just the loudest."

Through their tears, all three smiled at that.

Rose kissed Hyacinth's forehead.

"Time of Transition," Hyacinth said on a breath. Her gaze met Stormy's. "Get that son of a bitch."

Stormy nodded.

Hyacinth's chest rose. She looked at her two lifelong friends. "It's all about love." She exhaled.

Her chest didn't rise again.

Her fingers lost their grip on the wand, which rolled from her palm. It lay on the floor for a moment, then vanished.

20

JUSTIN'S GUIDE FOR THE ARTIST

•

Find the beauty in everything.

HUNTER WATCHED TENNYSON carry Hyacinth's body into her bedroom with Rose and Lily trailing behind. As if encased in ice, the others moved around the living room, aimless, lost, in shock. Stormy stayed beside him. He felt disoriented and as weak as a strand of spaghetti. He hadn't quite grasped what had just happened. *Hyacinth had died for him.*

He had to get up. He wasn't ready to stand, but he'd feel worse if he stayed on the floor.

He tried to push to his knees and almost didn't make it. Stormy's arms went around him, but she wasn't exactly unaffected by the ordeal either.

Together they pushed and pulled each other up and stumbled to the sofa.

"How . . . ? Why . . . ?" Reggie asked.

"The Oath," Hunter said. He waited for the tug, the pain that would prevent him from talking, but none came. He felt for the weight that bound him, the constriction that had settled on him when he had joined the Guard. They all had it. He couldn't find it, sense it at all.

God, Hyacinth had done it. But at what cost?

"What oath?" Kristin asked, snapping him out of his thoughts.

"The Oath of Allegiance. All Guards have to take it. It's a binding spell that prevents us from betraying the Council."

"By killing you?" Stormy said.

"If necessary."

"That's barbaric," Kristin said.

"Hyacinth removed it," Hunter said. He couldn't wrap his mind around her sacrifice.

"What do you mean removed it?" Reggie asked.

"I can't tell you. I only know it's not there anymore." Hunter dropped his head into his hands. "She took it into herself. And it killed her."

Stormy's hand slipped into his. He could still feel her strength from that weird connection thing they had shared. She and he and Hyacinth. Only Hyacinth was gone.

"All we saw was the three of you on the floor, your eyes rolled into the backs of your heads, and you seemed to be breathing as one," Kristin said.

"We couldn't separate your hands from one another." Jonathan stayed on the edge of the room as if he didn't quite trust Hunter. Hunter couldn't blame him. "It was as if you had all fused together."

"Yes, I'd like to hear more about this as well." Tennyson returned to the room.

Kristin ran to him. "Are they . . . ?"

Tennyson shrugged. "They're crying, but they seemed okay. They wanted to be alone with Hyacinth."

The women were crying here too. Hunter looked up. "I don't know that I can explain it."

Stormy jerked back as if struck, and she sucked in a loud breath. "We all changed into streams of energy or ribbons or something, and we weren't here, but we could feel one another and talk, although we weren't really talking." She shook her head. "I can't put it into words."

"Hyacinth went through me and found the Oath's stranglehold. She removed it. When she pulled free, her life force was weaker." Hunter couldn't face them. His gaze dropped to the floor. "I killed her."

"No, you didn't." Lily's voice came from the doorway. Her eyes were puffy, and her nose was red, but her head was erect and her gaze was fierce. "And she would hate to hear you talk that way."

Rose stood beside her, wringing a handkerchief in her hands and wiping at her face. "She was already dying."

Stormy looked up. "The cancer. I saw it when our life forces merged."

He had seen it too, but that didn't change the facts. The Oath had been killing him, but she had taken it from him, and it killed her.

Rose nodded. "She was diagnosed several months ago."

"But she was a fairy godmother. Why couldn't she use magic to help herself?" Stormy asked.

Lily came farther into the room. "Because despite our powers, we are still human, and we face some of the same issues that all humans do. And that seems to be the key concept that Lucas cannot grasp." A tear slipped down Lily's cheek. "When we defied the Council, Hyacinth had to stop her treatments for fear of getting caught. She felt great, but we knew the cancer was spreading."

Rose came in and sat on the couch. "Conceivably a doctor could have done the same thing the three of you experienced, but then the doctor would die. Hyacinth would never agree to that." Rose patted Hunter's knee. "You gave her a gift, young man. You allowed her to be useful, to save your life, to let her die for a reason."

Hunter frowned. "I didn't allow it. I simply didn't prevent it."

"As if you could. At our strongest we couldn't best Hyacinth in an argument, and you weren't in any shape to argue," Lily said. "We all saw what was happening to you."

"Hyacinth said she loved a Guard once." Stormy looked to the two older women.

Lily smiled. "It was 1941 and Hyacinth fell in love just after we were chosen. With the horror going on, we tried our best to protect the humans. The Council suggested that the Arcani needed to protect themselves first, but we didn't listen. We wanted to help the Groundlings as much as we could."

"There were days we came very close to harming ourselves," Rose said. "And still we couldn't save enough. There were so many, many Groundlings who suffered, and so few of us who could do anything."

"When Tony fell in love with Hyacinth, he helped as much as he could for the year they were together." Lily brushed another tear away. "But then the Council declared that the Arcani mustn't come to the Groundlings' aid. Many Arcani were dying in the war too, and the Council claimed they were trying to save them. We continued our work anyway, and the Council looked the other way since we were the godmothers. But Tony realized the Council was wrong, and helped us one last time."

"And that was all it took," Hunter said. "The Oath

would have activated the minute he made the decision. He had to know. We all know."

"Then why didn't you die when you let Kristin and me go?" Stormy asked, horror in her voice.

"I was in pain, but I still believed the Council was right. I just couldn't hurt you." He couldn't look her in the eye. "If it had been anyone else, I would have turned you in."

"And now?" Stormy asked.

"The Council is wrong." He waited for the pain again, even knowing the Oath was gone, but it never came.

"The Council asked me to sign the Oath," Reggie said quietly. "They never told me what it would mean."

Jonathan grew very still. His blue eyes turned frosty. "I will kill Sophronia the next time I see her. I could kill them all right now." He pulled Reggie into his arms and held her tightly. His shoulders lifted and dropped with agitated breath.

For a minute, nobody spoke. Then Kristin said, "I suppose we can't hold a memorial."

"No need," Lily said. "We've already taken care of it."

Rose sniffled softly. "We made plans together for this. Hyacinth is with Tony."

Stormy started to cry harder at that pronouncement. Hunter slipped his arm around her. They were linked now, somehow. She had seen into his soul, and she had not been frightened by what she found there.

"What do we do now?" Kristin asked.

Lily drew herself upright. "What we always do in times of crisis. We go on and save our grief for later."

Stormy stared off into space. "We get that son of a bitch." Her voice was hard.

Tennyson nodded. He picked up the tapestry. "I'll get to work on this." But he held his hand out to Kristin. "Help me?"

Kristin nodded, wiping a final few tears from her face. The pair disappeared to another part of the house where Tennyson had set up a library of sorts.

Hunter looked over the rest of the ragtag army. "We're going to need some help."

"Not now," Rose said. "You two look terrible. Go rest." She stroked Hunter's cheek.

The gesture surprised him. How could she touch him? Didn't she realize that he was to blame for Hyacinth's death? He had to make it up to everyone somehow. "There's too much to do, to plan."

Lily smiled at him. "Rose is right. I imagine you're impatient, but you've just been through an ordeal. You'll feel better if you rest for a while."

Hunter shook his head. "How can you stand to look at me?" he cried.

For a moment, Lily and Rose said nothing. No one spoke. Stormy moved closer to his side, but he stepped away.

Then Lily moved forward and cupped his cheek in her hand. "You are one of us now. Hyacinth made her decision. She chose your life. You should too."

"We loved Hyacinth," Rose added, "and we'll miss her, but she made the decision. We can't blame you."

"We trust you. As much as Hyacinth did. Now go rest," Lily said.

He didn't know how to react. He was used to taking orders, but from his commander. Lily's voice, while softer, held just as much authority.

Rose said, "You don't have the strength of a cotton ball right now. Stormy, show him where he can lie down. And you should rest too. We'll wake you if anything happens."

Stormy stood, and she swayed as she adjusted to standing. She needed rest, but he was fine. He'd just help her to her bed, and then . . . And then? He wasn't a Guard anymore. He wouldn't think about that.

He stood and for a moment his vision went black as the blood rushed from his head. She grabbed his arm. "I'm okay. I just stood up too fast."

"Uh-huh. Come on, Hercules. They're right." Stormy led him down the hallway to a small bedroom. The bed was tiny.

Stop thinking about sharing a bed.

Stormy pushed him gently toward the mattress. "We won't have as much room as we did in the Council Hall, but it will suffice."

God, she had had the same thought. But he had to admit the bed was inviting. He didn't have the energy to fight the suggestion of sleep any longer. He lay down on one side, and without another word, Stormy climbed next to him. She curled against his chest and stomach, spooning. His arm went naturally around her.

"We'll talk about everything later," she said, her voice distorted by a yawn. "But thank you for coming after us and helping. I am glad you're alive."

He didn't know what to make of those words, but she inhaled deeply and relaxed almost instantly. He didn't think he could sleep after everything that happened. He had just watched a godmother die for him, he had just betrayed the Council, and his guilt burned within him . . . but moments later, he had no thoughts.

STORMY DIDN'T KNOW how long she had slept. The sky wasn't dark, but it lacked the full brightness of day. They had slept for hours.

And then the pain hit her again. Hyacinth was dead, and she had nearly lost Hunter.

She had no right to think of him as hers, but she did nevertheless. Emotions ran unhampered through her, overwhelming her. She didn't think she had any tears left, but they gathered again in her eyes and leaked out, one after the other. No sobs accompanied the crying, just quiet sorrow spilling from her as if it just didn't have enough room in her body and had to come out somewhere.

Hunter moved against her and kissed the top of her head.

"I'm sorry." She sat up. "I didn't mean to wake you."

"You're apologizing to me? You saved me, remember? You and Hyacinth."

"Me? I didn't do anything."

"You're a great actress, but not a good liar." His hand reached out for hers.

Acting on instinct, her fingers twined with his. When they touched, her breathing calmed and her emotions seemed to settle. She looked at their clasped hands. It seemed to affect Hunter as well. His mouth lost its tightness and his forehead unwrinkled.

Curious, she released his hand. Almost at once a longing, a need arose in her blood. It wasn't overpowering, but sort of hummed just beneath her awareness. If she hadn't been looking for it, she wouldn't have noticed anything more than a feeling of slight restlessness.

He must have noticed the same effect. He didn't touch her for a few seconds, and then he took her hand again. Almost immediately she felt right, whole.

"You must have given me more than just your strength," he said.

She shook her head. "No, I think we just exchanged a part of ourselves."

He searched her gaze. "Our hearts?" Then his lips started to twitch.

A smile bloomed on her lips. "That is the cheesiest

thing I've ever heard anyone say, even if it is true." Her smile broadened.

He grinned back at her. "I know. I just can't do it. Doesn't mean I don't feel it."

"Thank God. I'd hate to think I'd fallen for someone who says that kind of thing."

"So you've fallen for me?" He cocked an eyebrow.

"No more than you have for me." She aimed her gaze right back at him.

Still smiling, he grabbed her and rolled her beneath him. "You are going to be such trouble. I can't wait." He kissed her, and her senses unleashed a delicious turmoil that was thoroughly exhilarating.

His hand slipped under her T-shirt and cupped one of her breasts. Immediately her nipple pebbled under his touch, lifting her to a higher level of arousal. Every contact of his hand sent sharp jolts of pleasure into her core. She gave herself over to the primal feelings taking control. She cupped her hands over his buttocks, lifted her hips, and molded herself against him. The tantalizing pressure only heightened the desire for more.

In a frenzy of eagerness, she pushed his shirt up and pulled it from him. She wanted her skin to slide against his, his chest to brush against her breasts, her hips to receive his. Anticipation flamed within her, heightening her frustration, heightening her desire. His fervor appeared no less than hers, for his hands worked at freeing her from her clothes and his own. At some point, he produced his wand and summoned a condom, a mere matter of seconds.

After a few frantic moments of disrobing, they lay together, naked, hot, and hungry. She didn't want to wait. There was urgency, forcefulness in his every movement, matched by her own. She wanted him inside her. Now.

She wrapped her legs around his waist to bring him closer. His mouth sucked at her neck, his tongue tracing circles there, while his hand kneaded and rubbed her breast. And more, all she could think was she needed *more*.

He reached between them and toyed with the sensitive bud that had her gasping in pleasure and aggravation. She rocked her hips to taunt him, his stiff length gliding along her, his heat stroking her to new heights, but still too far to satisfy her.

When he pulled away a moment later, she nearly cried out in anguish, but he rolled the condom over himself and then poised himself over her.

She didn't wait. She lifted her hips, and he pushed himself into her. Her entire body welcomed him. Already the quivering started in her belly, building in intensity, building to the release. He plunged into her again and again, and each time her body met his, determined to end the luscious ache that grew inside.

And then the ache shattered. Satisfaction and jubilation scintillated in every crevice of her body. Above her, Hunter's face constricted as he too found his release. Her body eked out the last of the pleasurable vibrations as Hunter relaxed above her.

He buried his nose into her neck, and she enjoyed the weight of him. "I didn't think I would smile today," she said.

"It's something we learn about in training. Sometimes, life is the sweetest when it's the hardest." He rolled from her. For an instant she felt bereft, but then he laid his hand on her stomach. "You know we're really going to have difficulty if we have to keep touching each other."

"I think it's nice." She snuggled closer to him.

"But hardly practical."

"No." She laughed. "My parents still like touching each other when they're in the same room, but they've been able to live successful lives despite being in love."

"I never said I love you." His voice lilted.

In a confident tone, she teased right back. "You don't have to." Stormy didn't need to hear it. She knew.

He laughed. "I always liked a smart woman." He rolled back to her and kissed her, gently, with awe, cherishing her. "I do, you know."

She smiled her answer, then felt a hint of mischief bubble up in her. "I think I'll keep you guessing for a while about my feelings."

He rolled back on top of her, and although he held himself in a position of dominance over her, no actual menace appeared in his demeanor. "You might want to rethink that."

Giggling, she lifted her head and kissed him. "Consider it rethought."

He dropped to his elbows and kissed her again.

A long while later, she sighed as she curled into his side, still maintaining a connection to him. "I think Hyacinth would approve."

"The real world is waiting for us out there." Hunter leaned back onto the pillow.

She nodded, loath to speak and banish this interlude, but knowing it had to happen.

Hunter swung his legs out of the bed, and she knew the moment had come. "We're going to need some help."

21

JUSTIN'S GUIDE FOR THE ARTIST

•

To find strength, you must allow yourself to be vulnerable.

DARKNESS HAD FALLEN by the time they walked into the living room. Six gazes shot to them. Traces of grief remained on the faces, and red rimmed most of the eyes.

"Do you feel better, dear?" Rose asked.

Much to her mortification, a blush crept into Stormy's cheeks. She nodded.

"I'm so pleased," Rose said. She smiled at Hunter.

Stormy felt that she had no secrets left. She looked around the room and found no blame or condemnation in anyone's expression.

"We've had news," Reggie said.

Hunter looked at her, and Stormy sensed the change in his posture. The warrior was back on duty. "What's happened?"

"The Council has appointed Lucas Special Council." Reggie shook her head. "They've moved him into the Council Hall and given him all the rights and privileges of a head Councilor."

Hunter's gaze narrowed. "How is that possible? The Magic appoints Council members."

"We received a note this afternoon. Apparently Lucas informed the Council of our attack on his house and convinced them that we attacked him because he's exposed our devious plans."

"That we want to take over the Council and rule both the Arcani and Groundling world." Kristin let out a soft snort of disgust. "He's convinced them we've provided an army of Groundlings with magical weapons."

"What proof does he have?" Hunter's gaze intensified.

A quiet fury erupted in Tennyson's expression. "He knows about Zack. Lucas led the Guards to Zack's house, where they found evidence of magic. Not surprising, since Callie lives there. She's a fairy."

Kristin's hand slipped into Tennyson's. "Callie has taken Zack and Jake into hiding. They'll be safe with the fairies."

Reggie's eyes glowed with anger as well. "The Guards also went to the bakery today. They tried to bully Tommy and Joy."

"But not for long." Jonathan smiled with schadenfreude. "Alfred took care of them. Never mess with a gnome."

Stormy glanced at Hunter. She didn't know how he'd take hearing that the Guards were bested, but she needn't have worried. He was in his element.

"Looks like they're upping the game." Hunter glanced around the room.

"Ian has been given a position as Lucas's aide," Reggie said.

"That doesn't surprise me," Hunter said.

"What about my family?" Stormy asked.

"We called and they're fine," Lily said. "They said not to worry, the Guard is there, but the whole neighborhood is watching out for one another. We gave them our Twitter name for communication. They'll contact us if anything happens. I believe Justin said something about being out in the open too long to hide now."

Stormy smiled. That sounded like her daddy.

Hunter turned to Tennyson. "Professor, how's that code coming?"

Tennyson smiled. "About halfway there."

"Good. Keep working on it. How long till they discover where we are?" Hunter threw the question to the others.

"Not long, probably," Kristin answered. "Now that they have Zack's name."

"Then we need to find a new place to stay," Hunter said.

The others didn't exactly relax, but Stormy noticed them instinctively deferring to the one man who had training in battle and strategy. Not that the others weren't competent, but none had Hunter's background.

"I have a few ideas. I'll get on it," Jonathan said.

"Okay." Hunter took Stormy's hand. "Stormy, you come with me."

"Where are you going?" Reggie asked.

"I have an idea, and I need her help."

"How will we let you know where we are?" Rose asked.

"Why don't we use the same idea as the Guards?" Hunter asked.

"What's that?" Stormy asked.

"Our insignia. We touch it with our wands, and we're in contact with our team. We can transport to their location."

"Brilliant," Lily said. "We just need an object." She looked around the room.

"How about this?" Rose waved her wand and five identical pendants on gold chains appeared. Each one was engraved with a hyacinth.

Stormy smiled. "Perfect."

Each of the godmothers stood by one of the pendants and touched her wand to it. Lily said, *"Semper in amicitia."*

Stormy slipped her pendant around her neck, and the others did the same. Always in friendship. It felt right.

Hunter said, "Okay, then pack up, take whatever's necessary, and move as soon as you can. Don't dawdle. They have a lot more men working on finding you than we have trying to get away." He turned to her. "Ready?"

She had no idea where he was taking her, but she trusted him. "Let's go."

They popped out of the house, and a moment later they stood in front of a neat condominium. The complex wasn't fancy, but appeared well maintained. Lights burned in the unit before them.

"Where are we?" she asked.

"Tank's place." He hesitated. "Tank thinks I'm dead."

"Excuse me?"

"Remember that list of names in the Hall? The minute I broke the Oath, my name disappeared from the scroll. That usually only happens when a Guard dies."

"But you didn't die."

"No, but that's only because no one has ever survived breaking the Oath before. Technically, a Guard's name disappears if he retires, dies, or breaks the Oath, which means death. I broke it."

"So Tank believes you're dead." She looked at the lights of the condo.

"He's my best friend and probably in a little pain

right now because the Oath is tugging at him for feeling regret at my death. At least I hope he's feeling some regret. We didn't talk about feelings much." He ran his fingers through his hair. "As long as you can hold, uh, bind him, he won't be able to report us, and he'll be safe from the Oath."

"Me?" Shock didn't begin to describe what she thought of this plan. "With my out-of-control magic? You want me to restrain him?"

Hunter grinned. "I can't do it. He knows all the Guard tricks. But you, you have godmother magic. Remember the naked spell and how I couldn't touch you?"

She did remember. "But I didn't do those on purpose."

"Exactly. They were from you, not regular magic. Stuff that others couldn't do. Well, now you need to do that on purpose."

Doubt assailed her. "What if I can't?"

"You can." He kissed her. "I have faith in you."

Her heart pounded.

"I'll be right beside you."

Well, that was nice, but that didn't guarantee she could do the magic he wanted.

"Just be sincere."

He wasn't helping. As she summoned her wand, she shot him a dirty look, then walked up to the door. Her hand shook as she rang the doorbell.

"Coming, coming." Tank's voice sounded slurred.

She glanced back at Hunter, but he just waved his hand at her. His belief in her should have given her confidence, but it didn't.

Tank opened the door and leaned against it. For a moment he stared at her, then his eyes widened. "You." He fumbled at his pocket, and then managed to pull out his wand.

She acted without thinking. Pointing her wand, she

said, "Don't move." And then she winced. She sounded like a bad movie.

Tank didn't move. He froze. Even his eyes didn't move. And slowly he tipped backward.

"Oh, no!" She waved her wand again. "Move, I mean catch yourself, oh hell." She covered her eyes as Tank smacked into the floor.

She ran to him. "I'm so sorry. That wasn't supposed to happen." She touched him with her wand.

Tank drew a deep breath and grimaced. "You are a menash." His hand shot out, missed her, tried again, and managed to grab her wrist.

"Let her go, Tank." Hunter stood in the doorway. His wand was drawn. "Get his wand, Stormy."

She grabbed it. Tank put up no struggle. In fact he was frozen again. But that didn't make sense. She hadn't done anything.

"You're dead," Tank said, still staring at Hunter.

Hunter shook his head. "Not yet."

"But thash impossible." Tank's face twisted into a mask of disbelief. "You're dead."

"And you're drunk." Hunter reached down and pulled Tank to his feet.

"Well, hell, yesh. My best friend died today. Only now you're alive."

"And you're still drunk." Hunter helped him to the couch.

"I've got to summon the Guard." Tank reached into his pocket for his wand.

"It's not there. We have it," Hunter said.

Stormy showed him his wand.

"Thash okay. I'm off duty anyway."

"No, it's not okay." Hunter held Tank's head. "Listen to me carefully. We've taken you prisoner, and you can't call the Guard."

Suddenly, Tank's face relaxed. "Thanks, man. It was beginning to hurt. Still does a little, but I think thash because I'm glad you're not dead. Even though you betrayed the Guard, man. How could you do that?" Tank screwed up his face until his nose was more wrinkled than a shar-pei's.

"I didn't, although the Council thinks I have." Hunter looked at Stormy and shrugged. Apparently, he hadn't expected Tank to be drunk either.

"You're with *her*." Tank pointed at Stormy.

Being pointed at was uncomfortable. A little alarming how right her dads had been about that. Pointing was rude.

Tank said, "She's the enemy." He reached for his wand, forgetting again he no longer had it.

"She's not, but we need to get you sober before we talk about it. You need some coffee."

"I'll do it." Stormy ran into the kitchen and found the coffeemaker. A short search yielded coffee and filters. She measured enough for a pot, extra strong, and pushed the button. She heard muffled sounds from the living room and frowned. Hunter was trying to get Tank to exercise. Was he making Tank do push-ups?

A few minutes later, she brought the pot of coffee on a tray with cups, sugar, and milk that she found after some exploration of the cupboards and fridge.

Tank was seated again on the couch, sweat dripping down his face. "You're cruel. I liked you better dead."

"Drink this." Hunter shoved a cup of black coffee into Tank's hand. "We've got our wands trained on you. Don't try anything like tossing the coffee on us."

"And I'm too drunk to succeed." Tank downed the coffee, and held out his cup for more.

Tank's presence of mind impressed her. That was probably why he was chosen as a Guard. Even drunk, he could follow Hunter's convoluted attempt to prevent Tank from violating the Oath.

An hour and several bathroom trips later, Tank no longer slurred, and he had lost that jovial quality the alcohol had loaned him. Now his gaze was sharp and hurt registered in his eyes.

"You want to tell me now what this is all about?" Tank examined Hunter. "You should be dead."

"I almost was." Hunter shook his head. "It's a long story."

Tank hissed as if he was in pain.

"That's the Oath," Hunter said to her. "Hold your wand on him and threaten him."

"I can't—"

"You have to. And mean it."

She understood why. It just wasn't easy. She pointed her wand at him. "Tank, if you could, would you turn us in?"

He nodded. "In a second."

She felt a surge of despair and anger. "How? It just isn't right." Her wand shook. "You will listen to Hunter, and not move from that seat until he's finished."

Tank frowned, wiggled a little, and then struggled to stand. He couldn't get up. "You can't do this."

"How do you feel?" Stormy asked.

"Angry. Disappointed. How could you go against the Council, Hunt?"

"I'm actually trying to save the Council now." Hunter launched into the story of Lucas and what he'd learned from the godmothers, old and new, and from Lucas himself. Tank listened without interrupting. He couldn't, actually. As soon as Hunter had started to speak, Tank's voice had vanished. He tried to speak once with no success.

Hunter reached the end of his narrative. "Now I need to ask you something." He looked at Stormy.

She shrugged and looked at Tank. "Can you talk now?"

Tank said, "I don't know. Okay, I can." He stood up. "I should report you now."

"You can't. We still have your wand," Hunter said. "One question, and then we're done, and we'll leave you alone. You've heard about what happened today. That the Council has embraced Lucas and given him a position on the Council? And that's not my question."

Tank nodded. "I was there. We were all there."

"Did you notice if any of the Council members were less than happy about the appointment?"

Tank thought for a moment, then he nodded.

"I need to speak with them, the ones who don't like Lucas." Hunter took Tank's wand from Stormy. "Listen to me carefully. Those Council members require your protection. *I* want to protect them."

"Her," Tank said. "There's just the one."

"Her. But in order to protect her from Lucas and save the Council, you can't turn me in. Do you know what I'm asking?"

Tank nodded. Hunter handed Tank his wand. Stormy held her breath.

Tank didn't touch the insignia on his shirt. He waited, took a deep breath, then grinned. "You are such an asshole, you know that?"

Hunter relaxed. "You okay?"

"Yeah." Tank shook his head. "I can't believe you found a way around the Oath."

"*I* didn't, and it cost someone her life. Now I'm just trying to make sure no one else pays." Hunter rubbed his face. "Too many people have died, and too many more will if we let Lucas take over."

"I'm not sure the Council member will want to see us tonight. I'm not even sure she's at home," Tank said.

"We'll wait."

STORMY HADN'T EXPECTED Sophronia Petros to open her own door, but their incessant knocking had brought the lady herself. She didn't appear happy. She looked over the trio on her porch. "Why aren't you dead?" Then she turned to Tank. "You've caught them. Congratulations. But I don't see why you brought them here."

"Where is your Guard?" Tank asked.

"I dismissed him." Sophronia shrugged. "Haven't you heard? We have a new order now. We'll be safe." The woman was too nonchalant, too blasé. She showed no fear. If anything, Stormy guessed Sophronia looked regretful.

"I think maybe you wanted one of us to come visit," Stormy said. "And you made it easier for us."

"Now why would I want to see you?" Sophronia said.

"I don't know, but we've stood here for a few minutes, and you still haven't raised an alarm." Stormy watched the woman.

After a few moments' debate with herself, Sophronia opened the door wider. "Come in, then. I might as well hear what you have to say."

"You're not afraid?" Stormy asked.

"No. After you've seen what I've seen, you learn that the monsters aren't necessarily the ugly ones."

Was that an insult? And then it hit her. Tank hadn't been the only one drinking tonight.

Sophronia showed them in to her sumptuous living room. The decor was mostly white and gold. Clearly the woman had no small children. "I suppose you want to sit down."

They sat, and for a few moments no one spoke. Sophronia blew out a puff of air. "Look. You didn't come here on a social visit."

Stormy swallowed past her jumpiness. "We need to know how you feel about Lucas—uh, *Luc*—LeRoy."

Sophronia arched a single, well-plucked brow. "You mean the new darling of the Council?"

Stormy eyed the woman. "You don't trust him any more than we do."

"What of it? I am merely one member of the Council." Sophronia picked up a glass from the sofa table and took a swig of the light brown liquid within. She didn't offer them any.

Stormy placed a hand on Sophronia's wrist to prevent her from drinking any more. Sophronia shot her a lethal look. Stormy ignored it. "Reggie told me what happened. You feel guilty because you didn't believe her when she warned you. But now you do."

Sophronia let the glass stand on the table and dragged her hand through her blond hair, leaving it tousled. "I don't do guilt."

"Nevertheless, you know she was right." Stormy waited for some kind of response and she finally saw it when the muscles in Sophronia's cheeks jumped. She was clenching her teeth.

"I don't know what you expect me to do. The Council has made its decision." Sophronia reached for her glass.

Hunter prevented her from drinking this time. "You don't have to do anything. It's enough that you are a Council member."

22

JUSTIN'S GUIDE FOR THE ARTIST

Noise and flash often cover shallow effort.

SLEEP, LONG IN coming, short in length, left Stormy feeling unsatisfied, restless. The pendants had worked perfectly, leading them to a small cottage in Pacific Beach. It belonged to a woman who did philanthropic work in Africa and wouldn't be home for at least another year. Jonathan said she owed him, and she had happily given him use of the house.

Stormy's stomach churned as if she knew she should be preparing for something that she couldn't identify, let alone prepare for. Knowing sleep was no longer possible, she tiptoed out to the kitchen. Could it really have been less than twenty-four hours since Hyacinth's death? A shudder shook her as she waited for her tea to finish steeping. The world was changing so fast. Too fast. Less than two weeks ago, her biggest problem had been choosing what color yarn to weave with. Now she was embroiled in a battle for control of the Arcani world. And possibly the Groundling one as well.

Reggie came in next. She smiled as she saw Stormy and grabbed a mug and filled her cup from the automatic coffeepot. "I thought I was the only one who kept bakers' hours."

"Not today," said Kristin, yawning as she walked into the kitchen. "It's mornings like this one when I wish I drank coffee."

Stormy placed her cup on the counter. "Do you feel it?"

"Like something is going to happen? Yeah." Reggie took a long sip of her brew, then closed her eyes. "Yesterday was such an awful day, and I think today's going to be worse."

Kristin nodded. "I know we're not supposed to have any precognition powers, but I feel it too."

They stood in silence, not daring to talk.

"Is it all right to be afraid?" Stormy asked.

Kristin put her arm around her. "I'd worry more if you weren't."

"It's just that . . ." Stormy paused. She felt a lump in her throat burn as it formed. Her voice dropped to a whisper. "I just found him."

"You love him?" Reggie asked.

Stormy nodded.

"Me too," Reggie said, and wiped a tear from her eye. "Not yours, mine." She gave them a weak attempt at a smile.

Kristin nodded. "When I first found out about magic, I thought life would be so easy. After the initial panic, I mean. Now I—" She stopped to calm her voice. "If I say I wish I'd never known, then I also wouldn't have met Tennyson."

Stormy really didn't know these women, but they'd

already been through adventures and heartache with one another. The beginning bonds of friendship had been formed, and she trusted them. The Magic may have thrown them together, but they were a team.

"Tennyson finished the translation last night. Late last night." Kristin looked at the other two.

"And?" Reggie said.

"He wouldn't tell me anything. He's still asleep."

"You know it has to involve all three of us," Stormy said.

Reggie nodded. "I was thinking the same thing."

"The Three Musketeers," Kristin said.

With as much magic as she knew, Stormy thought the three blind mice was a better description.

LUCAS GAZED AT his new chambers. He smiled. The Council had insisted on granting him these living quarters. For his own safety. The opulent suite of rooms suited him. But not perfectly. But for now, it was a start.

The sun poured into the room. It promised to be a beautiful day. Dmitri had brought his treasures from home. Well, one treasure. The rest could wait. He paused in front of the tapestry now hanging on the wall of his suite here.

They had tried to steal it yesterday. And failed. A great rush of satisfaction filled him. They might have taken two of the Gifts, but he still had one. Now he would have the time to study it and discover its secret. Now that the Council protected him.

He would have to move it, though. The sunlight would soon ruin it. Perhaps if he placed it under glass. But for now he enjoyed looking at—

The tapestry. It had grabbed Stormy's attention, as well it might have, but there was something more to her scrutiny. What had she seen? He'd asked himself that question dozens of times since that evening and never found an answer.

He leaned closer to the tapestry. Nothing. He could see nothing. Except a piece of lint.

He plucked it off, then frowned as he saw another. This was unacceptable. Dmitri should know better than to place the tapestry where dirt might damage it. He found a third mote. He was about to pick it off when he stopped. Small flecks dotted the tapestry. Although he knew he shouldn't touch it with bare hands, he brushed the surface with his fingers. A small cloud of dust rose from it. The tapestry felt . . .

Something was wrong. Stepping back, he viewed the image. Nothing. Yet the tapestry drew his attention . . .

His blood froze. The wizard's face lacked the detail it should. He leaned closer. It looked right, but the threads seemed too new. He combed the image for the other details. The woman's cloak lacked the richness of color that added depth. The ruby sphere didn't sparkle, and the staff was a simple stick without any detail of the carvings decorating it. This image wanted dimension. He grabbed the tapestry. The material was too stiff. It lacked the wear of time.

"Ahhhhh!" he screamed, yanking the weaving to the ground. "Dmitri!"

The door opened almost at once. Dmitri bowed. "Sir?"

"Is this the tapestry you found in my house?" Lucas pointed at the floor where the tapestry had landed.

For a fleeting instant, confusion passed over Dmitri's features. "Yes, sir. I brought it as you requested."

"This isn't my tapestry. This is a cheap imitation." Lucas kicked it.

Dmitri paled. "There was no other, sir."

"I am surrounded by incompetence." Lucas pulled out his wand.

Dmitri took a step back. "Is this a test, sir? Did you make a copy to see if I was discerning enough to serve you? If so, I have failed, my lord." He pulled open his shirt and bared his chest. "I deserve death. I would be honored if you killed me."

"Don't be absurd. I still have a use for you."

"Thank you, sir. You shall not regret this." Dmitri dropped to his knees. "How may I serve you?"

"They have Merlin's Gifts. I want them back. We shall have to lure them to us."

"How, sir?"

Lucas's nostrils flared. "We attack their weaknesses." His heart rate slowed, and he breathed easier. He knew exactly what to do. And the Council would help him.

"Tell the Prime Councilor I must speak with him immediately. Tell him I know how to catch the godmothers, and we must hurry."

Dmitri bowed again and left.

He would have Merlin's Gifts back. The *Lagabóc* only told how the first two were used. The *Lagabóc* didn't mention the tapestry at all except to say the Gifts form a weapon, but not how. Despite the presence of Tennyson Ritter, they wouldn't have had time to figure out how to use the tapestry. Lucas felt confident this was true. He had access to the same information as they.

Lucas walked to the window. Though he could see out, no Groundlings could see him. It was hidden from their view. Not for long. No more would the Arcani hide from those animals. No more would Arcani have to die for those creatures. No more would they suffer at the hands of the weak beasts. A new order would prevail, a new renaissance. And he would be at its head. "It's time. I only wish you could have seen it, Maman."

* * *

HUNTER SPREAD OUT a hand-drawn plan of the Council Hall. "Here are the residences. Most Councilors have their own homes, but there's always been a need for apartments at the Hall. Stormy lived in this one." He pointed to a square on the paper.

Except Tennyson, they had all gathered around the dining room table to plan their next move. Tennyson was still working on the final tweaks in the translation of the code, but they all agreed that the time to stop Lucas had arrived.

"Where do you think Lucas is staying?" Kristin asked.

"My guess is they gave him one of the nicer suites over here." He pointed to another level of the complex.

"Gee, they didn't give me the best rooms? What a surprise." Stormy let out a little note of disgust.

Reggie studied the plans. "The Hall is really extensive. How did they get so much room?"

"Gnomes built it. A lot of it is underground, extending through the cliffs." Hunter pointed to the first drawing. "That's all that's visible at street level. Shielding spells and regular Guard sentries protect the grounds. Down here is the transport room—the only room you can transport into or out of."

"They sure aren't going to make getting to Lucas easy," Kristin said.

"No, but they have never had a Guard with inside information working for the other side." Hunter drew in a deep breath. "That doesn't mean we aren't going to have a really hard time getting in there."

The computer in the corner pinged the arrival of a message. They looked at one another. The only ones who knew how to reach them were family or allies.

Rose walked over to check it. "It says, 'Stormy, call home now.' "

Stormy felt the color drain from her face. She grabbed her cell phone and turned the power on. The screen took interminably long to load. Then she punched in the number.

The phone picked up before the first ring finished sounding. "Ah, Miss Jones-Smythe. So lovely of you to call so promptly." Lucas's smooth, suave voice slithered over the connection.

Stormy nearly dropped the phone. She knew the others were watching her, but she couldn't feel anything beyond the panic that pummeled through her. "Where are my dads?"

"Right here. They're fine . . . for now."

Her knees collapsed. Someone had pushed a chair beneath her, so she didn't fall to the floor, but she didn't think she would have noticed in either case. "If you hurt them—"

"Then what? We both know the game has ended. The Council is here with me. As are the Guard." Lucas clicked his tongue. "It was a valiant effort, but you've lost. We are moving forward into a new world."

Hunter's hand squeezed her shoulder. She looked up. They were all staring at her, their faces filled with concern, horror, and sympathy.

"What do you want?"

"That's better. I'll be sure to tell the Prime Councilor of your cooperation."

"What do you want?" she said, louder this time.

"Why, you three. The godmothers. And the old ones too. The game is over and I've won."

"Fine."

"One more thing. Actually, three more things. Merlin's Gifts. You stole them from me. I want them back. All three of them."

So he knew about the tapestry.

"Bring them."

"Wait." Her mind whirled.

"What?"

"We aren't all here. I'll need some time to gather everyone together."

"You have half an hour. Don't be late." The connection ended.

That was when she let her pain swamp her. She clenched her teeth to keep from crying out. But she had to tell them. Every word hurt, every breath a chore. "Lucas has my family. He wants us in exchange."

"We should have insisted they go somewhere," Reggie said.

Stormy shook her head. "They wouldn't have listened. My fathers have always refused to hide."

"How much time do we have?" Jonathan asked.

"Thirty minutes."

Reggie draped her arm around her. "I can't believe you had the presence of mind to ask for time."

"I don't know how I did," Stormy said. The fear within diminished. Fury replaced it. "I want that son of a bitch."

A hot wind blew around her. Reggie took her hand and the wind increased. The lights flickered in the house. Kristin joined the link, and a red glow surrounded the women. The papers flew around them as if caught in a cyclone. Anything loose in the room—the tables, the chairs—rattled where they stood.

"There's the power of three," Tennyson said as he walked in. He smiled, but his eyes were red and a growth of beard covered his chin.

Jonathan grinned. "That's the most frightening thing I've ever seen."

Even Hunter looked impressed. "I'm glad I'm on our side."

Lily brushed a tear away. "You remind me of us when we were younger."

"The way I'm feeling now, I could join them," Rose said with a fierce set to her jaw. Her hands were clenched into fists.

Stormy broke the link of hands and the wind died. Her chest hurt, ached with pain. She dashed away a tear that escaped. "Damn it. We have to get Lucas."

"Then let's plan. We don't have a lot of time, but we have enough." Hunter swept the paper from the table and handed her a clean sheet. "We need to know the layout of your neighborhood."

Stormy started sketching. Art. Thank God she understood art. Her lines were true and confident.

Tennyson started talking. "I've finished with the tapestry. I know how to use Merlin's Gifts."

"And I have an idea too," Jonathan added.

"Good," Hunter said. " 'Cause we can use all the help we can get right now."

Twenty-five minutes later, they gathered to leave. A somber mood descended over the group. No one spoke. They all had their assignments. Tennyson and Kirstin stood beside each other, heads bent. Reggie clung to Jonathan's hand.

Then Jonathan yanked Reggie into his arms. She yelped, but he kissed her. He winked at her. "See you there." He popped out.

Tennyson smiled. "It's time. Be careful." The kiss was gentle.

Hunter moved to Stormy and took both her hands.

"We haven't even started yet. Don't let anything ruin that."

She smiled. He leaned forward, and he kissed her with more tenderness than she thought he was capable of. If she hadn't had enough crying in the past few days, she would have allowed herself a few tears.

The women looked at one another.

"We ready?" Kristin asked.

"No, but let's go anyway," Stormy said.

"We're right behind you," Lily and Rose said.

Stormy clasped hands with her fellow godmothers. Kristin nodded. "Let's go."

23

JUSTIN'S GUIDE FOR THE ARTIST

•

One's own worst enemy is often himself.

THEY ARRIVED IN the middle of the street facing Stormy's fathers' house. Stormy hoped they looked like avenging furies, but she had no idea if the pose worked. Inside she felt more like a flurry than a fury.

It was entirely too sunny a day for this confrontation. The sky was too blue, the wind too balmy, the air too clean. The absurdity struck her like a bad joke.

Guards lined the street and were positioned between the houses. At least twenty men watched them. The Guards didn't leave their positions. As Stormy turned around to assess their location, she noticed they never wavered in their focus. They were alert and ready for any movement. They looked formidable. God, she hoped this plan worked.

Lucas ambled out to greet them. An odd thought, really, but that's what he looked like—a host greeting his guests. Outrage simmered in Stormy. This was *her* home.

"I was beginning to think you weren't coming. Another minute and you'd have been late."

Ian stood beside him, along with the Prime Councilor. Ian looked like a favored hound happy to be at the side of his master, but the Prime Councilor looked less comfortable. His gaze darted between them, his shoulders hunched. He was right to be nervous. The idiot had chosen the wrong side.

Stormy stepped forward. "Where are my dads?"

"They're safe."

"Yes, yes." The Prime Councilor shuffled his feet and cleared his throat. "No harm has come to them, nor will come." He couldn't lift his gaze to meet hers.

"I'm supposed to trust you?" Stormy placed a fist on her hip.

"You don't have a choice," Ian said. "After your betrayal, you should be thankful Luc didn't kill them outright."

"Now, now, Ian. No need to be uncivil. We have won, after all." Lucas gave her a reptilian smile. His one-eyed gaze settled on Kristin and narrowed. "Kristin, you still look magnificent."

Kristin returned his gaze with icy disdain. "I'd say thank you, but I wouldn't mean it."

"Tsk tsk. You used to be more gracious. It must be the company you keep." He focused on Reggie and paused. "I am looking forward to paying you back for this." He indicated the eye patch.

"Really? Because I think it's an improvement. In fact I'm happy to give you a matching one on the other side." Reggie did unflappable well.

"Oh, yes, I shall delight in carving payment from you."

Only the slight tightening of Reggie's hand indicated her unease. Stormy wished she could give her a reassuring squeeze in return. Reggie said, "I'll send Jonathan your regards."

Her barb seemed to hit its target because Lucas flinched.

"Where is the monster?" Ian asked, then chortled at his wit. He laughed alone.

Lucas frowned. "There are only five of you. Where's the other one?"

"Beyond your reach," Lily said, her voice steady.

Anger blazed in his eye. The lines of his face hardened. "Did you think you could disobey me? I told you all to be here."

"You can't touch her. She's dead." Rose smiled. "She did enjoy thwarting you."

Lucas twisted his face into a caricature of grief, then sent them a look of disgust. "I can't say I'm not disappointed. I was looking forward to dealing with all of you personally."

"Lucas, it's not too late," Lily said. "You don't have to repeat your mother's mistakes."

The Prime Councilor glanced at Lucas. "Why are they calling you Lucas? And who is your mother?"

"His name is Lucas Reynard." Regal as any queen, Lily gazed across the space at the Prime Councilor. "And his mother was Elenka Liska."

The Prime Councilor gasped. "Impossible." He turned to Lucas. "Is this true?" Even Ian looked dumbfounded.

"Your reaction should tell you why I go by a different name," Lucas said.

"Well, yes, naturally so. Elenka Liska was a traitor. Her behavior has nothing to do with you," Ian said.

"My mother died for a noble cause. She tried to save the Arcani. She was no traitor."

Ian looked shocked and confused.

"You can't be that stupid, Ian," Reggie said. "On the other hand, maybe you can."

Stormy would have laughed at Reggie's words if the situation had been less serious.

"Stupid? I'm not the one captured today, am I?" Ian lifted his chin, then turned to the Prime Councilor. "She's just trying to distract you from our purpose here."

"I suppose so," the Councilor said, his brows drawn in confused contemplation. "But is it true?"

Lucas bowed his head. "Yes. Can you imagine the battles I have had to fight because of my heritage?" Lucas faced Lily with a hint of a smirk on his lips. "My mother was a great woman, perhaps misguided in her actions, but her heart was true to the Arcani. We shall not make the same mistakes she did."

"No, no, of course not," the Councilor said. He turned to the godmothers. "By the order of the Council, I hereby detain you and hold you as enemies of the Arcani."

With a flash from his wand, magic showered over the neighborhood. Stormy felt the tingle that confined them all to the compound. She could only hope they were ready.

"And now, I'll take back the Gifts." Lucas held out his hand.

"And now, we have a problem," Stormy mirrored his words, exaggerating her mocking tone. "See, we won't give up the Gifts. They are ours."

Stormy waved her hand. The tapestry appeared in her grip. She unfurled it and laid her hand on top of it. The missing stitches lit up as if fire glowed within the cloth.

The Prime Councilor stepped back. "Is that Merlin's Gift? What are you doing with it?"

"Parlor tricks." Lucas turned to Stormy. "Impressive. A pity your parents aren't here to see you show off."

She steeled herself against the flash of pain that jolted through her. She had to trust that her fathers would be fine.

"I can't place myself in such danger." The Councilor's gaze darted back to the safety of the house. "Perhaps it's time to call the Guards to—"

"No," Lucas shouted. "Not until they retrieve all the Gifts."

"All?" The Councilor gulped audibly.

"Councilor, perhaps you should go inside and see to our . . . guests. I can handle the women." Lucas didn't turn from them.

"Yes, yes. Good call." The Councilor retreated into the house.

Stormy's stomach curdled at the easy acquiescence of the Councilor. She watched his back as he hastened into the house. She had hoped that the Councilor would crumble, that his obvious unease would overcome his support of Lucas. That hope died as the door closed behind him.

Lucas's face shone with triumph. His glee at achieving dominance over the Councilor was palpable. Stormy tried not to let his confidence dishearten her.

Ian's mouth had dropped open at mention of the three Gifts. He finally remembered to close it. "They have Merlin's Gifts?"

"They stole them from me!" For an instant the urbane mask dropped from Lucas's face and revealed the hideous soul beneath. But then he regained control of himself and examined the tapestry from where he stood. "Lovely. So simple, yet elegant. Subtle. Unlike the overt brutality of the other two Gifts. This one was always my favorite. The most beautiful of the three. The greatest piece of art." Lucas moved toward the tapestry. He lifted his hand as if he were touching the weaving.

"I wouldn't try that, Lucas." Kristin pointed her wand at him.

He let out a low laugh as every Guard took a defensive stance. A score of wands pointed at the godmothers. He held up his hand. "Not yet, gentlemen."

Worse than the Guards' response to Kristin was their obedience to Lucas. The Guards remained in an alert stance, but lowered their weapons.

"Well, Kristin?" Lucas arched an eyebrow at her bravada.

Stormy wanted to slap the arrogance out of his voice, but her admiration for Kristin grew as a placid smile curved her lips. Kristin cupped her hand. "I believe you were waiting for this."

A brilliant red sphere appeared in her hand. It glowed almost as brightly as the tapestry.

Reggie's turn. The most petite of the three, she stood tall. Into her outstretched hand a long staff appeared. Intricately carved from a thick wooden branch, the staff seemed to exude solidity and firmness. Reggie's voice rang out over the street. "I bet you're not eager to retrieve this one, since it helped take your eye."

The three women lined up. Lily and Rose stood behind them. Lucas's eyes widened as he saw all three Gifts together. Ian looked as if he couldn't decide whether to run or stay and watch.

"*Opes,*" Kristin said. "For power." The sphere glowed even brighter.

"*Vires,*" Reggie said. "For strength." The staff radiated heat.

"Scientia," Stormy said. "For knowledge." The tapestry floated on the air.

"Tres omnes in uno," they said together.

Merlin's Gifts flew from their hands. Stormy held her breath as the orb slid onto the top of the staff and the tapestry affixed itself onto the wood like a shield. It stood upright like a sentry on duty.

"The weapon," Lucas said. Awe weighed heavy in his voice, and eagerness burned in his eyes. "With this I shall rule the world."

"It's not yours to use," Kristin said. "Any more than it is right for any one man or group to rule the world."

"Which is why we're here to protect the Groundlings and the Arcani," Reggie said.

"Because it's our job," Stormy said.

"You think you can stop me?" Lucas sounded incredulous. He raised his hand. "Take them."

Drawing their wands again, the Guards moved into alert stances. Half moved forward toward them, two for each. As the Guards approached, a new sound emerged. From behind the men, an enormous beast, larger than any man there, with a boar's snout and curved tusks broke through the line. Coarse orange hair covered his body, but speed made him little more than a large orange blur. The Guards scattered in his wake.

Ian screamed. "It's Jonathan!"

Stormy knew about Jonathan's other self, but had never seen him in his beast form before. It was hard to reconcile the beast with the handsome man she had gotten to know, but the look of love and worry on Reggie's face removed any trace of fear except for the man himself. Jonathan dodged wand blasts as he sowed confusion in the ranks.

From below, the ground trembled. A trench opened up beneath part of the line of Guards, toppling them into the earth. The gnomes had arrived. At the same time, flocks of fairies rose from the bushes and impeded the movement of several Guards. Callie and her troops sprang into action.

Hunter and Tennyson appeared from behind a house, followed by Tank leading a battalion of men. With Sophronia's aid, Tank had recruited a number of Guards. Since Sophronia was a Council member, her word was enough to secure their cooperation. They engaged the Guards from the other end.

And from the neighborhood houses, Stormy's other family emerged. Barbara and Conrad, Kazzy and his family, and all the other artists came out, wands brandished, ready to help.

In the space of a few seconds, the Guards realized they were under attack, and their strategy changed. Now that the surprise was over, their training kicked in, and they became the fighting machine they were renowned for. But confusion reigned as the Guards under Lucas's control recognized they were fighting their comrades under different orders.

Ian yelped and looked for a spot to hide, but Lucas grabbed his arm. "Get the women. They have the power. The others are just a distraction."

Ian's Adam's apple bobbed up and down, but he lunged toward them.

Stormy sent a bolt of magic toward him, and his wand flew over the house. "I really haven't learned control yet," Stormy said. She pointed her wand at him. "You don't want me to practice on you."

Ian pivoted, but Dmitri blocked his escape route. Lucas's servant threw up a protective shield around his master and himself.

"What about me?" Ian said. He clawed at the magical wall, trying to gain entry.

Lucas lifted his wand and, with a flick of his wrist, sent Ian flying to the other end of the neighborhood.

Odd. Stormy actually felt a little sympathy for the putz.

Lucas approached them. It seemed as if they faced only him. His lack of fear, his total disregard of the surrounding chaos, gave him a wild air. "You've made a valiant effort, ladies, but your distractions won't work. Even if you defeat these men, I have followers waiting only for my word."

"Lucas, your mother wouldn't have wanted this," Lily said.

"You know nothing about my mother," Lucas snapped. "You caged her up and forgot about her."

"We mourned for her," Rose said. "She broke our hearts as much as she broke yours."

"My mother never hurt me. She taught me strength. You believed you contained her. You couldn't. Her spirit was superior to yours, so you hated her. And she passed that spirit on to me."

Fierce pride and real pain blazed in his expression, but Stormy could summon no sympathy for him. He had created this maelstrom for himself, and she was ready to send him into it.

"And now this ends. I will take my rightful place in this world, the position my mother prepared me for. Give me the weapon."

"We can't do that, Lucas," Kristin said.

"Then you will die. But first you will learn to fear me." Lucas raised his wand and aimed it directly at the house.

"No!" Stormy started running toward the house, but Dmitri caught her arm. "Daddy! Dad!"

Lily and Rose had drawn their wands and were mouthing spells under their breaths, but Stormy watched in horror as the house collapsed on itself.

A bright light burst from the end of Kristin's wand and struck Dmitri in the chest. Dmitri's eyes widened. He stared at Kristin and smiled at her. He released Stormy, but didn't fall. Stormy watched in amazement as Dmitri, oblivious to the battle, bent over to pick a flower from the front yard.

Lucas merely laughed. "You will have to do better than that to stop me. An immaturing charm won't work on me."

Stormy's vision swam. Lucas had killed her fathers. She ran to the weapon and placed her hand on it. A moment later a second hand joined hers. Reggie. And then the third. Kristin.

Lucas's eyes widened. For the first time fear replaced the cockiness. The weapon stirred beneath their touch. Heat spread from the staff into their hands. Stormy felt power surge through her. She saw with clarity what she had to do next and knew the others had felt it too.

And then she dropped her hand and backed away. "I can't do it. I'm not strong enough to kill him."

Reggie relinquished her hold as well. "Restraint takes greater strength."

Kristin joined them. "I would do it for you, Stormy."

But Stormy shook her head. "I won't let us sink to his level."

"No one would blame you," Reggie said.

"I'd blame me." Stormy looked at them. "I can't kill him."

"Fools," Lucas yelled. "Idiots. You stupid, stupid women." He dashed to the weapon and grabbed it. "I have the will and now I'll have the power."

Merlin's Gifts let out a huge flash of light. Stormy scrunched her eyes shut, wondering what death would feel like. And she waited.

And waited.

She opened her eyes.

Lucas lay on the ground, his eye open to the sky, unseeing.

Stunned, she looked around for Reggie and Kristin, who appeared just as dazed as she. But they were alive.

From around them a voice sounded through the air.

"This is Council member Sophronia Petros. I demand all Guards cease their fighting immediately."

As if in slow motion, the Guards lowered their wands. The fighting trickled to a stop. A few of the fairies shoved a couple more Guards into the trench left by the gnomes, but fairies were like that.

From behind the farthest house, Sophronia marched out into the middle of the street. "Until we finish investigating this incident, all Guards are suspended. You are no longer bound by the Oath."

The Guards lost their aggressive postures. They looked as if they tried to make sense of what had just happened.

When Sophronia reached Reggie, she stopped. Sophronia looked at her. Reggie faced her without flinching. Sophronia then gave her a quick nod. "You were right. I do regret not listening to you."

Sophronia faced the crowd again. She waved her wand, and Stormy felt the confining shield lift. Sophronia's voice echoed over the crowd again. "There are wounded. Get them help."

The sudden end to the action didn't bring a sudden calm. The eerie slow-motion impression hadn't seemed to lift from Stormy's vision. She saw Tank help his friends to their feet. She noticed the gnomes disappearing underground. Groans from the injured rose above other noises. This was a battle scene.

Rose knelt beside Lucas. With her fingertip, she closed his eye. "Such a waste."

Stormy didn't know where to turn. She watched as Tennyson ran to Kristin and grabbed her. Jonathan sped over to Reggie, who, oblivious to his shape, hugged and kissed him.

Stormy's vision dimmed. She hadn't seen Hunter since she'd glimpsed him a few minutes earlier. And her fathers . . .

She let out a little cry and ran to the wreckage of the house. "Please, oh, please. Please."

She repeated her whispered plea over and over. Barbara and Conrad joined her. Their shocked expressions offered no hope.

"Please, oh, please." Stormy battled against the pain in her heart.

Beyond the house, the two studios stood undisturbed. The massive rock that Justin had used to distract the Guards jutted between the two buildings. As she stared at the rubble, her heart breaking, the once-beautiful, carved door to her studio opened. Her fathers stepped out. The Prime Councilor walked slowly behind them, his expression reflecting disbelief and shock.

With a cry, Stormy ran to her parents. For several moments none of them could speak. Stormy hugged and kissed her dads. Their presence alone lightened her heart, but it wasn't enough. Where was Hunter?

"How did you get out?" Stormy asked.

Justin was searching the faces of those around them. "That Guard of yours. Hunter. That was his name, right?"

"Hunter saved you?" she said.

"He broke in through the back door and pulled us into your studio." Ken let out a dry chuckle. "At the time I was annoyed that he smashed our door. I need to apologize."

"Yes," the Prime Councilor said. "He saved our lives. He is a hero. I did not realize he was a Guard."

"He isn't any longer," she said.

"You don't know what you're talking about. One cannot just leave the Guard. The Oath—"

"I know all about the Oath, and it seems to me you need to rethink what loyalty and allegiance means," she snapped back. Where was Hunter?

Her dads fell quiet as they picked up on her anxiety. She didn't care who knew she loved him. She just wanted to see him again. An unnatural silence filled her ears. She no longer heard any of the surrounding noises. Each passing moment brought more fear as she sought his face in the chaos without success. Her insides constricted and she found it difficult to breathe.

And then there he was. From around the end of Justin's studio, he walked toward them, holding Ian in front of him. Ian's hands were secured behind his back.

"I had to chase this one down. He was trying to get away." He handed Ian over to Tank.

Stormy launched herself at him. He caught her in his arms.

Between her tears of relief, she said, "If you ever scare me like that again, I'll kill you myself."

"Me? I wasn't the one with some magical weapon facing down the lunatic of the century." But Hunter clasped her close, and his arms gave her all the home she needed.

As he placed her on the ground, she lifted her face to his, and he kissed her.

Ken clasped his hand to his chest. “Looks like our baby girl will be moving out again.”

Justin laughed. “Good thing, because her room is a mess.”

24

JUSTIN'S GUIDE FOR THE ARTIST

•

Find the magic in everything.

THE AFTERMATH WAS messy. Slowly the entire story became known. At least a dozen Guards had been injured, two severely, but when faced with their comrades, neither side could use lethal force. It had saved the tragedy from being worse. Alfred had convinced the gnomes to support the godmothers, and Callie had led the fairies into the fight, but only after Zack promised to stay home. Six Guards led Dmitri, who had picked himself a bouquet, and Ian away and escorted the Prime Councilor to the Council Hall.

Only after all the wounded received help and everyone was taken care of did the godmothers and their companions return to the spot where Lucas had died. Merlin's Gifts lay on the ground, three separate entities again, as if the blast had torn them apart.

Stormy picked up the tapestry. A small tear marred

the corner, and a few threads had frayed along the edge. "I could repair this."

"I don't know if you should," Hunter said. "I don't know if anyone should touch those more than necessary. Power can do great things, but it can also do horrible ones."

"I think I agree," Kristin said. She picked up the ruby sphere. Sunlight shone through it, revealing a crack that hadn't been present before. She traced her finger along the minute imperfection.

Reggie was testing the fit of a piece of carving that had broken from the staff against the spot where it had fallen off. "We never did learn where Lucas got the Gifts."

"His mother found the tapestry in a castle," Stormy said.

"Does it matter?" Rose said. "He couldn't use them. He wasn't a godmother."

Clarity bloomed on Jonathan's face. "So that's why he died."

Tennyson frowned. "You want to explain it to the rest of us?"

Jonathan smiled. "Have you ever tried to do magic with Kristin's wand?"

"No," Tennyson said.

Kristin's brow puckered, and she handed her wand to him. Tennyson pointed it at a flower and said, *"Flore."* Nothing happened. Tennyson looked at Jonathan.

"I make wands, so I call myself somewhat of an expert. A wand focuses an Arcani's magic. Some wands fit better than others, but really it's a matter of taste. You can use any wand.

"But the wands of the godmothers are different. Hyacinth's wand vanished when she died." Jonathan turned to Lily. "Where did you get the wands for the new godmothers?"

"The Magic sent them," Lily said.

Stormy looked at her wand. It was unique—completely different from the wands of the other godmothers. In fact, all three of the godmothers' wands felt different somehow. Their intricacy, detail, and beauty were unmatched by the wands held by Tennyson, Jonathan, and Hunter.

"I have a top-of-the-line wand." Jonathan held out his. "Two, actually, but they don't compare to the ones you have. The Magic made those."

"Yes, I suppose so," Lily said.

He turned to Reggie. "Remember what happened when Sophronia tried to grab your wand from you?"

"I'll bet it was the same thing that happened when I tried to take Stormy's wand from her," Hunter said. When they all looked at him, he shrugged. "Hey, I was trying to do my job."

"Their wands are made by the Magic for the godmothers. They attack the people who try to take them. They don't work for anyone else." Jonathan looked at Merlin's Gifts. "When the Gifts were assembled, they really were nothing more than a giant wand."

"So Lucas killed himself." Hunter looked around at the destruction the man had wrought. "I can't say I'm sorry."

Rose said, "I can. I'm sorry for Elenka's suffering and anger. It produced his hatred."

"Yes, and right about now, Hyacinth would have chided you for being so soft," Lily said gazing off into the sky.

"Ha. She was the softest of us all. She just hid it well," Rose said.

The words sank in. Stormy looked at the tapestry she held, suddenly very glad they hadn't used the weapon. Any life was too great a cost, and the thirst for power had cost too many lives already. From the looks of Reggie and Kristin's faces, they were thinking the same thing. They already had great power as godmothers. They really didn't need something that would magnify its effects.

As if acknowledging their thoughts, the Gifts shimmered for a moment, then vanished. The women exchanged looks.

"Did you do that?" Reggie asked.

Kristin shook her head.

Tennyson said, "Try summoning them."

Kristin held out her hand, but nothing happened. She looked at Tennyson.

Tennyson nodded. "That's what I expected. According to the *Lagabóc*, the Gifts appear to the godmothers when they are needed. They appeared during World War II, but no one had the *Lagabóc* to interpret their use. Only the legend of a great weapon existed." He paused. "They're not needed now."

"So it's over?" Hunter asked.

"I think so." Tennyson looked over the neighborhood that appeared more like a battlefield. "Well, we still have to deal with the fallout, but I think so."

That felt right. Stormy thought about the pain, the anger, and the sorrow they had all suffered, and now a sense of peace and happiness stole into her. It was over.

Hunter looked down at Stormy. "I suppose I should ask you out on date or something. Now that I wouldn't be breaking rules."

"I might even agree." She grinned, and she stood on tiptoes to reach his mouth. Freedom flowed through her veins as he kissed her back. No fear, no panic, no anxiety. Only possibilities.

"Damn, and I thought she was my type." Tank's voice interrupted them.

Stormy stepped back and smiled at Tank. "Sorry about everything I put you through." She extended her hand.

"I can't say I enjoyed it all, but, damn, I'm glad I was on the right side of this thing." Before she could react, Tank grabbed her hand and pulled her into his arms. Dipping her slightly, he kissed her.

For a moment she was too surprised to move, but before she could push him away, he released her. Hunter was scowling. Tank squinted one eye at her. "Nothing? You sure, pretty lady? It's not too late to change your mind."

She recognized the glint in his eyes and laughed.

Hunter grabbed Tank by the neck, but there was no real strength in his grip. "Try that again, and you'll wish you had never gotten sober."

Tank just laughed. "I guess I have to find my own woman. So, you coming back to the Guards?"

Hunter thought for a moment. "I don't know yet. Right now, I just want to enjoy life a little. And I know a couple of guys who could use some help rebuilding a house."

Stormy's dads waved to them. She felt her face heat up. Clearly they had witnessed the entire exchange. It was one thing to have parents who were open about most things, but it was still embarrassing to have them witness your love life.

"And speaking of family, I need to see my parents," Reggie said. "I think Del will be happy to get home." She and Jonathan popped out a moment later.

"And you have a house to move into," Tennyson said to Kristin.

"Let's go. I can't wait to organize your bookshelves." Kristin kissed Stormy's cheek, and then she and Tennyson vanished.

"And we're going to visit Hyacinth and tell her all about our day," Lily said.

Stormy took Lily's hand and squeezed it. She already felt a deep bond with Reggie and Kristin. She couldn't imagine the hole that Hyacinth's death left in Lily and Rose's life. "Would you put some flowers on her grave from me too?"

"Of course," Rose said. "I think we'll get some hyacinths. That would have irritated her." Rose smiled and the two women disappeared.

Tank winked at them. "Duty calls. I need to report to the Council. See you around, buddy." He vanished with a quiet pop.

"Where are we going?" Hunter asked. He placed his arms around her.

"Well, I'm sure Barbara and Conrad will be happy to put us up along with my dads."

"No, thanks. I am not spending our first officially sanctioned night together with your fathers."

"I guess that leaves your place," Stormy said.

"Sounds good, but you know how small it is."

"I don't mind small. Besides, if we ever need more room, there's plenty of space in the compound. In fact, I think my dads will want to build us a house right here."

He didn't say anything.

She felt a little nervous. Had she assumed too much? They hadn't talked about commitment.

"Look, Stormy. I don't know."

Her stomach dropped. She clamped down on the disappointment that threatened to drown her.

"If I'm going to live here, that means I'll have to learn something about art. I'm going to need a lot of help. Know anyone who might teach me?" He smiled into her eyes, and she felt its warmth all the way to her toes.

"Don't worry. I know people with a lot of connections to the art world."

TEN DAYS LATER, the Time of Transition was ending. The names of the new San Diego Council members had appeared on the scroll, and Tennyson's was among them. He swore the first thing he would do would be to banish the Oath. The Guards would serve because they wished to, not because they were bound to.

The Prime Council in London had reviewed the events and promised to revise Council laws. They also decided to investigate the effect of Lucas's actions on the Arcani world and to form some sort of reconciliation with his followers. They named Sophronia as Prime Councilor in San Diego. Around the world in the Council Halls—Kyoto, Luxor, Budapest, Buenos Aires, Quebec City, San Diego—the names of the new fairy godmothers had been recorded and accepted.

At the newly repaired cottage in Mission Beach, the home of Rose and Lily, the new godmothers and the old gathered for dinner. The men were in charge of the food. They grilled steaks, veggies, and pineapple. Fresh bread from the Star Bright Bakery also graced the table.

"I could do this more often," Jonathan said at the end of the meal. "Good food, good wine, and good friends." He lifted his glass.

"I second that," Tennyson said.

Lily clinked her glass. "Ladies, I would like to propose a toast."

Rose beamed. "We're officially retired."

Lily sent her a small frown. "As Rose said, we're stepping down as of today, and I can't think of three more capable women to take our place here in this part of the world."

"May your life be filled with love and laughter," Rose said.

"May you find joy and give joy to all you meet," Lily added.

"And may all *your* wishes come true," they finished together.

Glasses clinked and cries of "hear, hear" filled the room.

"Do you think these three will be finishing each other's thoughts soon?" Hunter asked.

"Are you kidding, man? Haven't you heard them? They already are," Tennyson said with a laugh.

"We are in so much trouble," Jonathan said.

Stormy smiled with the rest of them, then looked a little concerned. "What exactly does taking over your positions entail?"

"You know. Getting out into the Groundling communities, listening for unrest in ours, and best of all granting wishes," Kristin said.

"I've never granted a wish."

Silence greeted those words.

She glanced around the table in a panic. "Remember? I saw wishes that day in Del Mar."

"The crowns?" Reggie asked.

"Yes, but I didn't have the chance to grant one." Stormy pulled her lower lip between her teeth.

"Gentlemen and ladies, you will excuse us for a few minutes." Kristin stood up and pulled Stormy to her feet. "We have an errand to run."

Reggie jumped up. "Where to?"

"The baseball game." Kristin linked arms with Stormy, and Reggie joined her on the other side.

Stormy's gaze darted between the two women who flanked her, but before she could speak, the familiar tightening of the lungs occurred and her vision grew black. A moment later they were in an isolated corner of Petco Park, and the Padres were playing. A roar from the crowd indicated some sort of action was happening.

Kristin and Reggie pulled her toward the stadium proper. As they entered the seats, their gazes were on the people, not the game.

Sprinkled throughout the spectators were children with their parents, some looking bored, some falling asleep. Baseball might be America's game, but no one could deny it got boring in parts.

A little boy sat in the third row up along the first-base line. He punched his glove and looked up at his dad, who was engrossed in the game.

Suddenly Stormy saw it. A tiny gold crown floating over the boy's head. She concentrated.

"I wish I could catch a foul."

She turned to other women. "Oh, no. I don't have control of my magic. Things go crazy when I use it."

They stepped in front of her. Kristin said, "Just trust your instincts."

Stormy shook her head. "People will see me."

"We're blocking you," Reggie said. "Go on."

Stormy pursed her lips, but drew her wand. She looked at the boy, then she looked at the game. And at once it felt right. The pitcher threw, the batter swung, and after a quick swish of her wand, the ball sailed high in the air clearly in foul territory. This was her forte, causing chaos.

The little boy's mouth dropped. Around him grown

men leaped to their feet in an effort to catch the ball dropping from the sky. They blocked the child.

But the boy held out his glove anyway, and the baseball landed with a loud smack right in the middle of the leather. His arm rose in the air, still clutching the ball in the glove, and his dad lifted him up. Then his image appeared on the Jumbotron, and he gave the world a toothless grin.

The announcer's voice came on. "I think we have a future big leaguer here."

The boy's eyes shone, and his excitement busted out of his smile.

Stormy turned to Reggie and Kristin, her own grin almost hurting her face.

"That was freakin' unbelievable! We have the best job in the world!"